CW00485625

THE MERSEY MISTRESS

SHEILA RILEY

Boldwood

First published in Great Britain in 2021 by Boldwood Books Ltd.

Copyright © Sheila Riley, 2021

Cover Design by The Brewster Project

Cover Photography: Shutterstock, Alamy and Colin Thomas

Every effort has been made to obtain the necessary permissions with reference to copyright material, both illustrative and quoted. We apologise for any omissions in this respect and will be pleased to make the appropriate acknowledgements in any future edition.

A CIP catalogue record for this book is available from the British Library.

Paperback ISBN 978-1-80048-574-7

Large Print ISBN 978-1-80048-575-4

Ebook ISBN 978-1-80048-576-1

Kindle ISBN 978-1-80048-568-6

Audio CD ISBN 978-1-80048-569-3

MP3 CD ISBN 978-1-80048-570-9

Digital audio download ISBN 978-1-80048-573-0

Boldwood Books Ltd
23 Bowerdean Street
London SW6 3TN
www.boldwoodbooks.com

I dedicate this book to Mums all over the world, who have the most difficult and most rewarding job on earth.

Come to me in my dreams, and then
    By day I shall be well again!
    For then the night will surely pay
    The hopeless longing of the day.

— —MATTHEW ARNOLD

She's gone!'

Ruby Swift's frantic words echoed and bounced off the perpendicular walls, carried up the medieval stone aisle of the village church and rang through Lady Rowena Ashland's head like a clash of cymbals. Rowena pivoted towards the hysterical interruption and knew.

She just knew.

Every moveable part of her body was rigid, petrified like granite, except for her wide, haunted eyes that gave a silent plea to Archie, who sat beside her on the hard wooden pew. His large, work-worn hand reached for hers and Rowena said nothing, her mind scrabbling to comprehend.

Turning her head she saw Ruby Swift, standing alone at the back of the Anglican house of worship. And a scream sliced through the fog in her head, galvanising her to move. Archie's ground-eating strides took over her own and the only sound was the click of her low- heeled shoes causing a reverberating echo in the stunned silence.

'She's gone, Archie!' Mrs Swift, Ashland Hall's housekeeper

and her most valued confidant had given up her own privacy for Rowena and Archie, wept as she told her nephew. 'He came in without warning, picked her from her cradle and left. No explanation. Nothing.'

'Who took her?' Archie's voice came as soft as his brown-eyed gaze, belying the bleached pallor of his handsome features. Six feet four inches of muscle, he towered over Rowena's slim frame as secrets swirled round them like spirits of the dead looking in on sins of the living.

'Reverend Harrington. He must have followed me from Ashland Hall and waited until you both left for church, unless he already knew where you lived.' Ruby told him as the three made their way back to the sandstone cottage at the end of the narrow lane. It was Christmas Eve. Grey marbled clouds sprawled low across the snow-flecked meadows, fields and hedgerows, with the potential of more to follow, and it was the first time Rowena had left the cottage since her daughter's birth ten days earlier. She and Archie had gone to the church to give thanks for their daughter's safe arrival and to arrange for Eleanor to be baptised the following Sunday.

'Leave this to me,' said Archie as he headed to his horse and carriage standing outside the cottage, and Rowena made to follow him. But he turned towards her, held her in his arms and whispered, 'you go inside, I won't be long.'

The first thing she saw when she entered was the empty cradle beside the fireplace and she headed straight to it, lifting the delicate white shawl she had spent hours crocheting while waiting impatiently for the arrival of her and Archie's beloved daughter.

'He warned me,' she whispered as if talking to herself. Holding the shawl to her lips she inhaled the newborn fragrance of their most precious gift.

'Who did?' Mrs Swift asked, easing Rowena into the fireside chair, 'who warned you?'

'My father,' Rowena answered as if in a daze, 'he told me he would take the child and send it away. He had that power you see. Not because he is one of the richest men in England. It is much simpler than that.' Rowena looked up into Mrs Swift's kindly features and she said, 'he can do as he pleases with me, as I am not yet twenty-one.'

'No!' Archie's aunt let out a gasp of surprise, 'does Archie know?' Eighteen-year-old Rowena nodded. She had told him when she discovered she was carrying his child, not knowing if Archie, her father's head horseman – but much more to her than that – would stand by her or take off in the middle of the night to avoid her father's wrath. But she had no need to worry.

'Archie would never leave me in the lurch.'

'But you cannot marry without your father's consent,' Mrs Swift did not feel it was her place to pry, but now understood why the two had woken her in the middle of a hot summer night and begged refuge – and absolute secrecy, which she gave unreservedly.

'He will never give me his blessing. You see, my father is a snob of the worst kind,' Rowena said, 'he dragged himself up by his bootstraps, granted, working and studying hard, he paid for his own education, even took elocution lessons to eliminate his working-class diction. Then he met my mother – the daughter of a shipbuilder – and the rest, as they say, is history.'

Surely he will see you and Archie are as much in love as he must have been.'

'Yes, he would - if he had ever been in love with anyone or anything that was not attached to money and power,' Rowena offered, 'but, you see, what my father had was ambition. He wanted to build the Ashland empire – and he did – when my mother received her inheritance. That way he could afford to bury his past under accolades and triumphs.'

'I don't understand,' Mrs Swift replied, removing her coat and taking Rowena's, ready to put upstairs before making a pot of fresh tea.

'My father does not want to be reminded of where he came from, a child from the Liverpool slums. Not fit to lick the boots of a man like Archie.' Rowena removed her hat and handed it to Mrs Swift. 'The only person who knows where I am is my sister, May. I wrote and told her about my baby girl... I was not aware she had lost the child she was carrying.'

'You mean to tell me that Reverend Harrington has kidnapped your daughter?' Mrs Swift's face was devoid of all colour.

'Not kidnapped. No.' Rowena told her, 'May lost her baby, and was told by a renowned Harley Street gynaecologist that she would never carry another, after complications almost robbed her of her own life. Giles Harrington, her husband, "suggested" they take Eleanor and raise her as their own to prevent any kind of scandal.'

'Oh, you are such a poor, poor girl,' said Mrs Swift, 'that is no decision for a new mother to make.'

'It is not a decision I would ever make, and I told Giles Harrington so when he wrote to me with his ridiculous recommendation.' Rowena clung to the precious shawl as if her life depended upon it. 'According to Giles, Father said I had two choices, the first was to give up my daughter and allow him and my sister to bring her up as their own—.'

'—And the second choice?' Mrs Swift asked, hardly wanting to find out, knowing how ruthless and ambitious Silas Ashland could also be when he had a mind.

'The second choice was for my daughter to go into Saint

Simeon's Home for unwanted and orphaned children, from where she would be sent abroad, once old enough, and reared in another country, unaware of who her family were.'

'So, you agreed to let May bring her up?'

'I agreed no such thing,' said Rowena, 'Archie and I are moving to Liverpool. I have some money and jewellery I managed to collect when I left Ashland Hall. Archie has his savings. We will manage.'

When Archie arrived back a few hours later, his face was ashen with anger and helplessness.

'I can't fight your father,' he told Rowena. Archie took hold of Rowena's trembling shoulders. 'He holds all the cards my darling, you are under the age of consent, and he could have you committed into an asylum. He has that power.'

'I smell a conspiracy.' Rowena felt her insides churn, 'May would never think of such a thing alone, she does not have the gumption. No, I see Giles Harrington's hand in this. With no heir to speak of, how on earth will he convince father to leave everything to May.'

'Your father said if you marry me while he is alive, he will disinherit you, too.'

'Let him!' Rowena lifted her chin feeling a steeliness stiffen her backbone. 'I will marry you, one day, Archie. But not while he is alive. I will not give him the satisfaction of respectability. He will lie in his cold lonely bed at night and know his daughter is living in sin.'

1

CHRISTMAS EVE 1910

Dressed warmly against the raw morning chill, Ruby Swift caught the woman's quick birdlike movements from the corner of her eye and, recognising her instantly, she placed the delicate lace shawl into her bag. Pursing her generous lips, she sighed deeply. A few moments more. That's all she had wanted.

'Mrs Woods, why are you skulking outside my door at this early hour?' Ruby's tone was sharper than she intended as she watched Izzy Woods grip the thin grey wrap around scrawny shoulders and she surmised the garment offered little protection against the biting wind coming in off the River Mersey.

'G'morning, Mrs Swift.' Izzy's small eyes streamed, and she wiped away wind-tears with her threadbare sleeve, sniffing loudly as Ruby emerged from the shelter of the overhead railway to cross the cobbled Regent Road. 'I just come from morning mass and wanted to see if Uncle was opening earlier today. It being Christmas Eve an' all?'

Everybody round the proud but downtrodden parish of Saint Patrick the Apostle called her beloved Archie, *Uncle,* because he owned one of the most important establishments in the North end of Liverpool. The pawnshop.

'You are too early, Izzy.' Ruby stood stiffly, breathing in the inescapable smell of lumber from the timber yards at Canada Dock mingling with acrid smoke from household chimneys, nearby warehouses, and factories. 'Christmas Eve or not, Archie will not open the shop before he has eaten breakfast. He has a busy day ahead of him, as do all of us.'

Ruby's schoolmarm tone rose above the foghorn bellowing off the river, and she regretted her impatience.

The much-needed pawnshop was the first business Ruby, once known as Rowena, and Archie opened when they moved into the district twenty years ago. The answer to many a poor housewife's prayer in this close, working-class community of Liverpool; its teeming back-to-back houses and courts housing the descendants of Irish, Catholic families, who came to Liverpool after fleeing the 1847 potato famine and set up home near to their workplace at the dockside.

A fleeting memory of yesteryear softened the rigid line of Ruby's shoulders, and her stiff demeanour relaxed, lessening the air of authority her standing in the community afforded her. Poor Izzy looked perished in her faded shawl, and Ruby felt acutely self-conscious of the difference between them. Her thick woollen coat, with its grey pelt collar matching the fur Cossack-style hat amply covering her dark curls, was a substantial barrier to the winter weather, keeping the cold squall at bay, unlike Izzy's.

No doubt the woman crouching in the corner of the hock shop doorway, hugging a couple of cheap pottery dogs, would go back to a cold, overcrowded tenement, her cupboards bare, and little hope of filling them without a visit to *Uncle* for a loan. Izzy would offer her prized but worthless ornaments as surety of payment, and Ruby knew they had been in the pawnshop almost as often as Archie.

The mother of a growing brood, Izzy's indolent husband had energy for only two things – the first to go forth and multiply and the second being the drink. Izzy was a prime example of why Ruby's beloved suffragist society was calling for women's emancipation. Women should lead the life they desired, and not that dealt to them by an overbearing spouse. One day, Ruby strongly suspected, wives and daughters would be their own person. Not the chattels of the men who purported to love them. Izzy deserved better.

'Archie will open up as soon as he has eaten breakfast,' she repeated. Ruby's words were softer now, almost apologetic in tone, as the dock road bustled into life. Even at this early hour, horses' hooves clip-clopped along the icy cobbles, their wagons groaning under the weight of the world's produce, and Ruby noticed Izzy shrink further back in the doorway, when she heard a passing policeman bid good morning to the barber, butcher, or greengrocer, already trading.

'I was hoping to get to Paddy's market before it gets really busy,' Izzy said over the noise of rumbling handcarts and wagons that worked this main road to and from the docks, all day, every day.

Ruby nodded, her eyes narrowing as she listened, trying not to judge. The local market would be heaving with hard-pushed women on the lookout for a bargain to brighten their Christmas table and bring a bit of joy, even at this early hour when traders were still building their stalls.

'Y'know what it's like when you've got little'uns,' Izzy said, and she quickly slapped her hand across her open mouth and was silent for a moment. Her words tripping over each other when they finally came: 'Well, *you* don't know what it's like to have little'uns... Obviously... I was only saying... I didn't mean...'

'I know what you meant, Izzy.' Ruby's understanding tone assured the other woman her tactless comment had not given offence. She and Archie could not raise a child in a place like this. Not that she'd had a choice in the matter. Her father and the cleric saw to that. Unlucky enough not to raise a child of her own, she knew the locals would give their eye teeth to know the full story.

To the prolific breeders of the dock road, her private life beyond the counter of the Emporium was meat and gravy to the likes of Izzy Woods. Minding other people's business gave little time to worry about her own troubles. But Ruby knew this woman, old before her time like so many, had a lot on her plate. And it had nothing to do with food.

'I s'pose you'll be run off your feet in the Emporium today?' Izzy's voice carried an almost imperceptible shiver and Ruby doubted the poor woman would ever step foot over the double-door threshold of the Emporium.

Her own business, larger than the pawnshop, was Ruby's pride and joy. The expanding commerce did much the same for her middle-class clients as the pawnshop did for Izzy, and Ruby knew if Archie's establishment was the poor woman's saviour, then Ruby's Emporium was the haunt of so-called *better* classes feeling the pinch, under the guise of shopping for glittering crystal or refined porcelain tableware – some of which had been brought from all corners of the world by hard-up mariners looking for a quick sale.

'I wanted to get to the market early before Mr Woods rises from his pit.' Izzy repeated while Ruby surmised, not without a stab of pity, he would sink Izzy's borrowed money into every alehouse along the dock road, given the chance.

Having lived and worked on the portside since she was eighteen years old, Ruby had spent the last twenty years getting to know every one of its inhabitants. But none of them knew the real her. The only people who knew were Archie, and Emma Cassidy, her loyal assistant who worked on the accounts of middle-class debtors in the Emporium's back office. A discreet cover for well-dressed businessmen who lived beyond their means.

Ruby's upper-class clients were selected only on recommendation. After the initial interview, Ruby offered the support that would save their good name, their business, or their marriage. With interest, of course.

A shrewd businesswoman, Ruby jumped at the opportunity to grow her business when a well-dressed young man had enquired if she offered loans. *Only on quality goods*, she quipped. The next day he had brought in a breathtaking Capodimonte vase, pledging it against a loan. She did not hesitate.

She gave the Capodimonte vase pride of place in the window, so Young Buck could see it every day from the carriage window as he made his way to the office. His repayment was never late, and Ruby could only imagine his beloved wife's gasp of delight when he presented it to her, *straight from the menders*, along with another fine piece on the day he paid off the advance of his loan.

And so, began one of the most discreet and lucrative loan companies operating under the guise of quality goods being sold at knock-down prices. Business boomed.

The overhead train approaching from Seaforth Sands ran towards Dingle in the south of Liverpool, giving passengers a clear sighting of the bustling docks on one side, and on the other, a bird's-eye view of the large double windows of her store, showing a fabulous array of expensive, cut-priced fancy-goods, which claimed the avaricious regard of young ladder-climbers who would rest their gaze on a previously selected piece, which could be bought on the never-never.

Paying off a little each week on a set of finest crystal goblets or the best china money could buy, the young office manager out for promotion, would not be ashamed to invite the boss and his good lady wife to dine. Even though he had insufficient wherewithal to do so. Discretion was Ruby's valuable stock-in-trade.

For the last eighteen years, she had put the vase back in the window many times. Sometimes, late payments inevitably meant the inability to pay the debt, and one of the more discerning, well-heeled members of the community would give pride of place to an exquisite piece of porcelain in her own windows by purchasing it, something poor Izzy would never be able to afford to do.

Ruby noticed the lingering look of hunger on Izzy's face as a fishmonger trundled his handcart through the damp air to set up his stall, while drovers moved cattle from docked ships to slaughterhouse, to butcher's shops and market stalls on this busiest day of the year.

When the day dawned fully, the road would be alive with dockers, riggers, shipwrights and scalers, carters, draymen, and trams. The local bobbies would pound their beat, immigrants would wander in a daze, looking for a cheap boarding house, and whores would hang off sailor's burly arms as they zigzagged their way from one alehouse to another, while hard-pressed housewives like Izzy did their best to make ends meet and hummed carols while the Salvation Army shook their tambourine, inviting one and all to *Rest ye merry gentlemen*.

'You'll catch your death hanging round here in this weather,' Ruby said as the pewter clouds, pregnant with the promise of snow, opened to release the first floating white flakes of the season.

'I might as well stay, now I'm here,' Izzy sounded deflated, her eyes dull watching all walks of life concentrate the seven-mile spine of the dock road and pass her by.

Another foghorn sounded on the river as the morning haze cloaked the Mersey and Ruby saw Izzy shiver uncontrollably – the woollen shawl she wore incapable of keeping out a draught, let alone the swirling blizzard to come – and she had a flush of Christmas spirit.

Opening the flap of her tooled-leather bag that held the whisper-soft shawl Ruby had fashioned with a crochet hook all those years ago, she drew out a crisp ten-shilling note and, looking right then left, she slipped the money into Izzy's cold, work-worn hand.

'Take this,' Ruby said, ignoring the gasp and startled look in Izzy's dark eyes. 'Tell nobody, you hear me? I don't want people to think I've gone lax.'

'Oh, Miss Ruby!'

Ruby watched the worry fade from Izzy's eyes, to be replaced with a tenderness that smoothed her prematurely lined face and Ruby's back stiffened. She was not known as a soft touch round here. But she knew what it was like to go without. By God, she did.

'I don't know how to thank you.' Izzy clutched the money tight to her shrunken bosom. And Ruby had a notion that nobody in their right mind would try to relieve her of the note if they valued their eyes.

'Keep that lad of yours under control. That's all I ask,' Ruby said, knowing Jerky Woods was a tearaway who would turn feral if he wasn't taken in hand. 'I saw him levering the cover off a grid round Queen Street last night.'

A cloud crossed Izzy's face and Ruby knew the lad was a wrong'un. But who could wonder when he had such a lazy article of a father?

'I can't do a thing with him.' Izzy wrung her hands, careful not to drop the money. The bunched skin round her eyes returned, her expression pained. 'He doesn't listen to a word I say. The only thing he understands is a belt round the ear'ole from his faader.'

'The boy needs encouragement, not a whipping. A steady hand.' Young Woods had no such person. No hard-working guardian he could emulate. Like Ned who looked up to Archie. Ruby felt heart-sorry for the woman who had reached a dead end with her eldest son. 'We'll say no more on the matter.' Ruby sighed, not wanting to take the good out of the money by bemoaning a woman already beaten. 'I hope you have a good Christmas, Izzy.'

'The same to you, Mrs Swift. God Bless you.'

'If we all had God's blessing,' Ruby threw the words over her shoulder as she headed to the discreet side door that ensured the customers of the pawnshop never met the clients of the Emporium and which led to the huge expanse of living quarters above, 'I doubt you would stand here waiting for the pawnshop to open, and I would be out of business.' Pushing the key into the shiny brass lock, she saw Izzy hurry in the direction of Paddy's market, eager to find a bit of Christmas cheer for her brood.

Once inside, Ruby did not take the stairs to the upper living quarters. Instead, she opened the door to the office at the back of the Emporium, went in and closed the door softly behind her as she walked through to the store.

Taking the cloud of ivory lace from her bag, she held the delicate shawl to her face, inhaling deeply. Imagining she could still capture that elusive fragrance. Whilst thrusting the memory of that other terrible Christmas Eve to the back of her mind, she placed the shawl on the glass shelf with reverential calm. Smoothing down the fine edging. Arranging the scalloped hem so it sat exactly right in the glass cabinet beside the till.

Something she had done every year since she opened the business.

There had been many enquiries about the shawl, but Ruby would never dream of parting with it. Telling the customers, they could have the clothes off her back. But the shawl was not for sale.

* * *

Entering the dining room in the spacious flat spread over two businesses below, the Emporium and the pawnshop, Ruby could see Archie was already seated, reading the morning newspaper whilst waiting for her to join him. A restrained Yorkshireman, Archie was disinclined to show his loving feelings in front of the staff, but Ruby knew her soft-hearted other half loved her as much today as he did all those years ago when her father took him on as his stable manager. Not that her father, the great Silas Ashland, would allow such a match. But his opinion was of no consequence any more.

'Good walk?' Archie asked as Mrs Hughes, the housekeeper, brought in a tray laden with breakfast accoutrements and Ruby nodded, swallowing hard, not yet able to speak as she sat down.

Every Christmas Eve, she walked alone to the Pier Head. She looked across the river to the place where her father had built his shipping empire. And every year, she took out the shawl, holding it close to her heart. Vowing that one day she would take the garment, the symbol of all she held dear, to her father. And she would show him all she had achieved without his help.

Archie silently reached for her hand in that unspoken understanding way they both had, and Ruby was contented. That small gesture told her all she wanted to know. They still had, and always would have, that unshakeable, impermeable bond.

'There is a mist on the river this morning,' Ruby said as unshed tears collected at the rim of her eyes, and she blinked them away. 'So, there wasn't much to see.'

'I'm glad,' Archie said, smiling to Mrs Hughes as she was about to leave the room. When the door clicked shut, he got up, went over to Ruby's chair, and kissed her, long and deep. 'I am so sorry we were not there that day. Things would have been so different if *I* had.'

'It wasn't your fault, Archie,' Ruby answered, knowing the subject came up every Christmas Eve. And was as painful today as it had been all those years ago. 'The blame lies at the door of my sister and that hard-faced cleric she married.' Pushing away her plate, unable to eat the breakfast feast Mrs Hughes had prepared, Ruby was certain she could not swallow a morsel.

'It is going to be a long day. You have to eat something,' Archie said, 'this is our busiest day of the year.' His troubled gaze never left her face, and Ruby gave him a reassuring smile.

'I am more robust than you give me credit for, Archie,' Ruby said. A signal to close the subject of their past and calm him. Their day would continue as it always did, busy and productive. 'Has Emma not arrived yet?' She decided she would try a piece of toast when Archie shook his head. 'That's unusual. She is never late.'

2

'Oh Mam!' sixteen-year-old Anna Cassidy cried as she rose from the table, leaving her two young brothers to finish their breakfast of porridge oats. 'What happened?' Anna hurried across the cosy room to the door where her mother, Emma, was limping badly and helped her to a stout brown leather chair near the fireside in the front room.

'I was on my way to the Emporium,' Emma told her daughter, 'I hadn't gone far, picking my way along the road as the gas lamp was out again. I didn't see the cover had been dislodged from the grid.' Emma winced in pain as Anna lowered her into the chair. 'I tripped over the iron cover, giving my ankle a nasty twist.' Surveying the damage in the firelight, Emma said, 'I doubt I'll be able to get to the Emporium today.' Her voice full of trepidation, she added, 'Today is payday and there is still shopping left to do for Christmas.'

'Don't you worry about that now, Mam,' Anna said, dragging the three-legged stool across the rag rug in front of the fire, 'we'll sort something out. You rest your leg on this.' She looked at her mother's ankle, which was already swollen to twice the normal size. 'It's going to be black and blue, Mam, you may have broken a bone.' Generous as the Swifts were with her mother's pay, in recognition of the responsible position she held, Anna knew this day's wages were needed if they were to have any kind of Christmas joy tomorrow. 'I'll take you to the Northern Hospital and let them have a look at it.'

'Great Howard Street is not far, I know, but I doubt I could walk even that short distance,' Emma said as daylight streamed through the window and brought her curious young sons from the breakfast table and into the front room of the terraced house that came with their mother's job. 'Just get me a cold cloth and I'll rest my leg.'

'It might do the trick to lessen the swelling,' said Anna, wanting to take the worry from the eyes of her young brothers, copper-haired James, and dark-haired Michael. Five-year old twins, who looked nothing like each other.

Hurrying to the scullery, she soaked a cloth under the cold copper tap before lighting the gas stove and making her mother a hot cup of tea, adding a little sugar for the shock. Anna went back to the front room, where her two brothers were huddled at their mother's feet in front of the blazing fire.

'I'm sorry to put you to all this trouble, Anna, love,' Emma said when Anna gently wrapped the cold cloth round her swollen ankle, 'you've got enough to do looking after the twins, without having to see to me as well.' Allowing a gentle sigh to escape her lips, she quickly glanced towards the arched wooden clock on the high mantlepiece. 'I've never been late in all the years I have worked for Ruby.'

'Mrs Swift will know something is wrong,' Anna said, knowing proud principles had stood her mother in good stead with Ruby Swift. Her mother's complexion had turned quite pale, and unshed tears glistened in her eyes. 'It's not your fault, Mam,' Anna's voice was soothing, 'I'll go along and tell the Missus what's happened.'

'Christmas Eve is ever so busy,' Emma said, as a worried frown creased her forehead. 'I can't let Ruby down today.'

'Don't give it another thought, Mam, I will take over your work if the Missus will allow it.' Anna knew Ruby was a canny, book-smart businesswoman. But so was she. A competent assistant at the twins' school, training to become a schoolteacher after being told she had the capability and proficiency. Her work ethic inherited from her hard-working mother who had gone out to earn a living for as long as she could remember. Mam had been working for Ruby Swift since Anna was a child on her hip. In the days when her father was away at sea, money was scarce, and nothing changed when he was killed after his ship sank. 'I will take over your duties today, please don't worry.'

'I knew that clever brain of yours would come in handy.' Emma gave a feeble smile and winced when Anna gently slid a cushion under her leg to make her more comfortable.

'Most certainly,' Anna said, knowing she had been fortunate to pass the matriculation examination to enable her to go to a good school, as had Sam, her twelve-year-old brother, and having finished her learning, Anna had been lucky enough to secure a position in the infant school her twin brothers attended. 'I'll call Sam,' Anna added, knowing her brother found getting out of a warm bed on a cold morning a bit of an unnecessary test of his obliging nature. 'He'll want to help in a situation like this.'

'I should have been more careful where I put my feet,' Emma told her daughter, who was putting a bowl of porridge on the table for Sam, after calling him from his bed. 'The street lamp was out, and I couldn't see the obstacle.'

'It is not your fault, Mam, I saw tearaways dislodging the

cover. Drink your tea while it is hot.' Anna had seen Jerky Woods and his cohorts interfering with the grid only the previous evening.

'You're a good girl, Anna,' Emma said, picking up her cup from the saucer. 'I don't know what I'd do without you and Sam. You are both clever and I do not want either of you going into service or serving behind a shop counter. I've got high hopes for both of you.'

Anna knew her mother had done her best for her four children, making sure they were respectable and all well-dressed and perfectly groomed, even if their clothes were bought second-hand from Ruby's Emporium. 'I'll go and let the Missus know what's happened, Mam,' Anna said, fastening her black button boots.

'I've to get the business takings into the bank before it closes,' Emma said, watching her daughter fasten the buttons on her good-quality jacket before pulling on a matching sage green tam-o'-shanter hat and marvelling at how efficient Anna was. 'Ruby won't want huge sums of money hanging round all over the place at Christmas.'

Anna looked to her young brothers before saying to her mother in a low whisper, 'Don't fret, Mam. I know you've been squirreling presents away for the boys, but I'll call into the market for the stocking treats after taking the money to the bank.'

'I wish you didn't have to go, you've enough to do.' Emma nodded to her five-year old twin boys, their thick shock of hair so like their older brother's, who were happily playing on the rag rug in front of the fire, oblivious to the complications unfolding round them.

'We all muck in together, Mam, that's our way,' Anna reassured her mother, who winced in pain when she moved her foot.

'I know you'd never ask anybody to do something you could do yourself.'

'I'm lucky to have four wonderful children,' Emma's marine-coloured eyes softened, and Anna, so like her mother, smiled.

'We may only have one parent, but we've never missed out on anything, especially love and care.'

'Be off with you,' her mother's cheeks grew pink and she dismissed Anna's sentimental observations with a wave of her hand. Then, she offered her daughter a pensive smile. Anna shared the same feelings when her mother's voice thickened with emotion. 'I wish things could be different, don't you?

'Pa would be so proud of you,' Anna said, knowing her mam missed her seafaring husband as much today as she did when they lost him five years ago, just before the twins were born. Then, Anna said briskly, 'I'll tell the landlord about that broken gaslight on the way to Ruby's. It should have been fixed ages ago.'

'You're a good girl, Anna.' With trembling hands, her mother sipped the hot tea, 'I do so hate to be a burden.'

'You are not a burden, Mam,' Anna gave her mother a reassuring smile.

'The turkey has been ordered—'

'—I'll call in to the butcher after I've taken the money to the bank,' Anna cut in. If she did not get a move on, she would never be able to catch up on all her chores.

'Please be careful carrying all that money – especially today.'

'I can look after myself if need be, Mam,' Anna tried to ease her mother's worry. 'Christmas brings out the best in most people and brings out the worst in some, but don't worry. Our Sam will help me.' She nodded to her twelve-year-old brother at her side, her greatest ally. 'He can pop into the doctor and ask him to come and have a look at your leg, while I go and see the Missus.' Anna wished she could take away her mother's evident pain.

'Indeed, you will not!' Emma's eyes widened. 'We will not be wasting good money on doctors. If you feel so strongly that I might need something, call into the apothecary, he'll give you a bottle of embrocation.'

Looking at the obvious swelling, Anna was not sure rubbing liquid would be enough to ease her mother's pain. However, she would not go against her wishes.

'I'll call into the fried fish shop on the way back.' Anna saw her brothers' expressions brighten at the rare treat.

'Oh yes,' Emma agreed, 'we'll have a nice bit of cod and some of those fried potatoes you young ones like so much.'

Anna knew her mother never wasted money on what she called 'lazy food', preferring, instead, to use hard-earned money on fresh ingredients. A wonderful cook, her mother made delicious meals from almost nothing and had taught her to do the same. 'You rest your leg, Ma, and boys...'

The twins looked up from their game of wooden, dolly-peg soldiers, whose battles were played out on the rag rug in front of the fire.

'Would you like to make paper chains and lanterns to decorate the ceiling?'

The twins gave a whoop of delight, nodding vigorously.

'I'll bring some coloured paper from the market. But you must look after Mama, be good and don't make a noise.'

Again, they nodded, assuring Anna they would be on their best behaviour.

'I'd better get a move on,' Anna said, 'I'll be back as quick as I can.'

* * *

Ruby lifted her head to see Mrs Hughes, the housekeeper, hovering near the door.

'I am sorry to disturb your breakfast, Mrs Swift,' Mrs Hughes's stiff tone told Ruby she had been inconvenienced, 'and I did tell her you were eating, but she says it's urgent.'

'Who is it, Mrs Hughes?' Ruby asked, and when the housekeeper said it was Anna Cassidy, she nodded. 'Show her in.' Ruby didn't mind eating breakfast in front of the daughter of her long-time employee, but her smile faded when sixteen- year-old Anna sidled apologetically into the room.

'I am so sorry to interrupt your breakfast, Madam.' Anna had never been privy to Ruby's living arrangements, and she felt uncomfortable, out of place, in the quiet opulence of brilliant white plasterwork framing the pale blue walls. How does anybody keep the woodwork so white in this mucky area, she thought, before realising she had not told Ruby why she was here. 'The thing is, Ma had a bad fall. Her ankle is very swollen.'

'Oh dear, that is bad news, especially today.' Ruby stopped eating, her mind working fast. There were several important accounts that needed Emma's attention today, which Ruby could not attend to, as the Emporium would be so busy.

'I can take over her duties in the office, if you wish, Madam,' Ruby's pause spurred Anna on, 'so you won't be inconvenienced.'

Her efficient manner told Ruby she was a confident, articulate girl who would be extremely helpful. 'I know Emma would not leave me in the lurch, especially on Christmas Eve.'

Nor forgo a day's wages. Anna kept that last bit of information to herself as she tried to keep her eyes from straying to the delicious food, reminding her she had not yet eaten. Instead, she concentrated on the luxurious pale damask curtains draped at the bay windows, a backdrop to the seven-foot spruce that filled the air with its exquisite pine perfume. Who could imagine such grandeur only yards from the bustling Mersey docks?

'Won't you sit down and have something to eat, a cup of tea?' Ruby asked, and Anna shook her head. 'I'm sorry to hear poor Emma is injured.' Obviously, the family would be dependent on her wages. But they were a proud family, never asking anybody for handouts, unlike some of their so-called betters, but she would ask anyway: 'Is there anything we can do?' She glanced across the table to Archie, who nodded.

'No, thank you, Madam, I have everything in hand.' Anna knew Ruby liked to be thought of as a tough businesswoman, but she was devoted to those who were loyal to her. Anna's heart beat a little faster.

Ruby knew that the family needed every penny, and to lose a day's pay would be a big disappointment to Emma on Christmas Eve. Her shapely eyebrows knitted together, and she was thoughtful for a moment. The office accounts would have to wait until after Christmas.

Without a doubt, the girl was intelligent enough to take on the accounts. Emma had worked hard to make sure her daughter received a good education. Nevertheless, discretion was the key to her success. Ruby knew she must abide by her promise of confidentiality to her clients. However, she knew Anna could be trusted to collect the rents.

'The outstanding rents must be collected, otherwise the tenants will think they have been given a Christmas bonus they could only dream of.' Ruby poured more tea into her cup. 'Do you think you could manage that?'

Anna nodded. She would do anything if it meant securing the day's wage for her mother.

'It might be Christmas Eve, but it is also Saturday. Ned and Archie never miss the football match and won't be able to collect rents this afternoon.' In the four years the seventeen-year-old had shared their home, Ned had brought much laughter and fun and was a steadfast supporter of Liverpool football club, while Archie was a dedicated disciple of the team across Stanley park at Everton. Each week, they went to the home game on match days, regardless of which team they supported. Unable to travel to away games because of working in the pawnshop.

'Our Sam will help me with collections,' Anna proclaimed with a smile, relieved she would be able to take the day's wages home to her mother, 'he will be my bodyguard.'

'In that case, here are the morning's collections.' Ruby gave Anna a leather bag containing a notebook of addresses and she secured the long strap across her body so it could not be snatched by any hoodlums on the make for Christmas.

Ruby and Archie had many business interests, Anna knew. Proof of what hard work and long hours could achieve, knowing when they came to the dockside, they had nothing.

'You are quite sure you don't mind taking over until your mother is better?'

Anna shook her head, knowing since her father died, her ma had not had it easy. She was the head of the family. Sam earned a few coppers here and there, usually carrying bags and boxes for a copper or two, while Anna earned a pittance, working at the school. And although Ma earned enough to keep her family fed and warm, there wasn't much left over for luxuries. However, their seemingly comfortable lifestyle brought out the green-eyed monster in some of the inhabitants of Queen Street, especially their next-door neighbour.

'I will do whatever is needed of me,' Anna said as the door opened and Ned Kincaid came into the room and nodded a greeting. The orphaned son of a gypsy fist fighter, Ned was taken under the wing of Ruby and Archie when his pa died in tragic circumstances.

Ruby caught the flash of surprise in Ned's blue eyes, aware of the creeping flush spreading across his strong neck. That meant only one thing, she thought, and Anna was the only person who had that effect on him.

'Hello, Ned,' Anna said brightly. But he just gave a fleeting smile, unusually quiet. And Anna wondered if, since he moved from the tenements where they had been neighbours, and she had moved to Queen Street, they'd naturally drifted apart from the childhood friends they had always been.

'When you've collected each rent, enter it into the book,' Ruby said, filling in the silence. 'Don't forget to sign your name.'

'Yes, Ma'am.' She had seen her mother do that when she had accompanied her years ago.

'Take no hard-luck stories,' Ruby ordered, 'there will be some who will try to wriggle out of paying – oh, and don't take a drink off anybody.'

'A drink?' Anna asked, her eyebrows pleating in confusion. 'What kind of drink?'

'Alcoholic,' Ruby told her. 'Some will engage you in conversation, ply you with eggnog or spiced rum, and before you know it, you have wished them all the best and left without collecting the money.' She tapped her nose with her forefinger, 'You've got to get up incredibly early to get one over on Ruby Swift. So be warned.'

'I consider myself warned,' Anna smiled, confident in her own worth when she caught the glimmer of a smile on Ruby's lips.

'Your mother usually does the accounts after collections. But, as it is Christmas Eve, we shall leave the accountancy work until we reopen.' Ruby liked the girl, who, some would say, had her head screwed on the right way. Anna's feisty nature reminded her of the girl she once was. 'Ned would usually accompany your mother to collect the rents, but the pawnshop is at its busiest on Christmas Eve.'

'And we can't forget the football match.' Anna gave a wry smile, knowing most men would go without a meal before they would miss the precious three-o-clock kick-off. 'I know every nook and cranny of the dockside. What is there to worry about?'

3

After collecting the morning's rents, Anna went to the apothecary for a bottle of embrocation for her mother and then to the fish and chip shop before hurrying home. She told her ma she was going to take over her duties until her leg was better, which was a blessed relief.

This afternoon she would go into the town centre to collect the business rents. Then after picking up Ma's wages, she would go to the market on the way home and buy the fruit, veg and meat for tomorrow. Ma had also reminded her to pick up treats for the twins to open in the morning. Knowing they would have money coming in put her mother's mind at rest and Anna liked being useful. They were in no position to lose a full day's wages, especially at Christmastime.

'Sam, do you think you could give me a hand to collect the rents this afternoon?' Anna asked before draining her teacup and collecting the empty plates from the table.

'Aye,' twelve-year-old Sam, more mature than his years, being the oldest male in the house, felt it was his duty to escort his sister, 'I've got to go into town, as well.' He gave a secretive smile, and Anna knew he had been saving hard for a Christmas present for Ma, and he had been looking forward to picking it up today. 'I will meet you at the Goree Piazza later,' Sam said as he went out of the door.

Anna removed the burgundy chenille tablecloth and spread last night's *Evening Mercury* on the bare wooden table so that James and Michael would be gainfully distracted making the Christmas decorations while Ma rested. She had bought brightly coloured paper with a few coppers her ma gave her that morning and cut the paper into strips and squares to make paper chains, and lanterns that would festoon the ceiling in celebration of Christmas Day.

Anna was beginning to realise just how hard her mother worked every day to keep their home warm and cosy and their bellies full. Feeling grown-up and dependable, she knew her mother had no need to worry. She was going to do all the things that Ma usually did to make Christmas Day special. This was going to be a Christmas to remember.

'I won't be long,' Anna told the small, floppy-haired boys who looked to her now, 'be good.' She had no choice but to leave her little brothers. They might not have much in the way of luxuries, but they had each other. 'Keep that guard up to the fire,' she told Michael, the more adventurous of the two, who nodded his head. 'If you go near the fire, the Catcher will come for you.' Anna knew Michael was terrified of the bogeyman who was rumoured to take wayward children from their families and were never seen again. She felt confident the warning would prevent her inquisitive young brothers doing anything dangerous.

Taking one last look round the kitchen, she was satisfied to see the boys busying themselves making decorations, with the smell of a Christmas plum pudding steaming on the hob in readiness for tomorrow. Maybe it was not the fragrance of Ruby's beautiful pine Christmas tree, nor the fireplace bedecked with dark green holly and plump red berries. Nevertheless, Anna thought, inhaling the clean scent of polished furniture, mingled with the steaming plum pudding, it was their kind of Christmas fragrance.

Holding on to her hat, Anna gave her brothers and Ma a hug and a kiss before lifting the latch. 'I'll be back as quick as I can,' she said brightly.

Closing the door behind her, Anna lifted her navy-blue serge skirt and tore down the back yard. And as she was short of time, she would have to use the shortcut through Olden Passage to take the morning's takings to Ruby and collect the afternoon business list.

'*Come to me in my dreams and by day I shall be well again...*'

Anna's voice faltered as she recited the Matthew Arnold poem, which Ma taught her after Pa died. Cutting through the passageway, she picked over lopsided paving stones, sensing she was not alone, and for some unknown reason fear pricked her scalp. Her ears straining for the slightest sound as a shiver ran down her back.

'It's the middle of the day,' she told herself, the morning's takings weighing heavy in the collections bag, but no matter what time of day the passage gave her the heebie-jeebies. Young tearaways congregated at the turning, just out of sight.

'*...For then the night will pay the hopeless longing of the day.*' She could hear the slight quiver in her whispery voice, feeling anxious as the tinny refrain bounced and echoed off the sooty red-brick walls as her footsteps picked up a pace, wishing Sam had come with her, even if it was only for some much-needed moral support.

Her marine-coloured eyes – the same colour as her mother's –

fixed on her feet straddling the gutter as rain and other *pestiferous* fluids flowed down to the grid. Anna's heart thrummed in her throat as she rolled the long word *'pestiferous'* over her tongue. She heard it used by the health inspector who visited the school. A *pestiferous liability,* he called the teeming dockside streets that housed Irish Catholic refugees who came to Liverpool looking for work and spread like oil into every crevice.

Her wandering imagination could not stall dark thoughts of what might lie at the other end of the passage. She stopped humming. All was quiet. Too quiet. And what weak sunlight there had been was dipping behind heavy clouds as she approached the loneliest part of her journey that made the fine hair on the nape of her neck stand up, her whole body on red alert when Anna heard a rustling sound she did not recognise. Her body tensed, and fear trickled through her veins like iced water.

She was out of sight of the main road, but, in the middle of her journey, she could not stop now. She turned and Anna could hear the thudding of her own heartbeat. Fighting to quell the rising panic, she pulled up the collar of her coat and kept her head down not noticing a fleeting shadow slip behind an over-flowing bin ahead of her.

When she heard the rolling clatter of a galvanised dustbin lid, Anna spun round, stiffening her back when the deafening sound echoed through the passage near the railway lines. Her cautious pace slowed, but she did not stop. She was tempted to turn back. But there were shadows there, too.

Anna's wide, cautious eyes searched the gloom for the source of noise as her dry tongue slid over the roof of her mouth and she let out a small mirthless laugh, her legs weakening when a ragged black and white cat sprang into her path.

'Stupid bloody moggie,' she hissed, her voice brittle as it

bounced back along the glossy-wet walls, and once more Anna pulled her collar up, as much to feel the security of the material as for its warmth.

'*Come to me in my dreams...*' She tried to continue, but found she no longer had a voice for the beautiful verse, the words seeming to cave in on themselves when she heard another voice.

'Stupid bloody Moggie...' The male voice, thick with menace, came at her from the end of the passage and Anna recognised the guttural tone instantly. Her heart slamming against her ribcage, she saw more darting images flit across both ends of the passage. The shadows were intent on trapping her.

Her parched lips fell open, but no sound came and every nerve in her body screamed in protest when she saw the bulky figure of Jerky Woods blocking her path. Around the same age as herself, Anna knew he was trouble. She cast a glance behind her to see street urchins approaching, obviously looking for a bit of excitement. There was no way out.

Tucking a honey-coloured curl behind her ear, Anna knew she must show no fear. She clamped her lips between her teeth, stifling a scream.

Stay calm. You can do this, she thought, feeling her stomach lurch. 'Holy mother of God help me,' the whispered words slipped from her lips as Woods emerged from the shadows and headed towards her, shoulder-barging smaller ragamuffins out of his way.

The wintry air hung heavy with menace, and Anna backed up until the heel of her black buttoned boot caught the edge of the gutter and she stumbled as Woods lurched forward to grab her. In moments, he was pushing her against the cold brick wall, his paw-like hands groping her shoulders, her upper arms. His warm, sour breath smelled disgusting and she flinched, her skin crawling at his touch. She must do something. She could not let him steal the money she had worked so hard to collect, walking the length of the dock road, up and down streets.

Woods was renowned as a troublemaker, who thought nothing of stealing what he could and brawling in the street, especially after the alehouses closed and he had sunk a few with his idle wife-beating father.

'I have nothing for you,' she said, knowing he was after money – or worse. Lifting her chin, Anna did not disguise her contempt.

'Oh, but you have,' Woods said. His piggy eyes focused on the brown leather bag whilst stroking her arm.

Anna knew if she was to escape, she must do something quickly. Leaning back against the cold, wet wall, she had only one chance of getting out of this nightmare situation. And while he was concentrating on endeavours unholy, Anna drew back her right leg. And with more force than she would dream capable of, she pumped her knee hard into his groin.

Knowing the powerful impact brought instant results, Anna was relieved when he let her go, doubling up and gasping. And an innate sense of survival filled her with a resilience she did not know she possessed. Anna did not wait until he got his breath back to make her way out of the passage.

'Don't just stand there, you bloody eejits. Go after her!' Woods screeched at the ragamuffins who followed him wherever he went, but Anna was quick and made a dash to the exit. While ill-clad urchins scattered to the streets, obviously wary of being within striking distance, when Woods regained his equilibrium. 'Don't think you'll get away with this, you stuck-up bitch.' Woods's voice, raw with anger and pain followed Anna out of the passage. She knew Jerky Woods would not forget this humiliation in a hurry and she would need to watch her step over the coming days but at least she had hung on to the money.

'Go hang your balls on the Christmas tree!' Anna shouted, her fear turning to exhilaration that spurred her on. Until she realised, she may have to walk back the same way later, when it was dark.

4

Sam could see no sign of Anna at their meeting place at the Goree Piazza. From his shelter under the canopy of soot-covered Portland stone in the shadow of the White Star Line building, he paced, trying to distinguish Anna's breathless approach amid the clattering hooves of passing carthorses on the cobblestones. Shivering in the perishing wind blasting in from the River Mersey, Sam dare not linger, it was too cold to stand still. He had not noticed the cold when he had been running back and forth, hailing hansom cabs or carrying Christmas boxes to the ferry boats for refined passengers who lived on the other side of the river.

Where was she?

Chased from the doorway more than once, he took a peep through the window and noticed the clerk coming round the desk. *Here we go again*, he thought, knowing if he moved from their meeting place to make a few more Christmas coppers, he would miss Anna. And that was not good.

'Go and hang round the taverns,' the clerk said, pushing his way through the door, his voice as cold as poverty, 'you'll pick up something there, for sure.' The contempt in his tone was not lost, and Sam scowled. His ma would be disappointed to see him treated thus.

It was customary for world-weary sailors, who had completed a long trip, to hit every public house on the dock road to gain their land legs, only to lose them again when they were filled with strong ale. Everybody was their chum while they had a pocketful of brass, especially at Christmas. If a young lad were fast enough, he could catch the coppers thrown down for the entertainment of sailors, who enjoyed watching the scramble of bare-footed boys fighting for the last farthing.

'I'm waiting for my sister, Sir,' Sam said courteously, showing he had been brought up properly. Ma made sure her family was always respectable.

'That's what they all say,' the snooty clerk pushed Sam from the step and he fell to the pavement. 'Be off with you, you're making the place look untidy.' He dusted his hands and Sam could feel his temper rise. If he were a bit bigger, he would... he really would.

Dragging himself to his feet, Sam pulled up his collar against the glacial squall. Still no sign of Anna. Hugging his jacket round his body and thrusting his hands in his pockets, he headed towards Commutation Row.

His head bent against the eddying wind, Sam weaved his way through the mass of busy shoppers eager to get into the large, brightly lit shops out of the icy sleet that suddenly began to rain down. Looking over his shoulder, he peered into the distance. With no sign of Anna, he would go and pick up his ma's Christmas present he had saved all year to buy.

Christmas would not be the same now Ma was off her feet, he thought. But his gift might go some way to bring a smile to her face and cheer her up. He imagined the look of surprise when she opened her gift, the thought spurring him on as he cut down Castle Street.

Aided by a strong wind at his back, he ran the length of Dale Street and on to Old Haymarket, racing through the grounds of St George's Hall, nipping between horse and carriages to the little jeweller's shop in Commutation Row just as the bell of a church clock struck the hour.

Blowing for tugs, Sam rested for a while on the door jamb, catching his breath. He was glad to see the shop was empty when he entered the dark interior and, proudly, placed the silver sixpence on the high counter. His last payment.

Every week since last January, he had completed many little jobs and ran hundreds of errands to scrape enough money to meet the weekly sixpenny instalments. He had saved enough money to pay off the silver locket and would have some left to give Anna, who could stretch a penny 'til it screamed. Especially when she went along to Cazneau Street Market and purchased the biggest, shiniest red apples.

Anna could charm even the frostiest stallholders with her open, happy smile and chirpy conversation, cheering the jaded traders who toiled from dawn 'til midnight. She might even manage to buy a small tree. And tangerines. His mouth was salivating at the thought. And some nuts for the little 'uns' stockings. A slap-up Christmas dinner would brighten everybody's day a treat. They would make it a Christmas they would never forget.

His mind was miles away as he waited for Mr Solomon to come out to the shop from his sitting room at the back. Letting out a contented sigh, Sam watched Mr Solomon shuffle in. Before he reached the counter, Mr Solomon slapped his forehead with the palm of his hand, turned round and shuffled into the back again, and Sam smiled, proud of the fact he had saved every farthing he earned, just for this moment. Returning, the old man waved a slim box in the air triumphantly.

'Here you are, young Sammy.' White-haired and bent like a question mark, he placed the box on the glass counter. Mr Solomon had worked in the darkened interior since he was a young boy, and Sam knew he was the only merchant who would allow a little tyke like him onto his premises. 'One man's money is as good as any other,' Mr Solomon announced as he opened the box and reverently tipped the contents into his tapered hand.

Sam's eyes dazzled at the striking silver heart-shaped locket. The pendant was obviously held in high regard by Mr Solomon, who placed it gently on the counter for Sam to inspect and admire it.

'For you, Sam, you are a good boy, and your mother will be so proud, Shalom.'

Sam's breath caught in his throat as he watched the silver chain coil round the old man's arthritic fingers, and his heart swelled so much he could hardly breathe. He could not wait to see Ma's face when she saw it, knowing she deserved to wear wonderful things.

'I will put it in a luxury box for you, my boy.' Mr Solomon smiled, and when he saw Sam's worried expression, he waved his hand as if swatting a fly and said, 'No charge. It is Christmas, after all.'

'Cor thanks, Mr Solomon.' Sam's eyes were wide as he watched the old man expertly arrange the pendant onto a white silk cushion. The inside of the pale blue leather lid was adorned with the same material. *Abraham Solomon High Class Watchmaker and Goldsmith* was written in swirling gold lettering, giving an added touch of opulence. This locket, in a magnificent box, was even fit for the new King's wife. So, it was good enough for his ma.

Securing the treasure into the waistband of his trousers, Sam patted his pockets. In his left was the money he had collected from carrying parcels to and from the ferries. And in his right, was the money to buy the twins some sugar mice.

Wishing Mr Solomon, the happiest of Christmases, Sam made his way to the door. Stopping outside as the old man locked it behind him, he heard a familiar, raucous chant and felt the hairs on the back of his neck stand on end. As if from nowhere, Jerky Woods stood head and shoulders over him, pushing him towards the busy main road.

'What ya doin' in there, Cassidy?' Woods demanded. 'This aint no place for the like's o' you.'

Sam did not have a ready answer, but he knew he had to protect himself, the money, and the locket. He had worked hard all year for this day. And he was not going to allow this thug to come along and steal it from him.

Sam did not see the first thump coming, but he certainly felt it... Fortunately, the attack did not last long, as Mr Solomon came out of his shop wielding a broom and chased the laughing bullies away. But it was too late for Sam when Jerky Woods and his mindless crew went up the street jeering, in possession of Sam's money. At least he had put up a fight and, slippery as an eel, he managed to secure the locket. Gingerly he touched his rapidly closing eye and felt the jelly-like swelling, grateful for Mr Solomon's fearless intervention.

'You come inside, and Mrs Solomon will patch you up, good and proper.'

* * *

Battling the wind-whipped corner of James Street and the Strand, Anna's eyes strained to catch a glimpse of her younger brother. Even in knitted mittens she had to lock her icy hands under her arms for warmth. To keep the blood running through her, she paced back and forth, gaining no comfort as the wintry sky darkened to the ebbing peel of the town-hall clock. It was growing dark and, shivering now, she felt the frozen air bleed into her bones. She had to keep moving to stop the vicious west wind slicing through her.

A deceptively delicate-looking girl, Anna's worried eyes scanned the hectic thoroughfare, as busy workers from the nearby offices passed her with barely a glance. Their heads bent against the arctic blast, they were wrapped warmly in good heavy woollen coats, hurrying to the warmth of their fireside. Likely as not, looking forward to some Christmas cheer.

If Sam had gone home, she had nobody to blame but herself. Angry tears threatened now, she wanted to bring good cheer to her ma and the two little ones. But if she did not get the money to Ruby before the bank closed... She began to pace again.

Unfurling a clasped hand from the scant warmth of her shivering body, Anna watched an old man light the gas mantle in the street lamp. And urging herself to feel optimistic, she was glad to see a golden halo of radiance light the icy drizzle. Anna wondered where young Sam could be. She had finished collecting the rent money and had been back here a few times, but there had been no sign of him.

'It's not like him to be late,' she muttered. Even though the glowing lamps looked cheery, she felt no comfort, nor even when the Salvation Army banged their drums and rattled their tambourines. Anna said a little prayer, although not for the baby boy whose birthday would be celebrated all over the world tomorrow. Her heartfelt supplications were for the safe arrival of her brother, and the need to get the money back to Ruby.

In the gloomy shadows of the shipping office opposite the River Mersey, she sighed, and a plume of white haze left her cold blue lips. The streets shrouded in a pall of smoking chimneys, while street traders, chestnut sellers, and hot-potato men competed to sell the last of their wares. No doubt eager for the warmth of their own home, as was she.

The music of the hurdy-gurdy in the distance brought no joy, as it usually would, and just along the road she saw the door of The Grapes public house open to release the smoky, boozy calls of intoxicated people within.

She could not tell how long she waited for Sam to arrive. Nevertheless, it was long enough for desperation to force her feet towards the centre of town and turn fearful hot tears to icy ripples. Something must have happened to him. Terrible images filled her mind. Even humble men grew desperate when cold empty bellies needed feeding, and Sam was an easy target. She shuddered.

Heading towards Preeson's Row, the street running along the line of the old castle ditch, Anna reached the bottom of James Street and she caught the plaintive signal of a departing train with dread weighing heavy in her heart. Then, as the whistle died away, she heard substantial boots competing with the clip-clop of horse's hooves that vied with the low rumble of handcart wheels crisscrossing the wet cobbled road.

In the shadow of Queen Victoria's monument, Anna turned. She took one look at her younger brother and gasped. Her heart going out to him when she saw his bruised and battered face. Huddled low in the confines of his jacket.

'Who blacked your eye?' she asked, forgetting the freezing air eddying up from the river.

'Anna,' Sam gasped, hardly able to get his words out, 'thank heaven, you're still 'ere.'

'What happened?' Cupping her brother's marble-cold face in her hands, Anna's fears were realised. 'I knew something like this would happen,' she cried, 'I was so worried.' She wrapped her arms round his shoulders, and he shrugged off her sisterly devotion, his own voice shaky but determined.

'I was attacked – and robbed.' He was obviously angry, kicking a discarded wooden orange box that flew, hit a shop wall with a dull thud and smashed to smithereens.

'Oh no. I knew it. I knew it.' Anna could not bear to think that the present he had worked so hard and saved for was now in the hands of an unscrupulous, cold-hearted thief.

'It was that bugger, Woods,' Sam said between gritted teeth.

'Jerky Woods.' Anna recalled her own run-in with him earlier. She leaned back under the lamplight to get a better look. Sam had a shiner all right. 'Are you all right?' she asked. Her first concern was for her brother. Although her distress about the robbery came a close second.

'Don't worry, Anna,' Sam moved from the confines of her arms and said in a deep voice, 'but he did get some of the money.'

'How much?' Anna's hands flew to her mouth to restrain the anguished gasp. He had worked so hard to save enough money for Christmas.

'He didn't get all of it.' Sam sounded jubilant.

Small he might be, but he was strong. He had to be. Living in the tough dockside streets, she knew that most of the people, poor as they were, still strived for God-fearing respectability.

Sam explained that he still had some of the Christmas tips…

'But we haven't got none spare now,' his voice was filled with disappointment.

'Haven't got *any* spare,' Anna corrected him, then assured him that it did not matter. Silently she vowed to find Jerky Woods and get back what was rightfully theirs. 'Sam, don't worry, we'll manage,' Anna felt their blessings must still be counted, 'Ma won't mind going without a present, as long as you are safe. He could have killed you.'

'I'm too smart for that,' Sam announced proudly, and gave her a little dig in the arm with his elbow. 'What d'you take me for, Anna?' Sam, full of the brotherly love he rarely voiced, managed a half-hearted laugh. 'I got a dig at his nose,' Sam said proudly, 'I weren't gonna let him flatten me without a fight... And Mr Solomon came with his broom, and scattered the lot of them.'

'Mr Solomon?' Anna asked, her face wreathed in concern, but Sam did not answer, and she knew he would say nothing until he was ready. 'As long as you don't run yourself into the main Bridewell,' she conceded, wanting to hug him and tell him everything would be all right and knowing he would never allow such a thing. Instead, she laughed and ruffled his thatch of dark brown hair, knowing he would scoff at any show of affection.

'Look,' Sam said, impatiently plastering his thick hair to his head and replacing his cap, 'I know collecting money is dangerous, 'specially today, and I'm sorry I was late meeting you, but I was in a bit of a bad way after the beating, and Mr Solomon took me to his wife, who insisted I wait until I was feeling a bit better. It took longer than I expected, that's all.' He put up his hand to quieten her obvious interruption. 'It's you I feel sorry for, carrying money round the dock road is perilous at any time of the year, not just Christmas. Ma did it, and now you've done it.' Sam gave a shake of his head. 'I was worried sick about you.'

'Aye, maybe,' Anna said. She had not thought of the situation like that before. Then, the mood changed when Sam motioned for her to follow him.

'I've got something to show you, but not here, being robbed once today was one time too many.'

Confused, Anna followed him, as he weaved his way through a warren of narrow streets round Custom House.

They had gone quite a way before he spoke again, and Anna knew her brother was doing his best to steer clear of the dreaded place on Brownlow Hill. The *workhouse*. Referring to it, when needs must, as 'the big house'. Given the choice, Anna would never speak of it at all. When poor people went in there, they hardly ever came out again.

'I've got a few more runs to do before I'm finished,' Sam informed her, knowing Christmas Eve tips were the best of the year. 'It would be a sin to pass up the opportunity to add to the family coffers,' Sam said, and Anna was grateful he was stepping up to help out. 'I won't be late home,' he added and, silently, Anna vowed to get back what was rightfully theirs from Jerky Woods. The fact that he was much bigger and stronger did not cross her mind.

As they felt their way along the narrow passage lit only by the flickering glimmer of a broken gaslight, Anna stumbled. Sam grabbed her hand to save her from falling over the bumpy flags that surrounded stone steps leading to a dilapidated lodging house and she gave a shaky laugh. 'What would I do without you, Sam?'

Anna knew that sometimes, stronger boys than her beloved brother would get to the big tippers first, nothing was guaranteed. Nevertheless, Sam fought for every customer. She felt so sorry for the work he had put in, only for a brute like Woods to take it from him.

'I reckon we've just got to make the best of it, for Ma's sake.'

'I reckon you're right, Sam.'

Anna did not like these mean narrow streets and huddled close to her brother. Even in daylight, the haphazard dwellings, accentuating the chaotic port streets, nestled in a maze of alleys and she was glad that even though her own home was modest, it was a palace compared to the hovels round here.

'You won't tell Ma, about me coming down to the river, will you, Anna? She will only worry.'

'I think she might notice the shiner, Sam,' Anna replied, and Sam shrugged, looking about him. Then, taking some coins from inside his jacket, he pushed them into her hands.

'There's enough there to buy the twins a little treat for tomorrow,' he said proudly. And in a moment of loving gratitude, Anna hugged him, much to his obvious embarrassment, when he pushed her away. Soppy girls.

'Oh, Sam, I'll buy them something nice when I get to the market.' Tears formed in her eyes.

'Well, you can turn the waterworks off for a start,' Sam's pragmatic tone forced a watery smile and Anna watched as, almost reverently, he took a slim leather box from his pocket and opened the hinged lid.

Holding out her hand, he put the box into Anna's palm and, her eyes widening, she could not form the words to ask where he had acquired such a valuable trinket.

'Remember when Ma saw that locket in the window of Solomon's jewellers?' Sam's voice came in short bursts as they stood under the gas lamp near the end of the alleyway and Anna remembered the day clearly. Ma was not one to covet material trinkets but said it reminded her of one their father bought her, which she had lost.

'Well, I bought it for her.'

Anna could hear the pride in Sam's voice. However, she could not help but feel a twinge of... Dare she even think it? Suspicion? Where did he get the money?

'I didn't steal it if that's what you're thinking.' Disappointment laced his words as he explained how he managed to afford the silver locket.

Anna sighed with relief. 'I know you wouldn't do a wicked thing Sam. But it must have cost a fair bit.'

'I only wish I had something to give you too.' He thrust his hands into his trousers and drew out the much-sewn pockets.

'As long as you are not hurt, that's good enough for me.' She fought the urge to hug him again as he put the box firmly into his waistband and buttoned his jacket.

'We're a right pair,' Sam said, letting out a low gurgle of laughter, and surprising her with an affectionate and welcome hug. 'I'll go down to the landing stage, there's bound to be a foreign sailor or two who needs directions to the Sailors' Home.'

'Go on, scat,' Anna said, as a warm glow of sisterly love flowed to her heart.

'I'll see you back home when I've earned a few more coppers.' Sam could not turn down the chance to ease their mother's worry.

He was halfway down the street when Anna called, 'I'll have fresh tea brewed.'

'We'll have a good Christmas, Anna, you'll see,' he called, waving.

'The twins will have something good to open tomorrow. Ma made sure of it.' Anna knew that Ruby gave her staff a 'Christmas box'. The yearly bonus, ranging from a few shillings up to as much as a week's wages, was reward for the work they did all year.

Five-years old was a lovely age to be, she reckoned. Still young enough to believe in the magic of Christmas and the wonder of what Santa would bring to every boy who had been good.

Looking straight ahead, she strode determinedly towards Ruby's Emporium along the dock road, comforted by the working men still lashing cargo on ships that had sailed from all over the world. Ahead of her lay the dark, forbidding passageway where

Jerky Woods had menacingly approached her earlier. And, although he had not laid a finger on her, the threat was there in his leering expression. Offering up a swift prayer of thanks that Sam was not badly hurt, Anna continued her journey, vowing she would see her day of that bully and no mistake.

5

Anna's stomach heaved for the second time that day when she recognised the menacing voice of the local bullyboy as she made her way towards Ruby's shop. She must keep her wits about her. Especially now. Otherwise Jerky Woods would take her down in an instant.

It had not been easy dodging his spiteful brutality. Anna had witnessed his cruel streak first-hand when he had poked a mongrel pup to death with a sharp stick. Then, laughing, he had kicked it round the dock road. She had tried in vain to stop his sickening cruelty, which brought the attention of his mother, who reprimanded him in front of his cohorts. And even though the awful incident had happened years ago, Anna had become the focus of Woods's ruthless nature ever since.

'What about a bit of a kiss under the mistletoe?' Woods waved the puny green plant of white berries above her head, his sugary words dripping menace, and Anna could, once more, feel the revulsion rising to her throat. She could not bear him touching her and, and judging by his coarse language, had a shrewd idea he would not stop at a kiss.

'Stay away from me! You thief.' Her words sounded desperate even to her own ears, but before Anna could hitch her skirt and run for safety, he grabbed her, roughly pinning her against the wet alley wall. So close she could smell the musty, unwashed stench on his clothing. With rising terror, she realised he would stop at nothing to get what he wanted. His hands were dragging at her skirt, trying to lift it. She tried to push him away, but he was solid. Unmoveable. Instinctively, she raked her fingernails down his face.

'Bitch.' Woods gripped both her hands, pinning them behind her back, and Anna tried to scream, but he pushed a huge palm across her mouth. She could barely take a breath.

'You think you're better than the rest of us.' Woods growled through his teeth as he banged her head against the sooty brick wall, and she heard a collective gasp from a group of street urchins who emerged warily from the shadows. All dressed in the same ragged ill-fitting trousers, feet bare, their faces hardly recognisable for the want of a wash.

'We keep ourselves respectable.' Anna shook her face free from his grip, refusing to be intimidated. She would always fight back no matter how strong he was. It was survival of the fittest round the Liverpool dockyards. If you were weak, you were done for. And she had no intentions of letting this guttersnipe get the better of her. Even though she knew that to retaliate would provoke him more.

'I saw your Sam in town. He ought to be careful,' Jerky Woods's voice was low and menacing. 'He doesn't know who's watching him.'

'He works for his money, not like some people.' The accusation in her words allowed Anna to keep a steady voice, but he clutched her jaw, squeezing her cheeks hard against her teeth.

Caught up in his vile show of intimidation, the pain was nothing to the humiliation she felt.

'His fetching and carrying must bring in a pretty penny when he can visit jewellers' shops, hey boys?' Woods looked over his shoulders to his unholy disciples, who murmured their agreement but kept their distance. When he turned back to Anna, apparently satisfied, he growled like a dog. 'Or maybe he skims a bit off for himself?'

Rage flooded Anna's body, giving her strength. *How dare he call her brother a thief!* Her pounding heartbeat spurring her on as her flinty eyes sparked contempt for this nobody who made it his business to make her life a living hell.

'You dare to say that to me?' Anna took a deep breath, her voice low, measured, she fought to stay calm, knowing if she lost her head now, the Lord only knew what she was capable of doing, after all these months of provocation. 'You have never done an honest day's work in your life, and you have the gall to call my brother a thief.' Anna knew she would have to control the volcanic rage building inside her. Common sense told her she was no match for Jerky Woods.

However, common sense was not her saviour right now. Her family worked hard and were respectable, and he had no right to discredit any of them, especially her Sam who did no wrong to anybody, and was the kindest, most caring boy a sister could wish for.

'I've seen him down the pier head, dipping into fine gents' pockets...'

'You liar!' Anna was too angry to be scared. 'My brother is no thief. Not like some I could mention.'

'Talking about me?' Woods's tone was menacing, but it had no effect. He had the money her Sam had worked hard for and she intended to get it back.

'When I tell Ruby what you did, she will run your ma out of town, raising a thieving hooligan like you.' Anna noticed his determined expression waver when she mentioned Ruby's name, knowing nobody, especially the poor of the parish, dared cross her. Ruby was a lifeline when nobody else would give the time of day. And Izzy Woods was a frequent visitor to the pawnshop. 'Sam worked hard to raise that money...'

'Pull the other one. It plays *Silent Night*,' Woods said, recovering his swagger.

'You know your own tricks best,' Anna countered, knowing he used brute force to get what he wanted. 'My mother raised us to be honest and upright.'

'If she is so good, why is she sending you out to collect rent money?'

'Mind your own business.' Why should she explain herself to the likes of him?

Woods lowered his face, his broken nose almost touching hers, 'I would not be surprised if she pinches Ruby's stock and sells it on the dock road.'

Anna felt the molten rage building. Her mother had never begged or asked anybody for money, even on her poorest day, yet Izzy Woods was in and out of the pawnshop like a fiddler's elbow. 'Your ma would hock her kids if she thought she could get beer money for your da.' Anna knew she had said a cruel thing, even before her head cracked against the brick wall, making her eyes spin.

'Stuck-up bitch!' Jerky Woods snarled through tight thin lips, his grip tightening.

Head-splitting pain made her vision blurred as Anna tried to scrape back the tangled hair from her face, aware of a tacky ooze running through her fingers. Her stomach lurched when she saw they were covered in her blood. She gasped as fear shot through her.

'You bastard!'

She would never routinely use gutter language. But this was not a typical situation. She must fight fire with fire, to get her point across. Anna aimed a powerful kick to his shin, making Woods curse. This thug would not get away with making her head bleed, calling her mother names, or stealing Sam's money. She went for him with all the strength she could muster.

In moments, Anna was grappling on the cobbled street, bringing untold shame to her family. But that was the last thing on her mind, as she lunged towards her attacker. Unaware a hush had descended. Her head was swimming, but still she made the effort to fight back. She was no quitter.

Gasping for breath, on the point of collapse, she was aware Jerky Woods had stopped fighting. He was lying motionless on the pavement.

'Run!' one of the urchins called, as some of his so-called pals took fright and made a dash for anonymity, through a labyrinth of courts and back streets, 'here's the jacks.' Everybody except Woods scattered at the mention of the local constabulary.

'I'll get you done for this,' Woods was now rolling on the floor, dramatically holding his head, and groaning loudly.

'You could do a turn on stage with an act like that,' a man remarked from the shadows. Climbing down from his horse, he watched Woods drag himself from the ground and he stopped groaning.

Anna let out a gasp of relief when she realised she had not killed Woods. 'I didn't hit him hard.' She could not yet see the man in the shadows. 'He's having you on. I have seen him take much worse. I was defending myself.'

'That's some left hook you've got there.' Ned Kincaid's admiration was clear in his familiar tone that made Anna slump with relief. They had been friends since their young days in Primrose Cottages, where the cramped, claustrophobic court dwellings with only one or two rooms to house large families was neither floral nor rural. Woods and his family lived at the bottom end near the midden, and Anna's family had lived next door to Ned at the other end of the courtyard near the water standpipe. But even in the poorest of courts there was a sense of community – unless your name was Jerky Woods. 'I reckon you'd better say you're sorry before she decides to have another go.'

Anna knew the bully would not argue with Ned. Nobody argued with Ned. And Anna counted her blessings. If Ned had not returned from the football match and made a detour when he did, Lord knows what might have happened.

'He pinched our Sam's money.' Anna could see Woods was not injured at all. He was playing for sympathy.

'Did he now?' Ned's voice was calm. A contradiction to the unwary.

'It weren't me, Ned. Honest.'

Destined to be a tough fist-fighter like his father, before he got under Ruby's steadying wing, Ned did not trust Woods, knowing his lies got him out of many a scrape, but not this time. His potent fist shot out and gripped Woods by the collar when he saw blood trickle down Anna's forehead, and overlooked the promise he made to Ruby as he landed a dig squarely on Jerky Woods's jaw. 'If you trouble Anna, or her family again, you will answer to me.'

Anna could see the vein throb in his temple, a sure sign Ned was struggling to hold his temper while Woods wriggled like a worm on a hook under Ned's strong grip.

'She attacked me.' Lurching and jerking, hence the nickname,

Woods used the tactics that usually got him out of trouble. But this time he was out of luck.

'Hand over the money you stole from Sam and be quick about it.' Ned's presence gave Anna renewed courage and, stretching to her full height, she felt ten feet tall.

'I haven't got no money.' Woods unwisely thrust his chin forward, his lip curling in a smirk and Ned hit it like a jackhammer.

'I aint scared of you.' Woods incredulous bravado fooled nobody. 'I could have him any day. He caught me on the 'op when I wasn't looking.'

Ned gave Woods a fearsome glare. Shutting the bully down immediately and impressing Anna no end. Then Ned calmly told Woods, 'Apologise and give her back the money.'

'What does *apologise* mean?' Woods was playing for time. A searing heat rushed to Anna's head. He could not get away with this.

'It means, say sorry,' Ned answered. 'Apologise to the young lady, or I will break you.' He was deadly serious.

'Who died and made 'er a lady?' Woods was unwilling to hand back the money he'd stolen.

'Say you're sorry to the young lady,' Ned repeated his request, screwing Woods's collar so tightly he choked.

'She's lying,' Woods gasped, turning the colour of a ripe plum.

'Say you're sorry to the young lady.' Ned's voice changed neither pitch nor tone as he raised another warning fist, watching the recognition dawn in the bully's piggy eyes, and he knew he had got the message.

'Sorry.' Wood's apology, although unconvincing, carried to his cohorts, who had returned to watch in a state of gleeful anticipation, their persecutor getting his comeuppance.

'Not good enough. She has a name. Use it.' Ned shook Woods until his teeth rattled.

'Sorry, Anna. It will never happen again, Anna. Honest, Anna.' The words sounded foreign coming out of his mouth. And his sardonic tone fooled nobody. But he said it. And what surprised Anna was witnessing Woods handing over the money he stole from her brother.

'You can leave him be now, Ned,' Anna felt braver, 'he won't be so quick to pick on the Cassidys in future.'

Ned released his grip, allowing Woods to land on a scramble. His boots sparking the cobbles in his haste to be free.

'Don't think you're getting away with this Cassidy,' Jerky Woods called from a safe distance, 'cause you aint.' The humiliation of being shown up in front of his cohorts burned deeply. Anna knew Jerky Woods would not forget this insult in a hurry.

'Ahh, go and frighten your mother 'til your father gets home,' Ned retorted with obvious amusement, watching the thug disappear up a back alley heading towards Queen Street. 'Are you sure you are all right?' Ned's eyes were filled with concern as he bent down to look more closely at the gash on Anna's head. 'Look at him, he's just an idiot, going in the wrong direction.'

'I am fine. He doesn't scare me.' Anna did not mean to sound ungrateful, because heaven only knew what would have happened to her if Ned had not showed up. 'But thanks ever so, Ned.' All she wanted to do was crawl away and lick her wounds like an injured animal. But first she had to get this money to Ruby. 'I can manage by meself now.'

Straightening her dishevelled clothing, Anna kept her eyes to the ground. She felt bad. She had behaved like one of those women who plied their trade at the dock gates, making Ned forget the promise he made to Ruby not to use his fists in anger.

'I'll come along with you if you like?' Ned sounded almost

cheerful, like the altercation had cheered him, but Anna did not want him getting into trouble for her.

'I'll be fine. He's all blow – full of hot air and no substance – and picks on people weaker or younger than himself.' Anna watched Ned collect the bay mare, knowing even if it galloped all the way to The Emporium, she would still be too late to get the money to Ruby before the bank closed.

6

The night had long drawn in when Jerky Woods grabbed his young brother by his frayed collar and dragged him away from Queen Street, heading towards the bustling market in Cazneau Street, known locally as *Paddy's Market*. He had done what he set out to do. But he did not feel as satisfied as he thought he would.

A rare glimmer of contrition forced him to think of getting his mother something for Christmas. He weren't gonna buy her a present or something stupid like that, but he would think of something that would make her so overcome with gratitude, she would forget he stole the last of the bread this morning. Another reason he stayed out of her way from the back-to-back courts he called home.

He eyed the holly and ivy-covered stalls as the smell of hot rum punch filled the air. He could just do with a hot bevvy to warm him, he thought, trying to push his encounter with Anna Cassidy and strong-arm Kincaid out of his mind. His humiliating defeat running like cold water through his veins. They were the reason he had done what he did, secure in the knowledge his hand had been forced...

'Here, watch who you're pushing!' he warned, as hurrying worshippers jostled him on the market pavement, eager to get to Saint Anthony's Catholic Church, the beating heart of the parish, while others scrambled for last-minute Christmas treats.

Eyeing the stalls with a view to what he could pinch, he ignored the competitive calls of market traders filling the icy air with the price of a pig's head or, if women had saved in the meat club, and were a bit flush, they could purchase a duck, a chicken or even a turkey.

His stomach rumbled as his hand shot out to snatch a crusty cob of bread off the stall and, even better, a fruit bun, having not eaten for hours. The tantalising smell of hot potatoes and chestnuts wafted on the cold night air. And although he still had some of the coppers he wrestled from Sam Cassidy, Jerky Woods had no intention of wasting them on food.

The worshipping throng headed towards the church and the strangest thought hovered in the back of his mind. He wondered if the church *would* fall if he entered, like his mother said it would.

Well, I ain't in no mood to find out, an' I don't need absolving, he thought as he sideswiped an apple from a fruit stall and put it in his young brother's pocket. No sense in getting caught with the contraband on his person if anybody saw him and called the *blackjacks*.

Another unsettling thought of Anna Cassidy and her too-good-to-be-true family entered his head and he grimaced, pressing full lips together as he cogitated. He'd liked the look of Anna when he moved with his family into Primrose Cottages. But she was stuck-up even then, and that was afore her ma took up working for Miss Ruby and got their selves that new three-up-three-down terraced 'ouse in Queen Street. She thought she were too good to talk to the likes of him. But she would soon find out she weren't nothin' special when she got home.

He had a good mind to go into the church, where the Cassidy family would be praying in the front pew or chewing the altar rails, thanking the Almighty for allowing them to move from the courts of squalor and want to the scrubbed steps and lace curtains of Queen Street. His scorn grew like a fungus and he dragged his young brother along beside him. Anna Cassidy was gonna be brought down a peg or two, an' no mistake.

Blowing out his ruddy cheeks, he released a slow stream of pent-up air and his eyes skimmed the burgeoning crowd of Mary-Ellen's, clad in their thick woollen shawls, jostling for a Christmas bargain. He din't want to think any more about the Cassidys, who thought they were better'n him just because they were well in with the local money lender, Ruby Swift.

'Can we go 'ome now?' Nipper cried as the bitterly cold wind sliced through him. Blowing warm air into his cupped, ice-cold hands did nothing to warm them before tucking them under his arms to try to bring some life into them.

'It's Christmas Eve,' Woods told young Nipper, his voice unusually spirited, almost cheerful, ignoring his young brother's earnest plea, 'we've got to get Ma something nice to open tomorrer.'

'What for?' Nipper asked his older brother.

'For Christmas, you clot,' Woods answered, eyeing the tantalising fruit stalls, and wondered if he dared risk pinching an orange, but the stall owner had his beady eyes to business, so Woods decided to wait a while. Next door, geese and chickens hung on hooks, the lively patter vying for attention among the bustle of customers who had left their Christmas shopping until late in the hope of a cheap deal. Their family had never celebrated Christmas because there was never enough money for presents. They had never been given a single present in their whole life.

'But we aint got no money.' Nipper was cold and hungry and miserable. He wanted to get off home but knew that was not going to happen when he was hauled off his feet and dragged along the wet litter-strewn pavement illuminated by the street's gas lamps.

'Who said anything about money.' Woods's eyes were bright, his words energetic. 'The traders are run ragged at this late hour, 'specially when the ould tails fall out of the alehouse all beer-eyed and sappy with Christmas bliss, joining in the Sally Army's soppy carols. They'll be paying no heed to the purse atop their shopping baskets.'

'Why did we 'ave t' go to Queen Street?' Nipper moaned, knowing he did not deserve the cuff round the head his older brother meted out.

'Because! That's why,' Woods said, biting down hard on the spent match clenched between his teeth, pushing all thoughts of Queen Street to the back of his mind when a welcome distraction sauntered his way. In the blink of an eye, his attitude changed. He gave Nipper a couple of pennies left from the money he stole from Sam. 'Get a hot potato, and while you're at it get Ma something off the second-hand stall. I'll see you later.'

Pushing back the peak of his flat cap to the back of his unruly thatch of dark hair, Woods sauntered with his usual rolling gait towards Lottie Blythe, a pretty girl who lived near the Cassidys in Queen Street.

'Well, as I live and breathe, if it ain't Lottie Blythe.' Woods's grin did not disturb the blackened matchstick hanging from the corner of his mouth. 'I was talking about you only a few minutes ago,' he lied. 'I asked Anna Cassidy if you had already gone to mass, or if you were going to the late one.'

'I am going to midnight mass, if you must know,' Lottie answered, feeling her cheeks grow hot, 'not that it is any of your business.' Her scornful words hid a sneaking regard for Woods's tearaway reputation, and she took a deep breath, trying to calm the little flutter in her chest.

'Here, let me carry that, it looks heavy.' He reached for her wicker basket and she automatically stepped back, heeding his notorious reputation and alert to the possibility of him running off with her Christmas shopping. There would be hell to pay when she got home to her widowed mother if she allowed that to happen.

Cocking her head to one side, Lottie pursed her lips and looked him up and down. 'I can manage. Thanks all the same.' Her voice held a hint of scorn, she was nobody's fool, and even though her mother was not well off, she brought Lottie up to have high standards, live a humble, godly life of servitude, go to mass, never answer back, do your best. And although Lottie was ripe for a bit of adventure, she had her sights set on somebody a bit more respectable than Jerky Woods. Biting her top lip, she saw the look of dismay in his eyes before he lowered his head. 'I didn't mean nothing by it,' Lottie said quickly. 'It's just that you can't... you know... there are some people who can't be...' her words trailed.

'Can't be trusted... Like Jerky Woods. Is that what you were going to say?'

'I didn't mean anything of the sort.' Lottie's voice rose to a squeak in her haste to rid him of such a notion while realising she was clutching her basket close to her body. Suddenly she thrust it towards him, almost knocking him off his feet. 'Here. Take it, of course I don't think that.' How could she be so hurtful. On Christmas Eve as well. He had a bad reputation, but he had never said a bad word to her. 'I've still got some shopping to finish for Ma.' She knew her mother would be apoplectic if she saw her only daughter conversing with a bad boy like Jerky Woods, or Jerry as she liked to think of him. Although she would never say his name out loud. Names were sort of, well, personal to a body.

Lottie liked to think well of people, and she had seen him round the market a few times. He was a rogue, but he always gave her a lovely smile and, given the chance, she was sure he was a truly lovely person.

He was smiling at her now and she loved the way his eyes crinkled in the corners. He had had a raw deal, that is all. He was misunderstood, obviously. And who could wonder? Her mother had told her all about that drunken father of his who would scare old Nick from the hobs of hell.

'That's so kind of you,' she said, vowing to light a candle for him at midnight mass.

'Don't mention it,' Jerky Woods tried to ignore her purse, sitting there among the cabbage and potatoes just asking to be taken. She bought two triangular bags of mint-balls and gave him a bag, which made his eyes shine with delight. 'Have you finished your shopping, now?' he asked, and she nodded. 'Fair enough,' Woods said, 'in that case, let me do you the kindness of walking you back home.'

He slipped her purse into his pocket as they cut through a throng of carol singers and a thrill of excitement coursed through his body. There was something he had to see in Queen Street...

The distant, dockland sounds of horse-drawn traffic and clanking cranes were a dying echo of the hearty yells and cries which during the daylight hours were evident in Liverpool's thriving port. Anna knew she would have no job if she were much later and her footsteps quickened.

'I thought Sam would be with you.' Offering her his clean cotton handkerchief, Ned indicated to her forehead with a nod and she wiped the small trickle of blood.

'It's Christmas Eve, people need their parcels carrying to a hansom cab, or even down to the ferries. He'll make more money tonight than any other night of the year.'

'The money will come in handy now your ma's off her feet,' Ned said, leading his horse along the dock road. He had always liked Anna, but suddenly she had turned into this arresting vision of womanhood that caused his heart to pound against his ribs and turned his brain to mush. He tried to think of something sensational to say. Then, looking out to the inky blackness of the River Mersey, Ned murmured, as if to himself, 'This is the beginning of the world.'

'Is it?' Anna did not have time to wonder what was on the other side of the river, because she was usually too busy trying to make ends meet on this side.

'One day I'll cross the water,' Ned said dreamily, 'and not just to the Wirral, or Ireland, or The Isle of Man. No. One day I'll travel much further than that.'

'Well, don't forget to send us a postcard.' Anna's crisp tone was tempered with worry. She could very well lose her job when she got back to Ruby's Emporium with the day's takings. She was truly thankful that Ned had got Sam's money back, but she had no time for daft daydreaming or romantic ruminations.

Reaching the Emporium, she felt a cold shiver of anxiety run down her spine. Ruby's other bay mare was still in its shafts. Head buried in a hessian nosebag at the end of his working day. Any minute now, Archie would come out and take the horse into the stable at the back of the shop. He would catch her with Ned. Moreover, he would ask all sorts of questions. Why was she late?

What time did she call this? Where was the money from the rent collections?

'I'm fine here.' Anna's mouth was paper dry, and she dipped her gaze, feeling more unsettled than ever, 'you don't have to walk me any further.'

'I don't mind,' Ned's usual easy-going manner returned, 'I've got to stable the horses.'

Looking up into his good-humoured face and taking in the flick of short dark hair under a flat cap, the peak of which did nothing to hide the shining warmth in his eyes, Anna wondered how he could be so casual about everything after the cruel blow he had been dealt in life. Losing both his parents before he was twelve years old and threatened with the workhouse before Ruby and Archie came to his rescue.

'You must go. If Ruby catches us together, again, she will think we have been...' Anna blinked rapidly, a flush of warmth spreading over her cold cheeks as she stumbled over her words. Unable to finish voicing her worry, she scurried to the large gates behind the shop.

'Like we've been what?' Ned overtook her and leaned against the whitewashed wall. He was smiling, aware he was embarrassing Anna.

'Get out of the way, you daft ha'porth.' She flicked her hand as if swatting a fly. If Archie came out of the shop now, she would die of humiliation. 'Be off, before someone comes out and catches you talking to me.' Turning on her heel, her back straight and proud, and her head held high, Anna pushed her way through one of the double gates and marched towards the back of the shop.

Leaning against the interior wall, she felt a bit giddy, and the sound of Ruby's footsteps on the scrubbed white floorboards alerted Anna to her employer's imminent arrival. Flinging the bag of money on to the table, she slipped her coat onto the nail at the back of the door. She eyed the bag of money. Ruby was going to want to know why she had not taken the money straight to the bank. It was no good. Anna knew she would have to tell the truth, that she was waylaid by Jerky Woods. Lying never did anybody any good in the long run. Wasn't that what her ma always told her. Be honest and you will not go far wrong.

Nevertheless, as she smoothed down her wayward hair, Anna noticed her head had started to bleed again and she quickly wiped away the dribble with the back of her hand as the determined footsteps grew louder and, taking a deep breath, Anna prepared for the moment when Ruby would tell her that she was not fit to do her mother's job.

Ned popped his head round the door. His eyes wide, he was just about to speak when a sharp intake of breath signalled her heart leaping to her throat. Anna gave a silent shake of her head, all the while keeping her eye on the adjoining door through which Ruby would appear at any moment.

'I'll walk you home,' he said in that maddeningly calm way he had about him, strong shoulders back, chest out, 'make sure you get home safely.'

Anna was just about to tell him she was not some helpless damsel in distress, when Ruby's footsteps gained momentum, almost at a trot.

'Is that you, Anna?' Ruby called, slightly breathless, obviously in a hurry.

Ma was going to be so disappointed. Anna knew she could not have picked a worse time to get beaten up. Christmas Eve was always a bit more expensive. She really needed the money this job brought in. She turned to tell Ned. But he was nowhere to be seen. Anna's heart hammered in her throat and skipped a beat when Ruby descended the two steps down into the office at the back of the Emporium.

'Oh, Miss Ruby,' Anna was going to have to play on the goodness of Ruby's heart, and stress that her mother had been a loyal and hard-working employee for many years, 'I am so sorry I didn't get the money to you sooner, but you see, I...'

'I don't want your apologies, girl.' Ruby's stricken face was unusually pale. 'You must hurry straight home. I have just heard the news... Your house is on fire.'

7

Barely catching the tail end of Ruby's warning, Anna spun on her heel, lifted her skirt, and ran as fast as her legs would carry her. Anxiety turning to terror coursing through her body, spurring her along the marketplace by way of the busy main road thronged with late-night shoppers hoping to get the best deal for Christmas.

Michael and James would be terrified, she thought. Poor little mites. She should never have left them alone. Aware of the pulsating thud of her own heartbeat vibrating in her throat, Anna gasped when a sharp pain bit into her ribs, but even though it was difficult to breathe, she could not let it slow her down.

A fierce wind blowing keenly up the River Mersey swept Anna along. People on their way to evening mass at six o'clock, stopped to watch her skidding on the wet cobbles in her haste to get back to her family.

'Please Lord, let them be safe.' Anna's rasping breath was painfully raw. Her arms were wrapped round her slim body, tightly holding onto the basket of groceries she had managed to buy earlier with the money her mother had given her, and paying no heed to the much-needed wages her mother had earned all week. Her only thought was for the safety of her family.

Before she even got through the viaduct at the top of Queen Street, Anna could smell the acrid smoke. And even though daylight had deferred to a night sky, she could still make out the thick, black smoke curling over the rooftops. Praying even harder, Anna pushed people out of her way in her haste to get back to Queen Street. But as she got closer, she felt she was trying to run through thick, heavy mud, her feet leaden. She could not get home quick enough.

Unable to face the result of her own neglect, her footsteps crawled to a halt. Anna did not want to see her burning home. If she did not see, her ma and her brothers would be safe. The house would be just as she left it. But as she stood silently on the cobbles that ran down the centre of Queen Street, amid the large throng of onlookers, the realisation of what was happening hit Anna like a slap in the face. She lurched forward, her feet skimming the cobbles. The crowd growing bigger. She had to get to the front. She had to get to her family.

No matter how hard she tried to elbow her way through, onlookers were reluctant to give way, pushing her back, determined not to miss anything.

'That's my home.' Anna managed to make herself heard above the noisy hubbub. 'Please, you must let me through.'

Like the parting of the Red Sea, the crowd separated and immediately cloaked her as she moved forward. A long line of neighbours were passing buckets of water from a standpipe or their own sculleries to the burning house. Anna's mouth slackened when she saw the flames licking her own front door.

'No!' she cried as the heat burst the wooden window frame, sprinkling broken glass on the frosty pavement, and she felt someone's arm round her shoulders. When she turned, she saw Lottie Blythe from next door. Her face ashen.

'If they do not get the fire under control soon, it could spread to our house!'

'Oh well, we can't have that,' Anna replied, her voice devoid of expression over the clang of the fire engine bell. When the vehicle screeched to a halt at the kerb, Jerky Woods was hovering on the periphery of her vision, watching the people of Queen Street slosh the house with bucket after bucket of water.

Jumping from the engine, the firemen unrolled their hosepipe and aimed a powerful spray of water directly through the broken window, and a hush descended on the crowd when an agonised scream rent the wintry night air and uncontrollable tears coursed down Anna's cheeks.

'Please help them,' she beseeched the firemen rushing forward towards the house, 'don't let my family perish. They would have been at mass if Ma hadn't hurt her leg,' she told Lottie. 'The twins had been looking forward to a visit from Santa and now their presents will be ruined.' The apples and oranges she had bought in the market rolled across the pavement as she dropped her basket. The toy soldiers in their red uniforms lay face down in the slushy snow. 'Let me through!' Rising panic made Anna's voice shrill.

She could feel the blistering heat spewing from the house and could clearly hear the wood cracking, fearing the worst when another sash window burst forth. Dodging the splintered glass in her effort to get closer to the house, Anna moved nearer while the crowd of gawping onlookers shuffled back – but not too far for fear of missing something.

'Out of the way now, miss. You can't go in there you'll be cooked alive.' A burly fireman pushed her to one side, aiming water through a broken window.

'I should never have left the twins alone,' Anna cried, hardly able to bear the horrific scene.

Just then a voice beside her said: 'Are you sayin' there's someone in there?' Wood's eyes, gleaming with ill-concealed fascination, were suddenly wide with something akin to horror. Given the chance she would have told him what she thought of his morbid curiosity, but she had no intentions of telling him anything, nor did he give her the chance when he turned from the house and legged it to who knows where? As the pungent, smouldering tendrils of smoke stung her eyes and caught her throat, she knew Woods was the least of her worries.

As time wore on, the flames died down and a trail of thick, black caustic smoke streamed from the place she had once called home. Her mind was in turmoil. *What had happened? The twins would have removed the fireguard to put on more coal. Had a cob of coal fallen from the hearth? Ma would not have been quick enough to prevent it burning the mat!* She never should have left them, especially when Ma was unable to care for them.

'Where's my mother, and my brothers?'

The firefighter shook his head but said nothing.

'My... brothers? Michael... James... Sam...?' Her throat was raw, her voice croaky. Someone took hold of her shoulders and she shrugged them off. Her gaze riveted on the smouldering shell beneath an icy silver moon. The blackened ruins of her home made worse by the thick fall of snow.

Peering over the shoulder of a neighbour, Anna tried to catch sight of what the firemen were doing. If her family were in hospital for Christmas, she would never forgive herself. Eyeing the stone steps that descended to the basement, Anna knew if she reached them, she could save Michael and James and her ma. If only someone would let her through. But someone bigger and stronger was blocking her path.

'Ned.' She gasped when she saw his face, blistered down the right side.

'You cannot go in there, Anna.' his caring blue eyes were vibrant against his soot-blackened skin. 'It is not safe. I tried to get inside, but the flames beat me back.'

'Where's Sam? He should be home by now.'

'I haven't seen him, Anna…' Ned quickly looked round, but there was no sign of Sam.

'I've got to get to Michael and James.' Her strained voice began to quake. 'I have got to save them. They will be terrified.' Scalding tears made clean tracks down her face and blurred her vision. Then, a suppressed hush descended on the expectant crowd when a brave fireman gingerly pushed his way through the charred remains of the blackened front door and into the house.

Anna had an overwhelming urge to scream. She gasped, realising she had been holding her breath. Determined to remain calm, it was nigh on impossible. Surely, Ma managed to get out of her chair to save them all.

'My dear girl.' Ruby's usually composed demeanour had gone, her face stricken. The new parish priest following close behind, made the sign of the cross.

As Ruby put a warmly protective arm round her shivering shoulders, Anna realised the evening mass must be over if the priest was here.

'Oh, you poor, poor girl,' Ruby said, before catching sight of the black-clad cleric holding on to his woollen biretta, his cassock billowing on the rising swirl of fresh falling snow. In his haste to see if there was anything he could do to help, he barged through the gawping observers.

'Oh here we go,' Ruby sighed, 'we've got the fire – he'll bring the brimstone, no doubt.' Anna could feel Ruby Swift's grip tighten. 'I've no wish to hear what he has to say, so let us get you out of here.'

Anna, rooted to the spot, looked up at the straight-talking woman. 'I'm not going anywhere until I find out if my family are safe.' If she could, she would have got inside the house and brought them out herself.

'Oh dear,' the new parish priest said helplessly, and Anna caught a look of futility spread across his pale face, while Ruby tried to shield her from the scene. Something stirred. There was a change of atmosphere. A collective gasp.

Pulling herself from Ruby's motherly clutches, Anna turned towards the burned-out remains of her home to see a stray mongrel cock its leg up against the railings, just as a fireman brought out a small bundle.

'He was tucked up in bed with his brother and his mother...' Anna clearly heard the fireman tell the priest. Her heart stopped for two beats. She watched as, almost reverently, he placed his burden on the ground, and she recognised the soot-covered body of her young brother.

Unable to contain the scream that fractured the freezing night air, Anna tore herself from Ruby's grip, hurling herself at the small body of copper-haired James. Dropping to her knees on the icy pavement, she stroked his lifeless face. Then someone laid her lifeless mother next to young James and Anna went to her. Her tears landing on Ma's blackened cheek and, tenderly, with a trembling hand, she wiped the tears away.

'Ma, wake up,' Anna sobbed, her voice barely a whisper. 'Ma, it's me. You are going to be all right. They've got you out.' Her eyes scanned her mother's beautiful face. There was not a blister or a blemish. Nor were there any signs her mother was breathing the frosty night air.

She cannot be dead! a voice screamed inside Anna's head, and erupted from her lips.

'Please wake up, Ma. The boys need you... I need you!' But her pleas went unheard as her mother lay motionless on the cold hard ground. A moment later, another limp body was placed beside his mother.

'Michael!' Anna scrambled to her little brother and she shook his thin shoulders. A small gasp of air rushed from his small lax body. 'He's still alive. I heard him breathe. He's alive.'

Father O'Connell moved her out of the way, and he put his ear to young Michael's chest. Moments later, he lifted his head and solemnly shook it. Clearly, little Michael was beyond anybody's help.

Barely aware of the small movement beside her, Anna lifted her head as untethered tendrils of honey-coloured hair stuck to her soot covered, tear-stained face, and her view was momentarily hindered as the crowd stepped back when the priest closed the pale blue eyes of her brother for the last time.

Ned, with tears streaming down his own smut-covered face, put his arms round Anna, who knew, with rising horror, that it was much too late for any of them. Gently he took her in his arms and rocked her, back and forth, as her agonised cries rent the night air.

Dazed, Anna could see the priest saying prayers over her mother's body, giving her extreme unction, before going on to give her young brothers the last rites too. When he had finished, she heard him say in that solemn Irish brogue so familiar in these parts: 'The boys would have been having their afternoon nap, asleep in their beds, they wouldn't have known a thing.' The gathered crowd gasped when he told the firemen without preamble, 'The remains can now be moved to a mortuary. It'll be a pauper's funeral no doubt.'

'Father O'Connell.' Ruby put her hands over Anna's head and ears to subdue any further thoughtless comment. 'If you don't mind.' Leaving her in Ned's care, Ruby returned to the priest. 'Is her dead family offending you, Father?' Ruby's nostrils flared. 'Should they be cleared away quickly, lest they offend anybody?'

The priest said nothing but went over to Anna.

A tortured sound of anguish sliced the freezing air, and it was not until she felt a stinging slap of pain shoot through her cheek, and saw Father O'Connell's look of furious disapproval, that Anna realised it was she who had been making the commotion.

'My family are gone,' she sobbed, her eyes wild. 'I never should have left them.' She felt sick. And to faint would be a blessing. Anna had no sense of anything outside her own grief and pain. Only vaguely aware of Ned's arms enfolding her, whispering soothing words, he shielded her from the prying crowd while Ruby ranted at Father O'Connell.

'How dare you raise your hand to that poor girl. She has lost everything. Her whole family. You, supposedly sharing the love of God, are nothing but a disgusting little man.'

'I beg your pardon, Madam.' Given his bulging eyes and slack jaw, the priest was obviously unaccustomed to being spoken to in such a manner.

'Call yourself a man of God?' Ruby was almost nose-to-nose and the priest took a step back and straightened.

'She was hysterical,' said Father O'Connor, 'she will make herself ill.'

'Is that so?' Ruby said in a low voice, not wanting Anna to hear the volleying diatribe.

'The church will look after her.' He took another step back as Ruby edged forward, and the gawping crowd found something else to spice up tomorrow's conversation.

'Oh no it will not,' the businesswoman's voice was steady, 'she is not being put in one of your institutions... You are not getting your hands on this one.'

'I doubt you have any say in the matter.' Father O'Connell grimaced, this woman was more than ready to do battle, he could see.

She paused for a moment before saying in the assured tone that had gained her both respect and notoriety in the parish, 'Anna is over the age where you can make her a ward of the church, Father.' Ruby stretched her straight back. A successful businesswoman who gave generously to deserving causes, she also funded many apostolic endeavours.

'These are poor people... Parish funds will pay for a funeral,' the priest countered.

Ruby, refusing to be beaten, leaned forward, 'Do not give it another thought.'

'The girl needs to be taken care of. She has another brother, I believe?'

'Mrs Cassidy was my loyal employee, I consider it my duty to take care of Anna and Sam.' Ruby, hands on hips, raised a defiant chin. 'Pay no heed, Sam will not be spirited away to god-knows-where, like some.'

'How dare you.' Father O'Connell sprayed saliva over the front of Ruby's coat, looking like he was about to explode. 'The children in our care are extremely well cared for.'

Ruby flicked the foamy spittle from her bosom, and the corners of her bow-shaped lips curled down in disgust. 'Tell me, Padre, what happened to Aggie Johnston's kids?' Ruby was aware the crowd was listening now and knew this was another added attraction to the evening's excitement. Playing to the crowd like a seasoned performer on the stage of the Empire Theatre, with a snap of finger and thumb, she said: 'Here one day playing happily in the street.' She watched the priest flinch. 'And gone the next.'

She looked to the crowd, 'That was two years ago, and poor Aggie hasn't seen hide nor hair of them since.' The fascinated gathering hung on every word. 'Poor sick Aggie went into the workhouse infirmary while her husband was away at sea.' She investigated the eyes of each bystander, knowing she would get a nod or a shrug, each one a customer of hers or, more likely, Archie's pawnshop. Turning, she asked: 'Do you remember, Father O'Connell?' His name sounded like a curse on her lips as, leaning towards him again, Ruby's dark eyes silently dared him to contradict her.

'Not that it be any of your business, woman, but I was told Mrs Johnson was gravely ill and not able to look after her children.' His Irish brogue became more pronounced. His face a raging puce.

'Is that so?' Ruby gave an unbeaten half-smile. 'You are new to this parish, are you not?' In time he would see things her way. 'But you will already know about my donations to the church.'

'For sure,' Father O'Connell spoke again, only this time his voice was not so sharp, fully aware that to offend Ruby Swift could result in parish funds being withdrawn. 'I understand your concern,' he said more placidly, 'however, I am not willing to discuss the matter in the street... Suffice to say...' He foolishly wagged his finger in her face. 'Church matters are none of your concern.'

'Then I will make them my concern.' Ruby threw back her head, giving the performance of a lifetime to the assembled crowd. She knew she had the upper hand and was not going to let this man get the better of her.

'The church does not profit off the backs of young children,' Father O'Connell spluttered, while Anna knew it was only because her ma's employer was so generous to the local churches that this priest did not summon the local bobby and have her carted away. He would have done so to anybody else who dared defy him. 'And I will thank you to keep your voice to a respectful pitch.' His growing, uncontrollable outrage was evident. Priests were feared round these parts. They were not belittled in front of their congregation by a heathen woman who had a stronger hold on his parishioners than he did.

'Go tell it to the King, little man,' Ruby countered – she had no time for religious conviction. 'You don't scare me with your threats of hellfire and damnation.' Ruby had her bellyful of the church years ago. The priest held no fears for her any more, she thought pragmatically. Those days were long gone.

Although grief-stricken, Anna could do nothing except watch in awe. She had never seen anybody argue with the priest – who really did put the fear of God into his worshippers. He, along with the rest of the clergy, had the last word. Even Bann Bateman did not argue with the priest, and he headbutted coppers. Nevertheless, they locked him up for that. But that was all well and good.

The firemen came over and said there was nobody else inside the house. So, where the hell was Sam?

Before anybody could stop her, Anna headed towards the smouldering house. They had not brought out Sam. He would have been home ages ago. In her desperation to find him, she hurried into the blackened husk. She had to find her brother.

'Sam. Sam can you hear me?' Her strident shriek echoed through the shell of her home. When Anna did not hear his voice, she feared the worst. He may be unconscious. He may be shielding upstairs, unable to get out as the fire had devoured some of the ceiling and floor. Inside the charred doorway, she heard a loud crack at the far end of the room and, grinding cinders beneath her black button boots she went to investigate.

Nippy as she was, Anna could not get out quickly enough to save herself, given that the new crack added to the many which had spread across the sooty ceiling like a spider's web. Looking up, she raised her arm to shield her head when part of the ceiling fell beside her and as it did a large chunk of plaster caught her arm and common sense told her the whole ceiling was in danger of crashing down. Hopeless and heartbroken, Anna was driven back. Angry with herself for so many reasons. She should have been home sooner. She should not have spent so long choosing the gifts for Michael and James. If she had been courageous, she could have made it into the house to save them both. But she was a coward. Sam would have risked his own young life to save them.

Leaving the house, she could see Ned and Archie trying to pacify Ruby and the priest, who were too absorbed in their own conflict to notice her sidle through the crowd of open-mouthed onlookers. Shattered beyond words, Anna wanted to be anywhere but here listening to people going through the tattered remnants of her life. In her muddled mind, nobody would miss her. It had stopped snowing and now icy daggers of hail stung her tear-swollen cheeks as Anna headed unsteadily along the dock road. She was going to find Sam.

8

Anna headed to the pier head, but there was no sign of her brother. She asked a young boy who had just carried Christmas parcels to the ferry for a grateful well-to-do lady, if he had seen Sam, and he suggested Anna look round the Seaman's Mission in Canning Place.

'That's your best hope,' said the urchin, earning a copper fetching and carrying for toffs who lived over the water. 'The Seaman's Mission might sound like a daft place to earn money,' he said, 'but it gives refuge to seafarers from all over the world and don't know the port. They just want a bit of peace from the dockside whores and seedy lodging houses and we show them the way, and because they're not used to the value of our money, we can earn a tidy packet.' All the time, the streetwise young lad kept an eye out for ferry passengers in need of a helping hand with their luggage, a hansom cab, or even directions. The port could be a dangerous place to the unwary.

The sky cast an eerie glow as a powerful wind blew more snow from the direction of the river, whistling and swirling up Paradise Street as Anna, hunched double, headed into

Whitechapel and was carried to the steps of the Sailors' Home, as the locals called The Seaman's Mission.

Pa told her this place had been erected from the subscriptions of ship owners and merchants to provide good, clean, cheap quarters. A sanctuary to sailors from the grog shops that advertised seamen could be drunk for a penny and blind for twopence. Sam could earn a pretty penny guiding foreign sailors to the safety of the Sailors' Home.

Anna was exhausted when she reached the door, only to be told women were not allowed inside. It was only a slim hope he would be here. Someone might have seen a young lad carrying luggage for a penny or two. Anna clung onto the hope with every fibre of her being as she huddled on the steps, her frozen fingers trailing twisted nautical ropes, dolphins, and mermaids under a crowned insignia on the iron railings. In her confused, devastated mind, she imagined what it must be like to be a mermaid. To let your cares float away and be dependent on nothing but the sea...

She did not know how long she had been sitting there, exhausted, ignored by most and scolded by others for blocking the steps. Praying on the goodwill of passing seafarers, she begged them to go inside to see if her Sam was in there. Some, worse for drink, were not in a friendly mood in the small hours of a raw Christmas morning.

Anna's misery plummeted to new depths, as darkness tightly wrapped its freezing grip round her, and she was startled momentarily when she was disturbed by a man hurrying up the steps. He did not give her a passing glance as his herringbone cloak brushed her cheek.

'Mister, 'ave ya seen my brother?' Bone-weary, Anna's voice was beseeching and barely a whisper, but she did not intend to give up. Someone must be able to tell her of her brother's whereabouts.

The man stopped at the top of the steps and looked down at her from beneath his wide-brimmed hat as if seeing her for the first time, taking in her slender frame before asking: 'Who is your brother? And why do you seek him, child?'

Anna forgot her tiredness and, suddenly alert, she wanted to tell the well-dressed man that she had not been a child for a long while. However, such a statement would surely give the wrong impression and she had had enough for one night. Raising her chin, she realised this man was the first to speak civilly to her. Other mariners had given her a wide berth. Most, she surmised, probably thought she was touting for business, proof if any were needed when the porter had moved her on twice. Trying to keep her voice level, she said, 'I have to tell him something... There's been an accident.' Anna felt uncomfortable under the stranger's steady gaze as she told her tragic tale, but she continued, nonetheless.

'That is catastrophic news, indeed,' he said sadly, 'I will go inside and enquire for you.'

'Would you, sir?' Anna sounded relieved. 'I'd be much obliged.'

He surveyed her once more before disappearing inside. Huddling into the railings, Anna shivered on the bottom step, almost too nervous to notice the chilly air on her face or the searing pain in her right arm.

The minutes stretched unbearably, her mind in turmoil. What if, by waiting, she had wasted valuable time? She should have gone back along the dock road. She should have asked the dock-gate bobby, a familiar figure round here, if he would help her find her brother. Anna was so desperate for news; her mind was playing tricks. The dock-gate bobby could not leave his post to go and help her. What was she thinking? But he could tell her if he had seen a young lad carrying a weary or drunken sailor's duffle bag to bring him to the safety of the Sailor's Home for a copper or two.

'Oh, please Lord,' Anna fervently prayed, 'I know I'm pestering, but please, let him be here.'

The door opened, and she turned sharply. The man in the wide-brimmed hat came out and her heart leapt to her throat.

'Is he here, Mister? Mister...?' Her voice rose, expectant, fearful. Nevertheless, her hopes dashed when he shook his head.

'I'm sorry, miss.' His courteous, sympathetic tone hurt more deeply than if he had kicked her down the steps. 'There's been no sign of the boy.'

'No.' Anna's heartfelt cry rent the freezing air. She did not think she was strong enough to take much more heartache and loss. Her throat constricted painfully, and the stinging tears welled and ran freely down her frozen cheeks. Unable to thank the stranger for his trouble, she turned blindly towards the river.

'Hold on a moment,' the man shouted, and Anna stalled. Turning, she watched as he fished in his pocket. He drew out some coins. That only meant one thing round here. And no matter how bad things got for her, it would be a cold day in hell before she stooped to selling herself to any man.

'Ta all the same, Mister,' she called over her shoulder, 'but I'm not for sale.' She hurried towards the river, disappearing into the swirling mist. She needed Sam now, more than ever.

* * *

The fire had died, and the gawping crowd had long since dispersed when Sam reached Queen Street. The true horror of the hellish image took a while to register in his mind. Unable to believe what he saw, Sam was mesmerised by the sight that met his eyes. Hands in pockets, he could only stand and stare in horror at the blackened shell of his family home.

'Tragic, aint it?' Jerky Woods blew into his cupped hands, his collar pulled round his ears in the freezing air that smelled of charred, damp wood and old smoke.

'What happened?' Sam could hardly speak the words. Terror holding him in its vice-like grip. Sickened by the devastating condition of his home.

Woods shook his head and shrugged. He could not bring himself to tell Sam his family were in there when the house went up. His guilt would not allow it.

'You said the Cassidys would be at early mass,' Nipper said and felt the grip of his brother's hand round the back of his neck.

'I said no such thing,' Jerky lied and, not meeting his brother's gaze, spat out the dead match.

'Ma couldn't go to mass because she had a nasty fall and injured her leg bad,' Sam explained to Nipper. 'Someone had lifted the cover off the grid, it was dark when she left for work this morning and the street lamp was broken.'

'Wasn't that the cover on the corner of the street?' Nipper asked his brother who gave his neck a none too gentle squeeze.

'That's a shame,' Jerky Woods said. His eyes looking anywhere but at the charred remains of Sam Cassidy's home.

'My family, what...?' Sam did not manage the whole question, terrified of the answer. He knew Jerky Woods missed nothing round here, if anything stirred, he was usually on the fringe and knew what was going on.

'It lit up the whole street.' Ten-year-old Nipper Woods's eyes were bright with ignorant disregard for Sam's devastation. 'Went up as fast as...'

Woods cuffed his young brother round the ear. 'Shut up, big mouth. He does not wanna 'ear that.' Woods's warning glare

silenced Nipper 'He doesn't want details.' Woods looked towards
the windows, usually illuminated with a cosy glow. Now they
were blackened holes, reminding him of lifeless eyes in an empty
skull. The fire took hold quicker than he expected and was well
under way by the time he arrived with Lottie.

Anna Cassidy really should not have made him look small in
front of his pals. Acting like she was better'n everyone. Lookin'
down her nose like he had just crawled out of a putrid chicken.
Well, she ain't lookin' down 'er nose now.

'Gerrof me. I didn't say not'n,' Nipper grumbled when his
older brother tweaked the short hairs on the nape of his neck.

'Keep it that way,' Jerky Woods ordered. His voice low and
menacing. 'It's a shame about your fam'ly,' Woods said over his
shoulder as he walked away, and Sam felt ice-cold water run
through his veins as he headed towards the blackened crust. How
could anybody survive such devastation?

Entering the house he had once called home, Sam turned
back towards the door on hearing footsteps behind him. But
there was nobody there.

Cinders cracked beneath his feet as he ventured into the
gloom. And if it had not been for a small chink of light from the
gas lamp outside, he would lose his way in this house he knew
like the back of his hand.

Shivering, he saw that most of the damage was near the
scorched frame of the front door. The rag rug his mother had
made was a blackened mess on the linoleum floor. Strangely, the
fireguard was still perched against the open grate. Sam got down
on his grubby knees and began to pray.

He did not know how long he stayed there. He could smell
the sweet scent of violets his mother always wore. And he felt her
short motherly nails gently scratch his tired head. Now crouched
on the floor, his legs tucked high up under his chest, his hands

protecting the slim leather box, as his eyelids grew heavy, Sam pictured his mother's delighted smile, when she saw the silver locket, he had bought her for Christmas...

* * *

Reaching Canning Dock, Anna barely noticed the web of skeletal masts and sturdy funnels of the ships moored on the river. A sharp pain bit into her side and stopped her dead in her tracks. She gasped for air, finding it hard to breathe. Maybe she should rest for a few moments, gather her thoughts, get some strength into her cold bones, and let the sharp pain subside.

Resting on an oak casket, she buried her head deep in her shoulder, trying to protect herself from the arctic squall. After a short while, she heaved her body from the casket, knowing she must not waste time feeling sorry for herself. Anna had to find Sam. Where else was there to look? She had searched everywhere she could think of.

Another hail shower forced Anna into a doorway of the Corn Exchange, a place that exemplified the ambitions of Liverpool merchants. Anna slid down the cold tiled wall. Her mind in turmoil, her eyelids heavy. The dockyards had fallen silent and there was no sound beyond the swell of the River Mersey hitting the dock wall. Ma was going to be so angry with her for letting Sam out of her sight. Their Christmas dinner was going to be ruined if he was not there...

9

'You, boy,' a stern voice called from the charred doorway of his burned-out house, causing Sam to jump with fright. He viewed the outline of the policeman with terror even though he had never been in trouble in his life. 'This is no place for you.' The constable's tone was a little softer. He knew the Cassidy family were a respectable lot who never got into trouble, they paid their way, and kept themselves to themselves. He had witnessed the tragic fire that took this little scrapper's family and rightly supposed the lad had nowhere else to go. 'On your feet,' the policeman said, 'it's a bitter night. You'll catch your death.'

Sam stumbled as he got up and the policeman caught him, stopping him falling over.

'What time is it?' He had no idea. 'What happened to my family?'

'Midnight mass has ended, so I'll take you to see Father O'Connell. He might have some news.'

Sam said nothing. His head full of questions but dreading the answers. Where was Anna? How did the fire start? Had his brothers tried to light his father's clay pipe that his mother kept after Da died at sea? Sam dare not ask the policeman how the fire happened. He did not think he could bear the answer.

* * *

Father O'Connell sighed deeply when he heard the ran-tan on the presbytery door. It had been a long and rather tragic day. Tomorrow, the most important day in the church year, would be busy and he had hoped to take to his bed with his cocoa. He was disgruntled to be interrupted at this late hour and blamed Father Furey for allowing the parishioners to call for the least excuse, at any time of the day or night.

'Who can that be, Father?' Mrs Jackson, the housekeeper, said as she put his hot cocoa on to the small round table at the side of his chair. 'It is such a pity Father Furey was called back to Ireland so urgently.'

'And very inconvenient,' Father O'Connell sighed. However, his low muttering did not go undetected by Mrs Jackson.

'Losing your mother is sad at any time,' Mrs Jackson said in mild rebuke, 'but even more so at Christmas, Father. I will see to the door.'

Father O'Connell raised his eyes to the ceiling. He could always depend on Mrs Jackson to put him in his place. When he heard the murmured voices in the hallway, he made his way out to see who it was and what they wanted.

'Hello, Father,' said the policeman, 'I am sorry to call so late, but I have brought this boy as he has nowhere else to go.'

The priest eyed the small boy accompanied by the local policeman, who could see only good things in some of these street urchins. On closer inspection, he recognised the boy as Samuel Cassidy and his tone softened.

'Leave him here, Mrs Jackson will see to him.' Father

O'Connell, being new to the parish, did not view these pocket-sized delinquents through such rose-tinted spectacles as Father Furey did. And his initial distrust seemed justified when, after a short conversation, he showed the policeman out without offering so much as a sniff of hot cocoa and returned to the sitting room, where Mrs Jackson held aloft a beautiful silver locket.

Father O'Connell could not ignore the glint of the silver locket in the beam of gaslight, nor the possibility this young boy had turned to sin. It was not beyond the realm of possibility he would succumb to the wicked ways of the common street urchin now that his family were gone.

'Where did a poor boy like you get money to afford such a fine thing?' Father O'Connell's unsmiling question was drenched in suspicion, making Sam's insides shrink when Mrs Jackson handed the locket to the priest and left the room. The box containing his beloved ma's pendant had slipped from the waist-band of his breeches when Mrs Jackson had taken him by the arm and led him into this pleasant, cosy room. But, on his return, the priest's expression was anything but warm.

'I b-bought it, Father,' Sam stammered, silently praying the priest believed him, knowing he would be in big trouble if he did not. 'I did extra jobs an' everything. It took me a whole year, Father... I got a receipt.' Sam emptied his pockets, but there was no sign of the receipt. 'I did get one. Honest to God.'

'Do not blaspheme, Samuel,' the priest's sharp voice made Sam flinch. 'Show me this proof of sale.' If the boy could produce the evidence, it would obviously prove his innocence, but it would not ensure a more lenient fate.

Sam pulled his pockets out of his short breeches, but there was no sign of the receipt, then he remembered. He had been so eager to show Anna their mother's gift, he left the jewellers in a hurry. Then Jerky Woods had waylaid him. So, when Mr Solomon had called after him, he had been eager to get away.

'The night has been one of pandemonium,' said Father O'Connell, who knew the boy would be hungry and cold, 'Mrs Jackson will give you something hot and nourishing.' The last thing Sam wanted was food. The thought made him feel sick. He wanted to find Anna. 'I will say special prayers for your family,' said the priest, 'and for you, to keep you on the straight and narrow.' Father O'Connell tucked the gift box into the pocket of his cassock for safekeeping. 'I will find out the truth when the shop opens after Christmas.' Until then, he knew Samuel would be better off out of harm's way. Somewhere the local tearaway, Woods, and his cohorts could not have any influence over someone so vulnerable.

He led Sam to the kitchen that smelled of freshly made bread that made his taste buds tingle and his tummy growl. Father O'Connell motioned for him to sit at the well-scrubbed kitchen table, and Mrs Jackson placed a plain white plate that held a slice of thickly cut bread slathered in potted beef paste and a glass of hot milk before him. And even though Sam was bone-weary and had thought he could not face food, he devoured the bread before him and warmed his insides with the hot milk.

When he had finished, Father O'Connell confirmed the nightmare news about his family, and his words, unhindered by maudlin sentiment, hit Sam like a ton of bricks. He knew the fire had claimed his home, but he did not want to believe it had also claimed his family.

'Anna?' Sam's voice was high-pitched with fear. 'What happened to Anna?'

'I will find out all I can tomorrow,' Father O'Connell told the distraught boy, 'but you must get some rest. When you have eaten, Mrs Jackson will show you where you can sleep.' He would not let the boy walk the streets. If young Samuel succumbed to the hyperborean weather, the priest suspected there would be a new face in heaven by the morning.

Sam went over the priest's words again as he followed Mrs Jackson to the small room at the top of the house where he was given a pair of too-large pyjamas from the charity box and, as he slid between the crisp cold sheets, he huddled into a foetal position and the tears began to fall.

* * *

'It is clear to me the boy will be in danger of going astray if he is left to his own devices,' Father O'Connell told Mrs Jackson, who nodded but said little for the moment. Having been housekeeper at Saint Patrick the Apostle Catholic Church for more years than she cared to remember, it was customary for her to join the priests after completing her day's work to discuss the day's activities before retiring to her own room.

'I worry about him turning to unlawful ways without the steadying influence of his family.' Mrs Jackson was a valuable source of parish information.

'I cannot allow that to happen.' Father O'Connell's elasticated principles gave him cause to believe their nightly conversations were not considered gossip. This woman seemed to know everything about everybody in the parish and she had an uncannily accurate opinion on all of them.

Her remark helped to make up his mind when Mrs Jackson said over her cup: 'I would not like to see poor Samuel go the same way as that unruly Woods boy.' Giving a customary shrug of her well-rounded shoulders, she had no idea that her off-the-cuff comment was going to change Sam's life in a way nobody would have suspected.

'Sam has nobody,' Father O'Connell said, staring into the dying embers of the fire, 'his sister is in no fit state to take care of him.'

'What about Ruby Swift?' the housekeeper asked. 'She has offered to take the lad in.'

Father O'Connell shook his head. 'I would not leave my cat in the care of that brazen woman, after what you told me about her,' he answered, 'I would not allow an innocent within ten feet of her.'

'Please don't let it slip that I told you,' Mrs Jackson said, knowing she had the ear of the successful businesswoman, who would cut her off in the blink of an eye if she suspected.

'You are certain that she and Archie Swift are living in sin?' Father O'Connell, still reeling from the housekeeper's earlier revelation, asked Mrs Jackson, who nodded her head.

'Father Furey is aware of the situation,' she said, 'although he does not condone it.'

'Nor does he condemn it, by the look of things,' Father O'Connell huffed, 'and I do wonder at his scruples, allowing this kind of thing to continue in his parish.'

'I'm sure *you* could never approve of such goings-on,' Mrs Jackson's tone was piously disapproving, 'even for the sake of the new church roof, to which she promised a hefty sum.' She watched him drain his cocoa cup.

'The new church roof, you say?' Father O'Connell looked thoughtful as he scraped back his chair and handed his cup to the housekeeper. Wouldn't it be a fine thing to report to the Bishop that they had enough money to replace the church roof. 'Nevertheless, that woman is not a fitting guardian for an impressionable boy.' Ruby Swift will not be the guardian of Samuel Cassidy if he had any say in the matter.

'Do you think he did steal the locket?' Mrs Jackson asked,

enjoying their discussion on this latest turn of events. It made a pleasant change not having to repeat herself over again, as she did with Father Furey, who had been deaf for years.

The younger priest looked doubtful. 'He has no proof he paid for it.' Quiet for a moment, he pondered, then said: 'No matter, I will ensure he is safely out of harm's way.'

'Are you thinking of Saint Simeon's, Father?' Mrs Jackson asked, feeling entitled to speak her mind.

'It is the right place to send a boy who needs rescuing from the sin of the streets, away from the guttersnipes and the vagabonds who roam abroad, causing mayhem and mischief.' He would not wait for Father Furey's return, to make sure Samuel Cassidy had a roof over his head and was taught good Christian values. 'Yes, he will soon learn to be an upstanding member of society there.'

'To think,' said Mrs Jackson, 'Saint Simeon's, built to save ragged and neglected children, is within viewing distance of one of the richest houses in England?'

He stretched to his full five feet six inches. 'And on that note, I will bid you goodnight, Mrs Jackson,' he said, heading towards the stairs.

'Good night, Father,' Mrs Jackson said, taking the cups to the sink. She had to be up again in four hours. If Father Furey were here, she would leave the cups until morning. However, she knew the new priest would not allow such a thing.

* * *

'Jesus, Mary and Joseph,' Anna said aloud when the early-morning peal of first mass bells alerted her, and she opened her blurry eyes. Unable to raise her damaged arm, she could not make the sign of the cross. Her arm had ballooned to twice its size, reminding her the ceiling of her home had crashed down round her.

In her distressed state, she had not noticed she was injured. But now, stiff, and frozen to the bone, Anna knew she must get up and move about and the continuing peal of the bells reminded her that it was Christmas day. The tragic events of the previous day flooded into her head. Ma and the twins were gone. She would never see them again.

The comfort of scalding tears was denied. Anna had cried until the well had run dry. And if she did not get moving, she would join her devastated family before the day was done. And what would happen to Sam? All alone. He could not cope. Her mind was in as much of a whirl as the raging blizzard. She would have it all to do now. Where did she start?

Her smoke-streaked coat had lost its buttons during the calamity and offered nothing in the way of warmth or comfort. As she dragged herself up, Anna felt her body grow too heavy for her legs. It was no good, she thought, she would have to stay sitting down for a little while longer... So easy to hug her knees to her chin for warmth. Her heavy eyelids drooping. Ever so easily, she drifted to a deep, dark place...

10

'I've asked everyone, but nobody has set eyes on either Anna or Sam,' Archie told Ruby when he came back from another search with Ned. 'Nearly all their family wiped out in one swoop.'

'It seems they just disappeared into the night.' Ruby paced the spacious living quarters which she and Archie had moved into with only a few bits of jewellery she owned and Archie's life savings. They had set up the businesses into a very profitable concern.

'I'll go out again when it gets light.' Archie knew Ruby would not rest until she had news of the young ones. 'You stay here in case either of them turns up. Anna may come back for her mother's wages.'

'Yes, Archie, you're right. We have to be practical, they have suffered a nightmare, but they will need money.' Ruby knew her customers, the rough and the refined, who bartered side by side in the neighbouring businesses of the pawnshop run by Archie, and her own exclusive Emporium, would be very willing to help in the search during the lengthening hours. In times of tragedy the whole community came together and did all they could to help find Anna and Sam.

'We've scoured the wharves and warehouses on foot,' Archie said, accepting a cup of tea from a worried-looking Mrs Hughes. 'It's time we got the horses out.' Archie's face was pinched with worry. It had been such a devastating night and he could not even manage a reassuring nod for Ruby. All he could do was hug her and hope for the best, knowing she would be reliving the time when they lost their own daughter... He looked at the clock on the mantlepiece. It was Christmas Day.

'I'll never forgive myself if anything has happened to them, Archie.' Ruby's voice sounded unusually frail. 'Emma was not just an employee she was our friend. The keeper of our secrets.'

Archie knew the locals thought Ruby Swift was one of them, just the way she liked it. It was good for business, she said many times. Little did they know she was as far from being one of them as it was possible to be. He had heard curious women gossiping in the pawnshop queue, when he was totting up a price on their old man's best suit. Pledged on Monday and redeemed on payday. *Lady Ruby*. If only they knew. Classy goods bought from her Emporium on the never-never and kept for best. When times were hard, the middle classes had the assets to hock. If the customers were unable to pay off their pledge, then the goods went right back in the window to resell... Ruby liked to keep things simple. By crossing a palm with silver, she knew anything was possible.

'Don't fret, lass, we'll find them and give them a home. For Emma's sake.'

Always caring, there was a veil of darkness in Ruby's dark eyes. Her typically robust expression held a hint of doubt that Archie had not witnessed for many years. Ruby was the bastion of strength to her customers whom she served with panache and unswerving dignity, but nobody saw the vulnerable side of her except Archie, who, for the past twenty-odd years, had been her right-hand man. Her muscle. Her mainstay.

'Ned and I will find them, don't you worry.' Archie put his arm round her slender shoulders and pulled her close. She was the most wonderful woman he had ever known, and he was utterly devoted to her.

'I love you.' Ruby's voice softened, and he nodded.

'Aye, lass,' he said in that tone of voice that would usually invite rebuke, but Ruby said nothing as a ghost of a smile crossed her lips.

'Please find them, Archie. I can't bear the thought of them roaming the cold streets on Christmas Day, or any day.' Ruby's voice took on that steely quality he knew so well. 'I owe it to their mother.' Ruby regained the business-as-usual facade. Only Archie saw the real woman. His Ruby, who understood people, young and old, rich, or poor. Her steely determination was what she depended on for her own survival. 'When you find them, bring them straight back here.' Ruby kneaded the back of her hand with her knuckles, then she began to take down the decorations from the pine tree. 'The shock will be too much for them to bear. They won't want gaiety and laughter when they will be in so much pain.'

'We will take care of them.' Archie's usually jolly face was grim as he pushed back his thick, steel-coloured hair from a worried brow.

Heading towards the door, Archie called to Ned, who was in the kitchen talking to Mrs Hughes.

* * *

'It doesn't seem right, having all the trappings of Christmas out on show when we've lost one of our own,' said Mrs Hughes.

'I expect Ruby will know the right thing to do,' Ned answered as he headed to the door, 'I also expect she's let her cup of tea go cold.'

'You're not as daft as you look either,' Mrs Hughes gave a wry smile, preparing another tea tray. Something told her today was going to be a long, unusual Christmas day unlike any they had known before. Aiming to keep busy she moved about the kitchen as she said, 'I'll make a fresh pot.'

* * *

'I heard the fire was started deliberate,' one of his customers, coming back from first mass, told Archie when they went to see if Anna or Sam had returned to the house.

'Deliberate?' Archie asked and looked at Ned, his eyebrows drawn together. 'How come?'

'Someone – I can't say who – heard Nipper Woods telling a lad from Primrose Cottage that he had seen someone push a lit match through the letter box.'

'A lit match wouldn't cause that much damage.' Archie's eyes took in the devastation of the blackened house, looking much worse in daylight against the whiteness of the snow.

'It would if it were on the end of a paraffin-soaked rag.' The woman's nostrils flared in disgust. 'Whoever did that wants locking up.'

'They'll get more than that if it's true,' Ned warned, his fists balled and his steely eyes cold. 'Come on, Archie, we've got to find Anna and Sam.'

* * *

'What's that over there?' Ned asked Archie, unsure if the bundle in the doorway of the Corn Exchange was human. He jumped down from the carriage before it stopped to look more closely. 'It's her, Archie! It's Anna!'

Pulling off his warm overcoat, he wrapped it round Anna's shoulders. She flinched, barely conscious, and his eye caught her badly swollen arm, relief flooding through him when he realised she was still alive. But she was in a bad way, he could tell just by looking at her.

Roughly he wiped his eyes with the pad of his hand, as Archie jumped down from the carriage.

'Anna, we've looked all over for you...' Archie said tenderly, 'everybody has been out looking.' He nodded to Anna's wounded arm, and Ned gently lifted it.

Gasping in horror, he mouthed the words, '*It's broken.*'

'Sore,' Anna managed to utter before her eyelids fluttered and closed once more.

'Help me get her up into the carriage.' Archie could hear the crackle in her chest. 'We must take her straight to the infirmary.'

'Here, let me.' Ned picked Anna up as if she weighed no more than a small child, and when Archie opened the carriage door, Ned climbed inside holding Anna close. He could not take his eyes from her stricken face and slowly shook his head and told her, 'I reckon if you get through this, you'll get through anything.'

Archie hurried to the front of the carriage and Ned tried to keep Anna warm. He did not know what he would do if he lost her. Gently stroking her pale, marble-cold face, Ned knew it was only Anna's help and Ruby's generosity that had kept him from feral activities, the like of which could have certainly put him behind bars. He gazed down at her unconscious form and could not prevent tears rolling down his face. Anna was the best friend any lad could have. He could not lose her. He could not.

* * *

Ruby paced the room, her anxious gaze fixed fearfully on the door, praying it would open and Archie or Ned would bring her news. Poor Emma. And those two angel boys. So small. So helpless. A funeral would have to be arranged, but she doubted Anna would have the means. As a loyal and trusted employee, the least Ruby could do would be to give Emma and her babies a respectable send-off.

Her mind wandered back to the time Emma came to enquire about work. Newly widowed with two young children and two on the way, she was willing to scrub floors to earn a crust and keep her children fed. Immediately, Ruby saw she had something about her when she speedily corrected another woman's calculations. Only a whisper from the workhouse, Ruby offered Emma a position immediately.

Emma Cassidy earned her money and was beholden to nobody. She had a good head for figures and was an asset to the business behind the large windows draped in fancy laced curtains that showed off Ruby's own private pieces. The ones that were never sold but showed good taste. It did not take long for women with a bit of brass to frequent her Emporium. Eventually, a select few, trusted customers were able to purchase items for a small sum each week, with added interest of course. Business boomed. Then, with Emma in the back office, some women could pay their dues in private. Small loans were arranged. To purchase something bigger perhaps. A bed. A sideboard. Maybe even a whole dining-room suite, which Ruby sold in the Emporium.

Expectedly, the men began to call. Bankers. Office managers. Doctors. Men who needed to keep up appearances but did not have the wherewithal to do so. After Emma's careful vetting, Ruby would invite them to call into the office, canny enough to realise that even better business could grow from middle-class social climbers who could ill afford the lifestyle they chose. Then, some would come back with a sad story of how they could not repay their loan. Sadly, for them, Archie and Ned would have to pay the debtors a cautionary visit, retrieving items to the value of that week's instalment.

It never ceased to amaze Ruby how many trusting wives, on the supposedly generous instructions of their husbands, gave away their best china, crystal, or silver to a worthy cause, while their spouse was at the office or the bank. The wives, proud of their beloved's generosity, gave lavishly to charity and parted with their possessions without question. Living in their country villas, they never saw their precious belongings up for sale in the bay-fronted window of Ruby's Emporium.

Distracted from her thoughts, Ruby heard the heavy tread of footsteps speeding up the stairs.

'We found her, Miss Ruby,' Ned told her, his face full of anguish. 'But we could not bring her back here, she has something called pneumonia.'

'Where is she now? I must go to her,' Ruby said, but Archie put his hand on her arm to stop her.

'She's in the Northern Hospital in Great Howard Street, but we were told Anna must have complete rest for the next forty-eight hours.' He did not tell her that the girl may not last the day.

Ruby's hands flew to her face and her colour drained. She had had a brother who died of pneumonia after falling into a lake. Slowly shaking her head, she closed her eyes, but the tears still came. 'We still have to find Sam.'

* * *

'The next few days will be critical to her survival,' the doctor told Ruby, who refused to be bound by procedure. If her charity donations were good enough for the hospital, she would insist on seeing Anna. But, alas, she was not allowed onto the ward and the only thing she could do to try to make things better was to have Anna moved to a single room, where Ruby hired a nurse to stay by her bed.

When they got back home, Ruby kept herself busy, removing the Christmas decorations.

'There will be more Christmases,' Ruby said, unable to eat the turkey dinner Mrs Hughes had prepared.

'An empty sack won't stand,' Mrs Hughes said, removing the untouched food. 'You won't be a blind bit of good to the girl if you make yourself sick by not eating.'

* * *

The following morning, the tweeny brought in breakfast, because Mrs Hughes was at early mass, and once again Ruby could not eat a thing as she worried about Anna and Sam. Poor Sam, what had become of him, she wondered as she sipped her tea, knowing the only sustenance she had taken since the fire was beginning to lose its appeal.

A short while later, there was a flurry of activity out on the landing and, after a hasty knock, Mrs Hughes burst into the room looking flustered.

'The fire was the talk of early mass,' she breathed, her face mottled by the cold weather and not a little excitement. 'Father O'Connell told me that little Sam Cassidy was brought to the presbytery by a policeman in the early hours of Christmas Day. Father O'Connell said he would take care of him for the foreseeable.'

'Oh, did he now?' Ruby felt the hairs rise on the back of her neck. 'Well, we will soon see about that.'

'Slow down, Ruby,' Archie said, his tone, always warm, soothed her. 'He won't come to any harm in the priest's house on Boxing Day.'

'Be that as it may,' she said, feeling calmer, 'but we will go and fetch him. I'm sure he must be at his wits' end worrying about Anna.'

'He won't be there for much longer,' said Mrs Hughes as she headed towards the door, 'Father O'Connell is taking him to Saint Simeon's.'

'He's doing what!' Ruby's stormy eyes widened. 'Archie, we are going to see the priest. And we have a funeral to arrange for Emma and the boys.'

'Please don't fret, my darling,' Archie said, 'we will sort this out.'

'Isn't it bad enough Anna won't be well enough to attend her family's funeral,' Ruby said, and Archie knew when she made her mind up about something there was no stopping her. Ruby liked nothing more than a good cause and this time, there was none better. 'Although missing her family funeral might be a blessing in disguise,' Ruby continued, as if having a conversation in her head, only for words to pop out of her mouth every now and then. A sure sign she was agitated.

Archie knew Ruby was still as beautiful today as that first time he'd set eyes on her all those years ago. Back then, he worked in her father's stables. She was a couple of years younger and had that wilful streak he admired. It did not take long for him to fall hopelessly, desperately, totally in love with her and that love had never diminished, growing stronger with each passing day. He would do anything for his Ruby. Even calling her by the name of his beloved aunt. Because that was how she wanted it.

'Sam must come and live here with us, there is plenty of room.'

'Of course.' Archie's eyebrows pleated and he looked troubled. 'Although, they may not want to live here when he finds out the truth. We don't live a conventional lifestyle.'

'Archie,' Ruby reached for his hand and her voice dropped to a whisper, 'you are such a worrier. The fact that we are not married is nobody's business but our own.'

His returning smile was cautious, when he recognised the haunted look on Ruby's beautiful face from old. He could have kicked himself for being so thoughtless. 'I'm sorry. Of course, they will come to live here, where else would they go?' Ruby liked everything to run smoothly and Archie did his best to make it so.

'You are so thoughtful, Archie,' she said, affording him the credit for the idea. 'I am sure Anna will settle in too once she is recovered.'

Giving them a roof over their head, Ruby felt, was the least she could do in fond remembrance of their mother. Just as they had done years ago for Ned, who was in danger of becoming a gypsy fist-fighter before an unlucky punch felled his widowed father.

* * *

When they reached the presbytery of Saint Patrick the Apostle, Ruby tapped her foot.

'Come on, come on,' she said, waiting for the door to be answered and, moments later, Mrs Jackson, Father O'Connell's housekeeper, came to the door and gave Ruby a pleasant smile.

'I'm afraid you've missed him,' said Mrs Jackson, expecting that Ruby and Archie had brought their customary Boxing Day donation to the parish fund.

'We've come for the young lad,' said Archie. 'Sam Cassidy.'

'Father has taken him to Saint Simeon's,' said the housekeeper.

Archie bid the housekeeper good day and guided Ruby down the winding path. He caught her when he felt her slump against him, and when she looked up at him, her face was colourless. 'You know I can't go to that place, Archie.'

'Don't worry, we will think of something.'

11

Sam felt his insides twist into a painful knot as he journeyed with Father O'Connell to Saint Simeon's Orphanage, situated thirty miles outside Liverpool, between the sea and the countryside. He barely noticed the golden sands at the end of the long trip and certainly felt no joy. None. How could he, when all his family were dead.

He had not slept a wink in the unfamiliar hard bed for the past two nights and when the priest's housekeeper put a breakfast of steaming porridge before him each morning, he could hardly look at it, let alone eat it. When it had grown cold and rubbery, Father O'Connell had nodded to Mrs Jackson to take it away. And the sick empty feeling in Sam's stomach was still there when they got to the iron barley-sugar-twist gates of Saint Simeon's.

'Here we are.' Father O'Connell, although not old, was stout in build and breathless as he clambered from the carriage outside the wide gates of Saint Simeon's.

Sam's disinterested gaze rested on the outstretched wings of the stone angels, looking down on him from the high brick pillars, and he wondered where his own guardian angels were during the fire.

Climbing down from the carriage, the three-storey building stood stark and forbidding against a pewter sky. The meticulous, perfectly laid-out box hedges stood in regimented squares, making Sam realise he had never seen so much greenery. And apart from the wide, double, wrought-iron gates, the rough, red-brick walls, higher than the tallest man, were surrounded by the frosty sprawling branches of huge oak trees. The cold shudder that caused his body tremors had nothing to do with the freezing weather.

'Come along, Samuel, do not dawdle.' Father O'Connell led the way briskly through a Gothic arch at the front entrance, where the smell of boiled cabbage permeated the vast foyer and caused the first stirrings of hunger.

'Wipe your feet, boy.' Father O'Connell nodded to the highly polished parquet floor that led to an oak panelled staircase. The smell of furniture polish mingled with the smell of the midday meal and Sam's stomach growled. But he doubted that, even though he was hungry, he could keep anything down.

Noticing the boy's colour drain, Father O'Connell moved quickly from Sam's side, lest he parted company with his innards. 'Do not disgrace yourself, Samuel,' the priest warned, 'if you make a mess, you will be the one to clean it.'

Sam sucked a long stream of air through his teeth, trying to control the urge to heave.

'They're all having their dinner,' said a petite girl with hay-coloured braids, standing, or rather leaning, against a door marked *Master's Office.* Sam reckoned she was about the same age as him.

'Who is having their dinner?' Father O'Connell asked, removing his black biretta.

'All of them.' The girl's tone suggested the priest had asked the dimmest question, while her thin shoulders offered a half shrug.

Sam could not help but admire her irreverence and worked hard to stifle a smile. He liked her on sight. Having only just met her, he felt he had known this little girl all his life. She reminded him of Anna, straightforward, spirited, her bright blue eyes taking in every detail of their arrival.

'Go and fetch the Master,' Father O'Connell said impatiently, obviously irritated by the girl, who was leaning her head to one side as if studying them.

'I can't do that, Father,' she shook her head. 'Mrs Hastings told me to stay here and not move.'

'Very well, is there anybody else who can attend to us?'

'Shall I go and find out, Father?' The girl with the hay-coloured hair contradicted herself, and Sam could not stop the snort of laughter that burst forth, obviously amusing the girl, whose eyes danced with mischief. She was being awkward, Sam could tell.

'Yes, do.' The priest watched her bob a curtsey in accordance with his wish.

'I'll just knock, shall I?' Without further ado, her small fist beat the door with a strength that belied her delicate stature.

A moment later, a tall, reedy man, wearing a white cotton napkin over a black frock coat, swung open the door and bent towards her.

'What is it, Daisy?' he asked, obviously put out at being disturbed when he was eating.

'There's someone to see you, sir,' Daisy said. 'He didn't give his name.'

'Daisy Flynn,' the master sighed, 'go and finish your dinner, and this time do it *quietly*.'

Sam noticed the last word was stressed and elongated. *Like the master*, he thought, briefly forgetting his troubles. Enjoying the exchange, he watched the girl scurrying towards the long corridor ahead.

'Mr Hastings,' Father O'Connell said without preamble, 'we spoke on the telephone, this is Samuel Cassidy.'

There was a moment's pause and then the tall man's eyes lit up.

'Ahh, Father O'Connell, so this is the new chap – Merry Christmas.' He held out a thin white hand and Father O'Connell shook it.

'Same to you,' said the priest in a dull voice, while Sam's eyes took in the beautiful manger by the far fireplace, its blazing embers giving the foyer a welcoming feel.

'Mrs Hastings and I would be delighted if you join us for luncheon?'

Father O'Connell leaned forward, his eyes aglow, and nodded enthusiastically. 'That would be delightful,' he said with more enthusiasm than he had shown since they left the priest's house.

'Daisy,' Mr Hastings called the young girl back, 'take this young fellow to the dining hall and ask cook to give him some hot food, he looks perished.'

Daisy ran back, took Sam's arm and bobbed another curtsey before leading him along the passage and down three steps, chattering all the time.

'So, where d'you spring from then?' Daisy asked, and when Sam did not answer she continued unabashed. 'Are you coming to stay here? We are having cabbage and boiled potatoes for dinner today... I wish it were yesterday, we got plum pudding yesterday, so we could cebra... I mean cebrelate... enjoy ourselves.' She giggled at her inability to pronounce the word *celebrate*, and Sam wondered if all the people in Saint Simeon's were as scatty as Daisy.

She opened one of the two doors and almost dragged him inside the large dining hall, where there were two long rows of tables, covered in immaculate white tablecloths.

'It doesn't always look like this,' Daisy explained pragmatically. 'The tablecloths only come out at Christmas and Easter.' In the middle of the rows at a top table, four adults were seated behind a beautiful display of dark Jackson ivy complemented by blood red berries. When Daisy let go of the door, it banged shut and all eyes turned to look at them, but nobody spoke, except Daisy. 'Miss. Miss. I have brought this boy for his dinner. The master said—'

'That's enough, Daisy.' A round woman dressed from head to toe in black got up from her place at the top table. 'Sit down and eat your dinner – *in silence.*'

Daisy's chin tilted upwards and she looked incredibly pleased with herself when she scurried to the empty seat at the far side of the hall, the heels of her black button boots echoing on the highly polished floor. When she sat down, Daisy immediately began whispering to a girl sitting next to her.

* * *

'Such a sad situation,' said Mr Hastings. 'Most of these children have been rescued from vile immorality and I dare say this one is no exception.'

The priest, enjoying the delicious food and drink, nodded. 'His mother was a widow,' he said, not taking his eyes from the plate, 'he has an older sister, but she does not have the means to care for him...' He sighed. 'There is nothing else for it... The boy cannot be allowed to roam the streets.'

'We can arrange something, as you know,' Mr Hastings said, taking his seat by the fire. 'Something that gives these poor wretches the chance to better themselves.'

'You mean the Child Migration Scheme?' Father O'Connell asked, and Mr Hastings, satiated after a huge roast dinner followed by a delicious trifle pudding, nodded through a cloud of cigar smoke.

'We have a party of children going out to Canada in January,' Mr Hastings said, 'would that be a problem?'

'Not at all,' Father O'Connell answered, 'the boy knows his family perished... What is to keep him here?' The move would keep the boy out of the clutches of that harlot, Ruby Swift. Father O'Connell knew all about Ruby and Archie Swift, living under the guise of man and wife when, in truth, they were living in sin. If they weren't so generous to the parish fund, he would have let everybody know of their evil ways.

'Quite,' said Mr Hastings. 'He can make a new life for himself and not be a burden on society, like some unfortunates.'

'I will sign the paper's immediately.'

And by the scratch of a pen, Sam's future was assured before his dinner had been eaten.

After Father O'Connell signed the papers, sealing Sam's fate and giving Saint Simeon's permission to migrate the boy to Canada, he said: 'Samuel is physically and mentally alert, you will have no trouble migrating him; he is an ideal example of a boy who will reap the rewards of Canada.'

'Canada is a young country,' Mr Hastings sounded eager, 'it is hungry for good, white British stock, an ideal training ground for boys who want to make something of themselves.'

'Although, I have heard *some* conflicting reports about the scheme,' Father O'Connell said, standing with his back to the high mantle, warming his well-cushioned backside.

'The arrangement does separate these poor wretches from their families. However, that is not always a bad thing given some of the families I have seen.' The guardian poured a generous measure of golden liquid into a crystal glass.

'Migration to Canada is a wonderful chance to make something better of their miserable lives.' Father O'Connell was convinced this was the best thing for the boy and did not feel the need to burden Father Furey with the details when he was grieving. 'It does sound the ideal choice.'

'Many children seeking refuge at our door have been rescued from sin and now enjoy a life of purpose.' Mr Hastings rocked back on his heels, his jutting chin giving an obvious show of self-importance. 'Some of these poor wretches had never breathed good clean air until they came here, their lungs clogged with smoke-fuelled fog and grime. And when they encounter the Canadian prairies all thoughts of their tough life back in England are just a mere memory.'

'You make the migration scheme sound like a winning ticket to the opening of the Pearly Gates.' Father O'Connell smiled and raised his glass of exceptionally good brandy. 'It is the ideal solution, a wonderful opportunity for this poor boy to make something of himself in a healthy country.'

Since the papers were signed, and the hands shook, all was well in Father O'Connell's world as he ambled to his carriage feeling very mellow indeed. Banging his walking cane on the roof of the carriage, he signalled to the driver that he was ready to go. And as the rhythm of the carriage lulled him, he decided a little snooze was in order, allowing his return journey to refresh him in time for evening mass. It really had been the most tiring day.

12

'Go and fetch your cap, Samuel,' Mr Hastings said in the drawing room of Saint Simeon's on a cold January day in the new year. Mr Hastings looked to the priest. 'Good journey?' He offered the chair by the fire, taking his seat opposite.

'The roads are very icy in places, and not for the faint-hearted in this weather.' Father O'Connell watched Sam leave the room before reminding Mr Hastings he had come straight from the funeral of the boy's family, and knowing Ruby Swift was still angry he had whisked Samuel away on Boxing Day without consulting her. He knew she was eager to care for the boy, but he did not consider her a suitable guardian.

'I did not feel it wise for Samuel to attend the family funeral,' said Mr Hastings, 'I believe the ceremony would have been traumatic, and unsettle the boy whilst adjusting to his new life.'

'Yes, I understand,' Father O'Connell said, knowing Samuel had not been allowed to visit his sister either. So, he was surprised when Mr Hastings told him on the telephone that Samuel may visit his sister in hospital today and asked if he would accompany the boy.

* * *

Sam was overjoyed when he learned from Mr Hastings that Anna was alive but even more so when he was told he could go and see her. His dark blue eyes were hopeful, knowing his sister had been at death's door a few times. He had been terrified he would lose her too. His stomach was doing somersaults when Ned Kincaid, muffled in a heavy coat and thick scarf, was waiting patiently, holding the reins in his gloved hands and waving to him before Sam climbed into the carriage.

Sitting opposite Father O'Connell, feeling very privileged, Sam could not wait to see Anna, and the sway of the carriage did nothing to sooth his overexcited nerves.

'Is Anna getting better?' Sam asked as they pulled up outside Ruby's Emporium. Seeing his mother's employer waiting for them gave him courage.

'I'm afraid not,' Father O'Connell said as Ruby got into the carriage, 'so do not be too shocked when you see her.'

Ruby nodded to the priest. Even though her heart ached for the boy with the pleading eyes, she could not bring herself to collect him from the orphanage. But Sam must see his sister; Anna was not recovering as expected.

'Will Anna be in hospital for a long time?' Sam was dressed in the outdoor uniform of Saint Simeon's Orphanage, she noticed, and looked very respectable in a brown woollen jacket, matching flat cap, rough grey shirt, brown corduroy breeches and heavy boots. Ruby thought Sam looked smaller than she remembered.

'We hope she will perk up when she hears your voice.'

'Anna has been very poorly,' Father O'Connell said in his plain-speaking Irish brogue, 'and she needs all our prayers.'

'I've got the angels and saints harassed with all the praying I've been doing,' Sam muttered, hoping the priest had not heard him when he saw Ruby hide a secret smile by looking out of the carriage window. 'But I'm glad I can visit Anna,' Sam said as they pulled up outside the soot-covered red brick building. It took every ounce of Sam's control and good manners to contain the urge to run on ahead. He was so eager to see his beloved sister. He so wished he could tell Anna, or even Miss Ruby, about his new adventure. But he was sworn to secrecy on the understanding he may visit Anna. But he would have liked to share the news that Mr Hastings had told him he had won a place alongside other lucky children to go to a new country called Canada.

It was going to be a fresh start. Great news for deprived children like him, Mr Hastings said. Although Sam had not realised he was deprived. So, when he was shown photographs of smiling Mounties on horseback, of brown bears standing upright on two legs waving from the other side of the camera, of pine trees and snow and mountains and lakes, his adventurous imagination was sparked as never before, and he could not wait to go. The prospects of a better life were astonishing, Mr Hastings said. He would have chances that he would never get living here. Anna would be thrilled for him, if only he could tell her. And she would join him out there when she was better, Mr Hastings told him.

'You cannot go onto the ward,' the straight-backed nurse looked very stern, and Sam's heart sank with disappointment. 'Your sister had a relapse overnight and is now sleeping heavily...' Sam could feel the tightening ache in his throat. Blinking rapidly to stem the threatening tears, he saw the nurse's eyes soften. Then, in a gentler tone, she said quietly, 'You may look through the window.'

'I won't disturb her, Nurse, I won't be a bit of bother. Honest...' He desperately wanted to try to make Anna aware he had come to see her. 'I'll sit beside her bed, hold her hand to show her... if she needs me...' But no matter how often he pleaded, the answer was the same. A definite shake of her head under a starched cap told him she would not allow him anywhere near Anna. Not even to give her a little kiss on the cheek.

'Why can't the boy sit with his sister?' Ruby asked as she marched up the corridor with Ned. How dare this chit of a girl tell Sam he could not see his poor sister?

'Doctor's orders,' the nurse said, but her high-handed tone did not scare Ruby.

'I pay the doctor. And I pay him well. So, run along and have a nice cup of tea while this boy slips in there to see his sister.' She nodded to the small private ward, 'He has come a long way to see her.'

Sam could see Anna through the large window. Her eyes closed and she looked peaceful in the iron bed. There was no colour in her cheeks at all, he noticed, resting his forehead against the glass. His finger trailed a small outline of the thin bed. He kissed the tip of his finger and placed it on the glass towards her lips. Poor Anna, she looked ever so ill.

'She's been like that since last night,' the nurse changed her tone when she whispered to Ruby, while Sam could not take his eyes from his stricken sister.

'Will she... will she...?' Sam's voice cracked, and he found he could not voice his fears.

'I've had enough of this, come with me, Sam.' Ruby put her hand on Sam's shoulder and led him in to see Anna. 'Something is preventing her from recovering,' Ruby told him, whilst the priest waited outside, 'I think the sound of familiar voices will do her the power of good.'

'They're doing everything they can...' Ned could barely get the words out, more scared than he had ever been, 'it depends on how much fight she has in her.'

'Nobody fights better than our Anna,' Sam said, sitting beside her bed with the conviction of one who believed in more than divine intervention. 'She can fight anyone or anything...' His finger traced the outline of her face and her plaster-covered arm and he looked up to the adults present. 'She can, you know...' His voice was barely a whisper, and he did nothing to check the tears rolling down his face, wondering if he would ever see her again. His Anna had always looked out for him and shared her jam butty because he was a greedy tyke who gobbled his own too quickly. His Anna who taught him his A, B, Cs... He was going to pray harder than he had ever prayed before. 'I don't think I could bear it if she were taken too.'

'As soon as she is strong,' Ruby said, watching him wipe his tears with the cuff of his jacket, 'she will come and live with us, and you, Sam. Would you like that?'

Her overbright voice was almost more than he could bear, and Sam nodded, unable to speak. Forbidden to tell Miss Ruby he would not be here tomorrow. He was leaving for a place called Manitoba on the other side of the world, first thing tomorrow morning.

'We must let her rest,' Father O'Connell said, urging him from the room to look through the window one more time.

'Ta-ra, Anna... I have to go now,' Sam's murmured words caused a cloud of condensation on the glass when he took one last look and noticed her thick lashes flutter. For just a single moment, she opened her pale eyes and looked at him. The ghost of a smile hovering on her lips. Then her eyes closed again. She was giving him her blessing to leave and make a better life.

Sam, led away down the long corridor by Ruby and Ned, looked back a thousand times, memorising every detail of the cabbage-coloured tiles and the smell of strong disinfectant that would linger on his clothes long after he left Liverpool. The flicker of Anna's fair lashes, the shock of freckles covering the bridge of her nose... He would never forget any of it.

'Father O'Connell has the silver locket I bought for Ma,' he said, when he caught Ruby's worried expression. 'I didn't pinch it, honest-to-God.' He crossed his puny chest with his right hand. 'Mr Solomon, the jeweller, will vouch for me. It might go some way to pay for her nursing, even...' He could not utter those dreadful words – *if she does not make it.*

* * *

Sam felt the tough leather of the blistering hobnailed boots cut deep into his feet as he lined up with nine other boys and ten girls. Daisy stood next to him as usual, looking very smart in her new tartan tam-o'-shanter beret, given to all the girls especially for the occasion.

They were also given a brown cardboard suitcase to open. Inside each was a selection of donated clothes, underwear, two handkerchiefs, a sewing kit – pins, thread, bobbin, a pencil and writing paper. Sam's eyes had widened. This was the first time he ever had anything to call his own. Everything he needed for the new world was inside the suitcase.

'At great expense,' said Mr Hastings as they gathered in his study, 'we are sending you, our cleverest, fittest, and most able-bodied young people to Canada. We expect you to make us proud.' He did not divulge the fact that the cost of fifteen pounds, paid for each child to emigrate, was cheaper than the twelve pounds per year it would cost to look after them under Poor Law rules, until they were able to make their own way in the world. 'You are expected to read these every day,' Mr Hastings told Sam when he handed him a copy of John Bunyan's, *The Pilgrim's*

Progress and a leather-bound Bible. Each of the other nine boys and ten girls joining him on the journey to Canada received the same. '*The Pilgrim's Progress* is an allegory.' Mr Hastings pointed a large ruler in his direction. 'Samuel, tell your travelling companions what an allegory is.'

'It is a parable, sir,' Sam said with confidence, recalling his favourite pastime when he and his siblings would sit round the fireside listening to their mother read stories from a well-thumbed copy of *Aesop's Fables*.

'That is correct. We have taught you well in the short time you have been with us.' Mr Hastings' smile was broad, obviously taking credit for his mother's work, but Sam did not dwell on the thought as Mr Hastings was still talking. 'You will be like the Christian who overcame many obstacles to reach the Celestial City. The story will encourage you as you embark on your journey to a new life. You have a place among the elite.'

Sam puffed up his chest, feeling suddenly proud.

'Not all are chosen to go to this new country called Canada. It will be a splendid opportunity for deprived children such as you.'

His chest deflated a little. His family might not have had much, he thought, but they were loved and cared for. Ma did her absolute best to keep the family together when Pa was killed at sea. And if she were looking down from heaven, she would see him do his best too.

Sam lowered his gaze to the floor, he swallowed hard and his chest tightened. Then he thought about this wonderful chance he had been given to better himself. A chance his mother and his brothers would never enjoy.

Anna will be thrilled, Sam thought. If only he had been able to tell her. However, that was impossible now. *I will do well, for the sake of my family and one day when I have saved enough money, I could pay for Anna to come and join me.*

Sam did not look back when he joined his fellow pupils as the horse-drawn omnibus pulled away from the orphanage. Heading for a new life.

13

Ned visited Anna the next day and sat beside her bed, listening to her shallow, rasping gasp, and he prayed she would survive. She had been like this since he and Archie brought her here four weeks ago. And not a day went by that he didn't sneak in to check she was still fighting to stay alive.

Even though she looked so ill, she was beautiful, cocooned in pristine sheets tucked under her chin by the competent nurse and, gently, Ned stroked her long, honey-coloured hair that fanned the pillow. Anna's fingers gently curved round his work-toughened hand and he tenderly kissed them. Something he would never dare do when she was awake. Poor Anna, if anything happened to her, he did not know how he would cope.

'I was hoping to see a change by now,' the doctor said in hushed tones behind him, and Ned spun round. He had been absorbed in willing Anna to wake; he had not heard anybody enter the room. He found it hard to concentrate on anything except his stricken friend.

'Will she... will she...?' Ned found he could not voice the fears that kept him awake at night, knowing Ruby and Archie were just as anxious. *Please fight on, Anna*, he silently pleaded, unable to imagine a life without her. 'You've got to make her well, Doctor.' His whispered words were hoarse as he wiped his eyes with the pad of his thumb to try to stop the tears welling, but it was no good, nothing could stop them.

'I will do everything I can...' the doctor said, putting his hand on Ned's shoulder.

Looking at her now, it was hard to believe there were so many days when Anna had shared her hopes and dreams for the future with him, because that was all she had to share.

'Would she be better at home?' Fear laced Ned's voice. He had heard stories of people who never came out of these places alive.

'She is receiving the best possible care,' the doctor replied as a nurse dabbed Anna's raging forehead with a cooled flannel. She had been in and out of consciousness for a long time. 'Sometimes, the mind needs to close down to heal the body.'

'It has been weeks.' Ned was desperately impatient for her to get better. 'I thought she might be stronger by now.'

'She experienced more suffering than we will ever know,' the doctor said, 'and even though her body is healing, the mind is a mystery.'

'We can only wait and pray,' Ned said just as Ruby came into the room, and he got up to give her his seat.

'We'll beg help from the big man upstairs,' Ruby told Ned. She had once believed in a higher deity. Although not any more. But she knew Ned believed. And she would not deride his faith. 'As long as the middleman keeps his sticky beak out of my concern.'

Her thoughts turned now to Father O'Connell and his overbearing attitude. From the moment they met, Ruby and the priest had clashed. The mistrust was obvious on both sides, they would never agree on anything.

'We have to believe she will pull through,' Ruby said, trying to remain positive. 'As soon as Anna is well enough to leave here, she is coming home with us.'

'She will fight this.' Ned's heart soared, knowing Ruby was going to give his best friend a home.

'I am going to write to Father Furey, who is the parish priest, after all, and I shall inform him that his stand-in has incarcerated young Sam at a time when he needs people round him upon whom he can depend and trust.' Ruby, looking at Ned, could plainly see what she had suspected for a long time: Ned Kincaid loved Anna Cassidy with his whole being. Ruby recalled the way his eyes lit up when Anna walked into a room. And how he teased her to hide those loving feelings. His conversation always included her name. *Anna said this, Anna said that, Anna thought this, Anna did that.*

Ruby knew true love when she saw it and Ned Kincaid was displaying all the signs. Looking at him now, Ruby could tell Ned was full to the brim with suppressed sorrow, he would stay here day and night if he was allowed. Hardly taking his eyes from her, only nodding, unable to speak, but Anna needed her rest and so too Ned. Ruby advised they leave.

'We will come in again, tomorrow, Anna.' Ned reluctantly got up and, for just one moment, she opened her pale eyes, and for the first time in weeks Ned heard her speak.

'*Stay safe, Sam... Stay safe.*'

'Anna, it's me. Ned.' He looked to Ruby, and they hurried back to sit beside Anna willing her to open her eyes again. But she fell silent, so still, Ned worried he had imagined it.

'Maybe the crisis is passing,' Ruby said, letting him know he had not imagined Anna's whispered words. 'Anna seemed to grow stronger after Sam came to visit. I will ask Father O'Connell to fetch him again.'

Ruby's unstinting dedication to Anna over the last weeks had been a revelation to Ned. She even helped the nurse to bathe and change Anna's nightclothes, and change the bed, and when she was at her worst, Ruby stayed with her all night. The older woman could not have done any more if Anna had been her own daughter.

'Archie is speaking to Matron, Ned.' Ruby went on. 'We want to bring Anna and Sam home. Sam is not a juvenile delinquent, his poor mother did the best she possibly could for her children, and I have a duty to her to make sure her offspring are well cared for.'

Ruby's eyes were full of concern when Archie entered the little side ward, and he silently nodded, Ruby sighed. All was well with the world when Archie was beside her.

'We can apply for Sam to live with us,' Archie said. 'If anybody can win them over, you can,' he added, knowing Ruby would do everything in her power to persuade the orphanage to release the boy into her care.

'I doubt that very much, Archie, the new priest took an instant dislike to me.' And she thought she knew why; he had obviously heard about her and Archie not being married. 'I would much rather deal with Father Furey, but he is not due back from Ireland until next week so I have no choice but to deal with that unapproachable man of the cloth,' Ruby said with new-found determination, 'but it doesn't mean I cannot communicate with Father Furey. I will send him a telegram first thing tomorrow. But before that, I will try one more time to persuade Father O'Connell to allow the boy into my care.'

* * *

'I would take the best care of Sam. You must let us care for him. For his mother's sake and for his sister's well-being.' Ruby was unaccustomed to begging, finding the situation unnerving when she went round to the presbytery of Saint Patrick the Apostle.

'Sam is the only person Anna has left,' she added. She was going to do all she could to reunite brother and sister.

Father O'Connell lifted his hand to silence her. 'Samuel is at an impressionable age,' he said, unwavering, 'he would be too close to unsavoury influences.'

Imagining a double meaning in his words may be a sign of a guilty conscience, Ruby matched his direct gaze. How dare he insinuate that she and Archie were unsavoury influences. 'Would you care to elaborate, Father?'

Archie was concerned for Ruby's blood pressure when he stepped forward, knowing she was not averse to telling the priest exactly what she thought of him, which would not help matters.

Father O'Connell spoke again, addressing Archie more favourably than he did Ruby. 'Your dedication to this unfortunate boy is admirable, Mr Swift,' Father O'Connell said, lifting his chin and looking down his elongated nose, 'but you cannot save every poor child.'

'I understand that,' Archie replied. He suspected the lifestyle he and Ruby chose to live did not meet with Father O'Connell's approval.

'These children are different, they are respectable and good-living,' Ruby cut in. 'I owe it to their mother to take good care of them.' She was desperate to reunite brother and sister, knowing Sam was safe in her charge might give Anna the strength to recover. 'Emma Cassidy was more than our employee she was a valued friend.' The only friend Ruby had when she arrived here all those years ago.

'Perhaps you feel guilty because they were running errands

for you instead of being at home caring for their injured mother?' Father O'Connell's voice held more than a note of accusation and Ruby felt her heart sink.

He was right. She did feel responsible. If only she had not insisted they collect money on Christmas Eve, the brother and sister would have been at home with their family and none of this would have happened.

'Might I remind you,' Archie's voice was determined, strong, 'my wife paid to have the church roof mended, and she has donated a considerable amount to the Children's Fund.'

'Your wife, you say?' Father O'Connell looked doubtful and Ruby placed a cautioning hand on Archie's sleeve.

'We will do all in our power to get Sam back.'

'Be that as it may.' Father O'Connell waved away her words as if swatting a fly. 'But the situation is out of my hands. In the absence of legal guardians, he has been made a ward of the church, as is fitting for a young Christian boy.'

'But why?' Ruby gasped, horrified that all this time Father O'Connell did not mention, nor even hint, that Sam was being made a ward of the church. 'I offered to take the boy in.'

'He was in possession of a rather valuable silver locket from Mr Solomon's jewellers, and without any proof of purchase, Mr Hastings and I felt it wise to steer the boy on a path to living a good, wholesome life away from savage influences...' He stopped suddenly. He had said too much.

'And how do you propose to do that?' Ruby's eyes darkened. 'By teaching him how to bow and scrape and obey rules without question. To cower him into submission?'

'I have no wish to answer that, Madam,' Father O'Connell said. 'Suffice to say, the situation is now out of my hands – without proof of the boy's innocence, I had no choice but to make the final decision.' Father O'Connell felt he had the upper hand.

He was not going to allow this brazen woman to influence a young mind.

'I will get the proof you seek.' Ruby knew nothing of the locket before Sam told her. But she did know Manny Solomon. 'I do not believe for one moment that Emma Cassidy's offspring are anything but honest and upstanding members of this parish, and I will not have her children's name besmirched by a new broom like you.'

'You are such a busy woman,' Father O'Connell's tone was skimming mockery. 'How would you make time to raise a child?'

Ruby's pulse raced and her nostrils flared, she did not trust herself to speak for a moment, with good reason. When she eventually found her voice, her anger hit the priest right between the eyes. 'How dare you?' Ruby's voice was barely a whisper when she stepped forward like a hunting cat, untamed and dangerous. 'You sanctimonious little upstart. How dare you tell me what I have time for? If I want to raise a thousand children, I will!' She watched Father O'Connell step back towards the fireplace and a thought struck her. Evil souls burned in hell. And greed, to her way of thinking, was the biggest evil of all.

'We will go to Saint Simeon's and speak to Mr Hastings,' Archie said as he took her hand, supporting her arm in a bid to keep it from swiping a man of the cloth.

'I have somebody I need to see, first,' Ruby informed him.

* * *

Ruby sat at the side of the counter in Mr Solomon's dusty jeweller's shop, while Archie stood behind her, watching the old man poring over the huge account's ledger.

'Here it is,' Mr Solomon said on a sigh, drawing his arthritic forefinger down the page, 'this is all the proof Sam needs to show he bought the locket honestly.'

The page bore Sam's name, with the jeweller's signature next to fifty-two payments he made over the last year. Then, at the bottom of the page, written in perfect copperplate handwriting were the words, *Paid in Full.* He also went to the back of the large book, and in the cardboard pocket his fingers sought the piece of paper he knew would be so important to Sam's future.

'This is the receipt he lost when the young tearaway, Woods, cornered him on Christmas Eve. I recued Sam and his receipt, but he forgot to take it with him when he left the shop.'

'Manny Solomon, I could kiss you!' Ruby said, waving the receipt triumphantly in the air.

Mr Solomon stepped back, a twinkle in his eye. 'I would be incredibly happy about that, but my good lady wife would not be so pleased.'

* * *

'We will go to the superintendent of the orphanage and tell him there is proof Sam is not a juvenile delinquent,' Ruby's breath hitched a little and she exhaled in a series of short bursts. Her determination to bring Sam home overshadowed her fearful reaction to visiting the orphanage. 'We will demand he leave that place immediately.'

As a successful businesswoman, Ruby was accustomed to getting her own way. Something many women were demanding these days. She enjoyed a life that would shock those who lived, worked, and shopped in this part of Liverpool. And Archie knew she felt it was her duty to give the Cassidy children a home, as they had with Ned. These young people may not be her own flesh and blood, but they had managed to quickly claim a piece of her heart.

'We will go to see Father O'Connell first of all, and show him the proof of Sam's innocence,' said Archie, 'then make arrangements to go out to Saint Simeon's to collect the boy and bring him home. If anybody can persuade Mr Hastings to let the boy come back where he belongs, you can.'

Archie knew Ruby had written to Mr Hastings and had done everything in her power to persuade the guardian to release the boy into her care, but he was adamant, Sam was too close to unsavoury influences in his own neighbourhood. Archie suspected there was more to Mr Hasting's decision, believing Father O'Connell had his finger in this particularly unsavoury pie and surmised that the orphanage superintendent may have been making enquiries about him and Ruby.

Just over an hour later, Ruby and Archie returned to the rectory with the evidence of Sam's honesty.

'Father O'Connell is out for the morning,' Mrs Jackson told them. The housekeeper remembered the day when Archie Swift brought Ruby to the dockside. It seemed such a strange set-up. What with her being so refined and him being – how could she put it? – a bit rough round the edges.

Following Mrs Jackson's gaze Ruby turned to see a carriage pull up outside the presbytery, she hurried towards it. In her hand, she carried the receipt for the locket and waved the proof of Sam's innocence under Father O'Connell's nose as he got out of the carriage.

'You have something that rightfully belongs to Sam Cassidy, and I intend to take it back to him and prove his innocence.'

'The silver locket?' The priest looked undaunted. 'I will get it for you.'

Moments later, he was back and handed Ruby the locket.

'I'm afraid this makes no difference whatsoever to the outcome of his fate. The arrangements have been made,' said Father O'Connell with a self-satisfied sigh.

Memories of the helplessness she had once felt in her father's house lay heavy on her shoulders. The church had been involved that time, too.

14

'Won't you reconsider, Father?' Ruby reached for Archie's hand, and Archie gritted his teeth to stop himself from saying something he might regret, when Father O'Connell shook his head, his face grim. 'There is no going back. Take comfort in the fact you saved him from the workhouse.'

'It sounds final, Father?' She was appealing to his better nature. 'But this isn't the end of the matter, I will rescue Sam.'

'We did everything we could.' Archie's brown eyes, usually dancing with good humour, were now hooded in disappointment when the priest closed the presbytery door behind them.

'It wasn't enough though, was it, Archie?' Tears ran freely down Ruby's pale cheeks as she straightened her back and lifted her chin. 'Archie, take me to Saint Simeon's. Sam must be allowed to visit his sister to help her recover.'

Moments later the priest appeared with his hat and coat looking determined. 'I will accompany you,' Father O'Connell said in his typical no-nonsense tone.

'There is absolutely no need, Father,' Ruby replied with fire in her eyes, but sadly, not in her heart. What did the old goat think she was going to do? Run away with the boy and never bring him back. Voicing the words silently in her own head, Ruby realised that the idea did not sound so preposterous.

'How is Anna coming along?' Father O'Connell made a small stab at conversation and was visibly shocked at Ruby's words, said in a determined voice which was usually reserved for erring customers.

'She is desperate for the company of her family, to heal and grow strong. But mark my words, you people will not get away with this. *I* will raise Sam to be a fine, upstanding member of this community, not the church.' Ruby knew she was inflaming an increasingly septic relationship with the local priest. It was no secret that she no longer trusted religion. With good reason, she thought. However, she did not dwell on the subject during the rest of the silent journey.

* * *

Pulling a huge hood over her bowed head, Ruby had her hand on the handle of the carriage door in readiness to alight.

Storming from the carriage, Ruby knew the winding gravelled footpath would be flanked by pretty flowers in summer, planted by the inhabitants of this house of detention no doubt, but now in the deepest of winter, the frozen borders were devoid of any cheer, as she now felt.

She gave a loud ran-tan on the black lion's head knocker. Tapping her foot impatiently, Ruby strained to hear footsteps approaching from inside, averting her gaze from the neighbouring mansion house, Ashland Hall. The enormous sandcoloured residence of one of the world's most successful shipbuilders in England. Ashland Hall had once been her home. And was the reason she did not want to visit Saint Simeon's Victorian soot-covered orphanage, which stood only a couple of acres to the west.

'If this is all too painful, I will take you back,' Archie felt wretched, he promised Ruby she would never have to come back to this area again. Ruby shook her head.

'I must do this for Emma.' Ruby no longer had any contact with the mighty Silas Ashland, or the financial powerhouse that was his shipbuilding empire situated on the other side of the Mersey and to which she had once been heiress. But she pushed the thoughts to the back of her mind as she had done for the last twenty-odd years, when she noticed Father O'Connell following closely behind.

When there was no answer to her knock, Ruby turned the large bronze handle on the front door and stepped inside with Archie.

'Madam, please slow down.' Unbuttoning his dark overcoat, the priest's hurrying footsteps echoed behind as they made tracks across the expansive hallway. She had no wish to be in this place any longer than was necessary.

Her stomach churned as she inhaled the strong smell of lavender floor polish, able to see her reflection in the linoleum as her hand trailed the curved oak balustrade. How many novice skivvies had bruised their knees to cleanse the sins of their ancestors? she wondered acidly.

'Just as long as you know, Father,' Ruby threw the words defiantly over her shoulder as she marched along the draughty corridor, 'your church may think it has Sam in its clutches, but Anna is in my care now. The timely reminder stilled any further comment on Father O'Connell's lips.

With the lightest tap of her knuckles, Ruby opened the door to see Mr Hastings sitting behind his huge desk. Looking up, he was obviously surprised at her audacity. Although he did not protest when she stepped forward without invitation.

* * *

'Sam Cassidy is a smart boy,' Ruby said, 'he is brave, honest and has no business being here.'

'I agree with you.' Mr Hastings' voice was low and placid, his posture straight, shoulders back, chest out.

'I will fight you people to get him back where he belongs.'

'Do not rush in where angels fear to tread, *Mrs Swift*,' Father O'Connell said in a low voice, behind her. Nevertheless, Ruby was not listening. She refused to be intimidated by a man who put the fear of God into the less enlightened parishioners of the Vauxhall parish.

'Indeed,' Mr Hastings said rising from his desk to stand before a welcoming fire blazing in the grate.

'Mrs Swift wanted to see the boy,' said the priest, hovering just inside the door.

'We would take every care of him,' Archie said in that calm, authoritative way he had about him, 'and raise him as a man to be proud of.'

'Be that as it may,' Mr Hastings's words sounded a little smug to Ruby's ears, 'but the matter is out of my hands.' The balding man spoke through white whiskers fashioned into a handlebar moustache.

'What do you mean?' Ruby had a strong sense of foreboding. She knew what these so-called benefactors were capable of. To some, children were a commodity to be bartered to the highest bidder, little more than a slave market where children, no taller than a tabletop, were taught to cook and sew and tend the needs

of *their betters*. 'We told Father O'Connell we will take the absolute best care of Sam.'

'Your enthusiasm is admirable, *Mrs* Swift.' The articulation of
her status was not lost on Ruby and she gave Father O'Connell a
withering glance as Archie came to stand by her side.

'However, we did not feel your living arrangements were, shall
we say, compliant with our views on child-rearing.'

'Would you care to elaborate?' Archie drew himself up to his
full six feet four-inch height. Head and shoulders above the two
men before him, his posture erect, his muscles tense. His steely
gaze challenging. Ruby had only ever seen him like this once
before today. When their daughter had been taken. Reaching for
Archie's huge hand, she opened her mouth to speak when Mr
Hastings raised his hand to silence her.

'There is no point in pleading the boy's case, Mrs Swift. Sam is
not here,' Mr Hastings explained, 'did Father O'Connell not tell
you?'

'Tell me what?' Ruby felt a cloud of foreboding rest on her
shoulders and shot the willowy Mr Hastings a venomous glare.

'Samuel Cassidy has been sent to Canada along with forty-
nine other children – twenty from Simeon's.' For a heart-stopping
moment, the room was completely silent.

'Canada?' Ruby arched a questioning eyebrow to Father
O'Connell. She knew children were sent to the colonies, of course
she did.

'How dare you!' Tears of anger and frustration ran down
Ruby's pale cheeks. 'You had no right.' Her eyes flew to Archie,
who looked murderous in his silence. 'No right at all.'

'We had every right,' Mr Hastings told Ruby. 'The boy is an
orphan. We did what we thought was best for him.' Even as he
stretched to his full height, the superintendent was still nowhere
near the commanding presence of Archie, and Ruby had to physi-

cally hold him back when Mr Hastings added: 'Father O'Connell signed the consent forms himself.'

Ruby felt nauseous. Her offer to raise Sam with his sister had been completely disregarded. The priest had listened to her pleas and promises and said not one word about his involvement in this disgusting practice. Her voice was low, controlled and gravelled when she addressed him. 'Father Furey would never have treated us like this.'

'But Father Furey is not here,' Father O'Connell told Ruby who lowered her head and closed her eyes to try to block out this terrible news, all the fight knocked out of her. Once again, Ruby felt the loss of a child for whom she cared so deeply. Without another word she and Archie left Saint Simeon's Orphanage and headed to their carriage.

Looking into Archie's pale eyes that usually danced with good humour, Ruby could see they were hooded, as if he were in pain, and she knew exactly what was going through his mind.

Archie remembered the time, all those years ago, when he curled his strong fingers round her hand and took her from her family home. 'We did everything we could,' he said, hoping the strength she had garnered over the last twenty years would stand her in good stead.

'Once again, Archie, we were too late.' Ruby's hand gripped the box that held the silver locket, and in the other she held the receipt that proved Sam was a boy of good character. A respectable boy. A boy who should be with his family. Not sailing to a place on the other side of the world where he had little chance of seeing his beloved sister ever again. Ruby knew that feeling so well.

'Are we not going to wait for Father O'Connell and take him back to Liverpool?' Archie asked as they settled into the carriage.

'Let him walk,' Ruby answered staring out of the carriage window.

* * *

'I have heard good things about the lives of children sent to Canada.' Father O'Connell said breathlessly, when Archie allowed him into the carriage, unable to force him to walk the thirty miles back to Saint Simeon's, but he knew, if looks could kill, Ruby would step over his cold dead body without another thought.

"You stole Sam and sent him away to another country?' Her face darkened, concentrating. Comprehending the enormity of the situation. A cat stalking a mouse. 'How dare you!' she was incandescent with suppressed rage. 'From some of the reports I have heard, this is tantamount to child slavery.'

Archie gently rested restraining fingers on her arm as the priest, spoke again. 'As you know, my good woman,' Father O'Connell said with the air of one who was not accustomed to being interrupted, 'exploited children seeking comfort at the door of the church and rescued from sin are not sold into slavery.'

'I have heard about the practical advantages,' Ruby's voice was barely controlled, 'for children who are orphaned, homeless, starving on the streets, and who have nobody to turn to. But that boy is not Sam.'

'The poor wretch will have a chance to make something better of his miserable life,' Father O'Connell said, and Ruby shook her head.

'He had a life here!' She refrained from calling him *Father*, as would be expected. 'I know the scheme is a wonderful opportunity for poor children to make something of themselves in a healthy country. I am not disputing that. What I am questioning, is your right to send him overseas when he has family here.

Family who can look after him. Family who did not give permission for the boy to be sent away.'

'Canada is a young country,' the priest spoke to Archie, oblivious to Ruby's plea, 'hungry for good, white British stock.' He was not going to let this woman dictate what he could and could not do with his little charges, no matter how much she gave to charity.

'Or perhaps, Father O'Connell, what you have failed to disclose, is the fact that it is cheaper to send children away to another country than to bring them up at the rate payers' expense, am I right?' In some cases, Ruby had discovered, some of the children were not even orphans. 'There is no need to send him to a foreign land on the other side of the world.' She knew adults who had never stepped foot outside Vauxhall Road, let alone travelled thousands of miles away on a ship.

Ignoring her protest, Father O'Connell lifted his hand to silence her. 'Your dedication is admirable, Mrs Swift, but you cannot save every poor child in the parish.' He lifted his chin and looked down his nose. 'Everything is arranged.'

'What do you mean?' Ruby demanded, her heart beating faster now. 'When is he leaving?'

'I cannot divulge that information.' Father O'Connell stretched his neck and thrust his chin forward without looking to Ruby, 'Suffice to say the reason Samuel had been sent away is because he was in the company of a known tearaway, I had no choice.'

'Had? You say you *had* no choice.' Ruby, who did not suffer fools, looked threateningly at the priest now, and Archie laid his hand on hers in case she got a little carried away.

At that moment Mr Hastings appeared at the carriage window. 'I'm afraid you are too late,' he said, 'the boy sailed early this morning. Did you not say, Father O'Connell?'

'It slipped my mind.' Father O'Connell watched Ruby closely. She said nothing.

Then, shuddering visibly, Ruby motioned to Ned, for them to move on. She could not get out quickly enough.

When she got to the Prince's Landing Stage in Liverpool over an hour later, she saw the Ashland Line's R.M.S Sunshine heading for the horizon. She had missed the royal mail ship that was carrying Sam to Canada by five minutes.

15

Horse-drawn omnibuses had conveyed the children of Saint Simeon's to the Prince's Landing Stage as Sam sat quietly looking out of the window, watching the green countryside disappear to be replaced by the soot-blackened ramparts of the dock road. His neighbourhood. He recognised the many streets where he had once played as a youngster and the ghost of a wry smile lifted his face. Had he ever been young? He found it difficult to recall. His childhood seemed unremarkable. But he grieved the family he lost and mourned the life he could have had. *I hope the journey I am about to take will change all that.*

Several ministers of various Christian churches had gathered on the dockside and committed the boys and girls who would be leaving on the next tide to the guardian priests. Sam craned his neck, his eyes rising up and up. He thought the huge ship was bigger than the White Star Line shipping office, Goree Piazza, where he arranged to meet Anna on Christmas Eve, the day that his life changed. He had never seen a ship so big. He leaned back to try to catch sight of the top deck.

All round him had been hustle and bustle, porters running

up and down gangways, luggage and people were loaded with expert efficiency as he waited for the order to board the ship with Daisy and the rest of the children from Saint Simeon's. Now the time had come, Sam could not get away quick enough.

'*Ta-ra, Ma, Ta-ra, Anna,*' Sam silently mouthed the words as his eyes lingered on the newly built Liver Building as it shrunk on the horizon. The majestic building had taken three years to complete, and swallowing the tears that threatened, he wondered if he would ever see it again. Sam leaned over the railings of the ship to see the stern of RMS Sunshine leaving a huge trail in its wake, recalling the top-hatted men of importance bidding them a final farewell amidst hearty shouts and cheers.

He tried to think of anything that would prevent him dwelling but failed. Nothing could end the torturous memories of the good days when he had a family.

But he had no family here any more. He had been chosen to go to this wonderful far-off land called Canada, Mr Hastings told him. He had to be strong. He was one of the lucky ones. He was making a new start. When the ropes had slipped beneath the water, he felt his heart sink with them.

'The water looks different from this high up, doesn't it?' Daisy said, peering over the ship's rail.

'It certainly does, Dais.' Slowly, and with agonised patience, he watched his beloved homeland disappear in the distance and he kept watching until the Liverpool waterfront had shrunk to a dot on the horizon. Then it was gone.

Even the gulls had not ventured this far, he thought, listening to the crash of water against the side of the ship. The masters, the guardians, and priests were of the same opinion. A little tyke, like him was not fit to live in the country of his birth and should be deported to a place he had never even heard of mere weeks ago.

The children travelled in steerage with two hundred Irish refugees, and as many Russian Poles, who were in a filthy condition and appeared destitute. Sam felt rich in comparison, although he did not have much either.

By the time he viewed the long tables and sat at the wooden forms to eat his first dinner of Irish stew, rice pudding, coffee, bread, and butter, Sam was more than satisfied. Later, he joined the other boys, who had a tug of war on the deck, which his side won.

After prayers at seven o'clock, when he prayed for his family as did every other child from Saint Simeon's, he devoured a bowl of hot gruel before bed. The sea air had certainly sharpened his appetite.

It had been an eventful day with much to think about, and Sam looked forward to curling up in his bunk and going over the happenings of the last few weeks. He had a new life ahead of him now, and he must be strong.

The following day's sail was choppy in foul weather and everybody was seasick, including the masters. Sam doubted he would ever eat again when the smell of a plain breakfast of bread rolls and porridge sweetened with treacle assailed his nostrils. But Sam had no stomach for it.

'If I survive this journey, Dais,' he told the girl with the hay-coloured hair as mile-high waves enveloped the ship, 'I will survive anything.' He grabbed Daisy's coat as she suddenly slid across the sloping deck and saved her from being lost over the side of the ship.

'Inside now!' one of the guardians called and Sam crawled back to his cabin. There were six wooden bunks, each with a straw mattress and a grey blanket. Hammocks accompanied the bunks for the bigger boys, who complained that they should have proper beds.

However, Sam soon discovered the despised hammocks proved a far superior kip than the bunk he had just been thrown out of as the ship pitched and rolled in the Atlantic and continued for the next few days. The situation got so bad that even when his favourite meal of beef and potatoes, followed by plum pudding was put before him, Sam found he still had no stomach for it.

The miserable seasickness was not helped by the location of his cabin over the works of the ship and the steering gear. The drone of the propeller shaft kept him awake at night, while the smell of hot oil, steam, and no ventilation made him nauseous, until Sam felt he could take no more.

His stomach heaved when the storm died down, and he dragged his grey blanket from the bunk, clearing out of his cabin to find somewhere quieter to sleep. Under a pitch-black sky with the wind howling round his pyjama-clad body, he discovered a spot by the ventilation shaft in a quiet corner of the deck. And, settling himself down for the night, Sam huddled beneath his grey blanket for warmth and quickly nodded off.

The following day, the boys were ordered out of bed to wash and dress, the weather had eased somewhat, and they had a run on the deck before breakfast. Even though Sam's life had never been easy, he did not think battling a stiff wind while running round the deck of a surging ship was the best start to the day. The masters said it was to preserve self-esteem and ensure discipline during the long days ahead.

'Another hour or so kipping would have done my self-esteem the power of good,' he told Daisy, who giggled behind a curled hand. 'I think we have to do this, to stop us throwing ourselves over the side and swimming home.'

* * *

'Hello there, you,' Daisy said in that melodic Irish voice when she joined Sam at their usual meeting place at the ship's rail after lunch. The sun shining behind her gave Daisy an ethereal quality.

'Hiya, Dais,' Sam said, quickly wiping his eyes with the pad of his thumb. He was catching the last weak rays of the winter sun, his eyes red-rimmed. 'That salt breeze doesn't half sting your eyes,' he told her.

'It stung my eyes this morning, and once yesterday afternoon,' Daisy, a good friend since he went into the orphanage, said in her singsong voice. Her clear blue eyes, mesmerising, Sam's heart lurched. 'This is so exciting, don't you think?'

'Yes Dais, it is exciting.' But Sam did not want it to be exciting. He did not want to experience the thrill of adventure and look forward to a new life in a new country. Nevertheless, against his will, he did feel excited. And treacherously guilty for feeling that way. His brothers would never be lucky enough to feel like this, he thought, and the realisation brought with it an emotion he could not explain, reminding him of a time he let young James take the blame for eating the biscuits which Ma baked for Sunday tea. They had been cooling on the kitchen table. He could not resist. One led to another, and before he knew it, they were all gone. Ma blamed James, and his little brother did not snitch, taking the scolding with a strength that belied his tender age. Sam could not look him or Ma in the eye for hours. In the end he could stand it no more and gladly took the punishment that he hoped would banish the feelings of guilt and show his young brother that stealing does not pay.

He told Daisy the tale, turning in her direction he had to keep hold of his cap for fear of losing it over the side on the high wind.

Daisy's inquisitive eyes lit up her heart-shaped face; he could tell her anything.

'Mam couldn't afford to keep me.' Daisy shivered, rubbing her arms over her woollen coat. 'It was hot that afternoon when Ma took me to the orphanage... June or July, I think. It doesn't matter no more.' She gave a melancholy smile, and Sam saw her puny shoulders give a half shrug. 'She told me I had to be a good girl and not to give cheek.' Daisy's fair eyebrow raised with an as-if-I-would expression, which made Sam laugh for the first time since they last spoke. Daisy was the funniest little girl he knew and when she mimicked her mother with a wagging finger, he thought she could tread the boards with an act like that.

'*Don't answer back now, Daisy, d'you hear me?*' Daisy said in a broad, Irish twang and her eyes widened. 'Well, o' course I heard her, she was standing right there in front of me. I'm not deaf.'

Sam could not help himself, his spirits lifted, he threw his head back and laughed. but only until Daisy's voice, solemn now, dipped.

'I didn't see her leave,' Daisy continued, 'I just heard the door close. Her heels clicking away on the old linoleum. I went over to the window. So, I could see her when we waved goodbye.' Daisy nodded her affirmation. 'I saw her hurrying down the long path. She did not turn round. A man was waiting at the gate.' Her eyes suddenly opening wide in horror, her voice full of indignation, 'He kissed her. Right on the lips. In broad daylight an' all.' Daisy shook her head. 'I never saw him afore.'

And, looking out to sea again, she said, 'Ma promised she would come back for me at the end of the week. But she didn't. Nor the next week, or the one after that...' Her voice trailed off and Sam could now see the pain she rarely showed, hover behind her eyes as she started to hum a hauntingly beautiful tune.

Suspecting Daisy's constant chatter stopped her dwelling on

her situation, Sam realised he was not the only one who was hurting. Unintentionally, he wondered how a woman who was supposed to love her daughter above all else, could desert her. He could have listened to Daisy all day, she was a tonic was Daisy.

'She put me away because she din't want me no more,' Daisy said eventually, 'she never was coming back to get me. I got in the way, I s'pose.'

'Don't say that, Dais...' Sam was surprised at how quickly she touched his heart.

Nevertheless, Daisy shook her head, making her tam-o'-shanter wobble. 'I wasn't the type of kid a ma could love,' she said with an uncomplicated air of certainty born of neglect. 'I wasn't pretty or clever. Ma told me so – all the time.'

'Hard-hearted cow,' Sam muttered under his breath. He had the urge to put his arm round her, but he had the feeling Daisy would not thank him for it.

'It comes to something when your own Ma calls you an ugly spud, doesn't it?' Daisy made a brave attempt to smile, but it did not quite reach her eyes.

'You are not ugly.' He felt angry at the coldness of this poor girl's heartless mother. 'You are pretty.' He did not feel the least bit embarrassed telling Daisy. Not like he did when Anna said soppy things. He wanted to make her feel better, and to see that cheeky smile again. 'Don't you ever forget the sun shines from your eyes, Dais.'

Her overbright eyes glistened at the compliment. Then she lowered her gaze.

'Are you waiting for them to walk off your feet, Dais?' Sam asked eventually at the lengthening silence between them, seeing the concentration on her face as she studied her stout brown leather shoes and Daisy laughed.

Turning away now, Sam leaned against the ship's rail, his cap skewed, listening hard to try to hear the distant cry of seagulls. He was quiet for a long while, recalling his own loving mother and his twin brothers.

Liverpool had gone. So, too, his beautiful Anna. How he wished he had stayed by her side that day. Even now, if he closed his eyes and inhaled deeply, he could still detect the faint smell of disinfectant and it reminded him of his older sister. Suddenly he felt more alone than he had ever done in his whole life.

'I'm sorry if I upset yer, like,' Daisy said behind him. When he turned, Sam saw that she was suddenly as bright as a button. As if their former conversation had not taken place. She had a smile as wide as the ocean and gave him a playful dig with her forefinger and said, 'I won't make you sad again... Shall I sing to you?'

'You didn't upset me,' he said, knowing if Daisy could recover quickly then so could he. He smiled. 'Go on, give us a tune, Dais...'

Resting her chin on her knuckles, Daisy batted her eyelashes, and, in a pitch-perfect voice, she sang, 'You'll have rings on your fingers and bells on your toes...'

Sam suspected he would have taken his chance with the fishes and tried to swim back home if it had not been for Daisy. For, it was her company and kind-hearted way of looking at life that made the days fly by. With her, he could share his thoughts and dreams for the future. He was going to get a respectable job and make lots of money, enough to raise a good family.

Sam took hold of her small hand in his, 'You know what, Dais,' he said, 'I like talking to you, I can tell you stuff, I don't have to keep everything locked inside my head.'

'If you kept all those ideas in your head,' Daisy laughed, 'it would get so big it would explode.'

Sam would never be lonely in Canada when he had her by his side.

* * *

Moments later they were jolted out of their reminiscence when there was a commotion from the other side of the ship. A young lad, much younger than Sam, climbed onto the ship's rail, and before anybody could stop him, the child jumped. Daisy screamed and Sam ran across the deck, dragging at the buttons of his woollen jacket, flinging it across the deck and hopping as he tried to drag the heavy boots from his feet, while the ship rolled and bounced. He must save the boy.

With no thought for his own safety, Sam climbed the rail to reach the stricken child when he lost his footing and slipped, his leg dangling over the side of the ship and his scrawny body quickly following as he felt himself slipping towards the water.

Suddenly he felt a tug on his shirt collar. Then two huge hands slipped under his armpits and he was dragged back to safety.

'We've got to save him!' Sam cried as hot spikes of adrenaline coursed through his veins when he tried to make another bolt for the ship's rail and, once again, he was pulled back.

'There is nothing we can do,' said the young priest. His face had lost all colour and he looked as if he was going to be sick, but instead he leaned down and said in a low voice that commanded Sam's attention: 'If you go into the water you will be killed. Or eaten alive by sharks. We cannot risk another life. It is tragic, but we have lost him to God's care. We will pray for the repose of his troubled soul.'

Even though the R.M.S Sunshine dropped anchor and ship's company searched for the stricken child, there was no sign. When the young priest said mass, there was not a dry eye on deck.

16

'If he'd had the receipt to show the priest, he would still be here,' Ruby said to Archie as she entered the small room at the hospital.

Anna had overcome her crisis and was growing stronger by the day and as she opened her eyes, she could see there was something different about Ruby today.

'Who would still be here?' Anna asked, sitting up when Ruby and Archie came to visit her as they did every day.

Ruby tried to lift the straight-backed chair to move it closer to Anna's bed when Archie stepped in and placed it easily.

'There is something I have to tell you...' Ruby's face was full of concern as she twisted the gold band on her finger, while Archie, standing behind her, put his hand on her shoulder and Ruby looked up at him.

She must broach the subject of Sam's exile to Canada and knew she had to try to find the right words. However, none would come.

'What do you have to tell me?' Anna gripped the starched white sheet, rubbing the back of it with her other hand. Shifting in the narrow bed, she stared at Ruby, suddenly afraid the woman was going to say she would not be visiting any more. She did not know how she would cope alone without her daily support.

Ruby's dark eyes scoured the white tiled wall. Her gaze resting on the long sash windows that let in plenty of light and fresh air, illuminating the perfectly made-up row of beds in the ward next door. But there was nothing to inspire words that would soften the blow. Concentrating on the stiff-collared nurses bustling and fussing over their young charges, Ruby knew she was delaying the time when she would have to give Anna the worst news possible. Her last remaining relative had gone from her life and she may never seem him again.

'Miss...?' Anna swallowed hard when Ruby took her hand, and a cold shiver of fear made the fine hairs on the back of her neck stand on end. Only yesterday, the doctor said she would soon be ready to go home. But she no longer had a home to go to.

'You asked me why Sam did not come to see you...' Ruby's words faltered, and Anna nodded, afraid.

'Please do not tell me something terrible happened to Sam as well.' She had a gauzy memory of him looking at her. It may have been a dream. She could not say for sure. His forehead was pressed flatly against the window. He was making shapes on the glass with his finger... He looked so worried...

'He won't be coming to see you any more,' Ruby said, unable to look the girl in the eye. Her words faltered, and she took a deep breath before saying, too quickly, 'He's gone away.'

'Gone away? Where to?' Anna could hear her own despair.

'Sam was taken by the church to Canada.' Ruby explained. 'He is being given the best possible chance, trained in a trade that would give him a good start in life.'

Anna felt like she was outside her own body watching Ruby, Archie, and herself. The only proof she was alive was her thundering heart hammering in her throat.

Anna felt like she had been slapped. Trying to make sense of this information, she said nothing. She could not. The words would not form the questions. She had heard of this Canada, of course she had. The country was one of those pink bits on the large map on Saint Patrick's school wall. There was a vast expanse of blue water between England and Canada.

'Canada is thousands of miles away,' Anna's voice was barely a whisper. Then, the reality of the situation dawned on her. She could see Ruby's lips moving and she tried hard to concentrate. Having no home suddenly did not seem quite so important after all.

Ruby tried to be as sensitive as possible, but the news obviously came as a great shock to Anna whose face drained of any colour, so she did not go into great detail about the Child Migration Scheme and Canada needing farm labourers, or England needing to reduce its child pauper population. 'He's going to make a new life,' she said, hating herself for sounding like Father O'Connell, who explained that the wide-open spaces of Canada would be good for the boy. 'He is going to be someone.'

'But he already is someone.' Anna's body shook under an avalanche of pent-up anguish.

'They say you can pick gold off the streets...' Ruby made a stab at lightening the mood, but it was no good.

'And who are *they*, may I ask? If you are as influential as people say you are, could you not persuade the authorities to keep Sam here?'

Ruby flinched. 'You are right, and I understand completely what you are going through.' Sam may have gone to a better place, but that did not make it right. Not when he had family here in Liverpool.

'I will never see him again.' Anna knew she should not take her sorrow and frustration out on Ruby. She was angry with

Father O'Connell, who no doubt encouraged Sam to go to Canada. She was angry with Mr Hastings, whom Ruby had told her about, who put stupid ideas into her brother's head. Moreover, she was angry with herself for being so weak, unable to get better more quickly.

'Oh, Anna, do not upset yourself, you will make yourself ill again,' Ruby said with a tenderness Archie had not heard for many a long year, and her eyes implored him to do something. He went to fetch Ned.

* * *

'Sam came to see you before he left...' Ned said, dropping down so he was at eye level with Anna, resting on the heels of his boots.

'Did he know I wasn't going, Ned?' Anna's eyes were red and swollen with crying. 'Did he not want to stay here with me?'

'He could not miss this chance to better himself.' Ned did not tell Anna that Ruby had done everything she could to keep her brother here. The revelation would add salt to her wound.

'I have no family now,' Anna cried.

'You have us...' Ruby said looking up to Archie, who nodded. 'If you want us, that is. It's all arranged.'

'Thank you, Miss Ruby.' Anna would be thankful because that was the way her mother raised her. But still all she wanted was her Sam. Anna knew that Ruby and Archie had paid for the funeral of her mother and her little brothers. Ned told her so a few weeks ago. Holding her hand, he'd described the marble headstone with all their names on. His voice low and full of empathy, which Anna did not want – '*You can visit the cemetery any time.*' He had assured her. *Archie and Ruby did not give her family a pauper's funeral. Ruby had been so kind to her.* 'I am grateful, it's just... just a lot to take in... I will work hard to pay back your kindness.'

Ruby looked puzzled. Then she smiled. 'I'm not only offering you a job, Anna, I am offering you a home.'

'A home?' A home with Ruby, Archie and Ned was kindness beyond anything she had ever imagined. 'I don't know how I will ever repay you.'

'Ruby will think of something.' Archie smiled, and Anna's stiff shoulders relaxed.

Anna felt overwhelmed by this latest news. Pulling up her knees to her chest, she circled them with her arms and buried her face when Ned put a comforting hand round her shoulders.

'We'll look after you.'

'Please don't be kind to me.' Anna wiped her eyes and blew her shiny red nose, distracted from her confused thoughts when she saw Ruby rummaging inside the carpetbag which she carried everywhere.

'It's in here somewhere,' Ruby said and then took something from her bag. 'Here it is.' She handed Anna the oblong box. 'Father O'Connell had it for safekeeping. Sam wanted you to have this.' A little white lie sweetened the pill when Anna's eyes widened.

'Ma's locket! Sam was going to give her this for Christmas.' Fresh tears welled. 'Sam saved hard all year to buy this,' Anna replied, taking hold of the precious box.

'He is the most honest and thoughtful of boys,' Archie said, 'I expected nothing less.'

'This will remind me of my brother's kindness, not that I will ever forget,' Anna said as Ruby fastened the silver locket round her slim neck, 'I will wear it always, until Sam returns to tell me of his great adventures.'

17

'I can't believe I was sick for so long,' Anna said when Ned and Ruby helped her up the stairs to the living quarters above the Emporium.

'You will recover better out of hospital.' Ruby told her and Anna nodded.

When she saw her new bedroom, Anna gasped. The room smelled of fresh flowers and the pale lemon wallpaper with pink roses matched a frilled bedcover and made her think of sunny summer days, even though it was only February.

'Is this for me?' Anna asked Ruby and Ned smiled, nodding his head as he put her small suitcase on the chair near the window.

'It's a bit girly for my taste,' he said with a wink, 'but it's all yours.'

'I've never known such luxury,' Anna said 'although my bedroom back at Queen Street was comfortable and clean, it was nowhere near as plush as this. Nor was I lucky enough to have fresh flowers in my room.' A wave of betrayal sliced through her excitement when she thought of her poor mother. 'But I'm not ungrateful' Anna said quickly. She loved her family with all her heart. 'Ma did her best for all of us.'

Rubbing the arm that had been released from its gypsum plaster cast only yesterday, she appreciated everything Ma did for all of them. Anna caught sight of a gold filigree photo frame on the bedside table and on closer inspection it held a photograph of her whole family, taken before Christmas last. Ruby had commissioned it as a special Christmas present.

'It is precious,' Anna gasped in wonder, her words barely audible. Her family, buried six weeks ago, were as close to her now as they would ever be, and this was the best gift she had ever been given. She did not feel the tears rolling down her cheeks as she gazed at her family for the first time since that awful Christmas Eve.

Archie and Ruby had organised everything while she was too sick to go to the funeral. They were so kind and nothing like the people who served behind their own counters.

'If only I had been a bit stronger,' she said eventually, Sam, my beloved Sam, would never have been shipped off to Canada.'

'Archie and I did all we could to stop him being sent away,' Ruby said, her tone apologetic, and Anna realised what she had said.

'No, I don't blame you,' Anna said touching Ruby's arm, 'I'm sure you did everything you could. It is me I am angry with. If I had ignored Jerky Woods taunts, none of this would have happened.'

'You are not the one to blame either, Anna,' Ned did not tell her he lay the blame squarely with Jerky Woods. 'We feared you would not make it.'

'Ned stayed by your side every chance he got,' Ruby told Anna. 'But we will leave that conversation for later, I'm sure you must be starving,' Ruby was in her element when she had somebody to fuss over. 'I will leave you to get settled. and will ask Mrs Hughes to bring tea and some of her delicious, toasted crumpets along with some much needed news of the outside world.

Everybody was kind and sympathetic, Anna knew. And she should have shown her gratitude better. But these people were not her family and she doubted she would ever see them as such.

'I think I will take a walk back to Queen Street, tomorrow,' Anna told Ned and Ruby when she came into the sitting room a short while later, Archie was out on a collection for the Emporium. 'If I don't get up and stretch my legs soon, I'm sure I will lose the use of them,' Anna told Ned. 'A little stroll can't do any harm.'

'Ruby doesn't want you upset, none of us do.' Ned's furrowed brow told Ruby he was worried.

'I'm stronger than I look,' Anna said from the sofa in the sitting room. And although she felt she was able to do anything at all, she was amazed at the amount of energy it took to leave hospital, unpack her meagre belongings and cross a room. Before long, her eyes grew heavy.

Anna was aware there was somebody else in the room and her head shot up from the brocade cushion it had been resting on. Ruby and Ned were nowhere to be seen. She could not believe she had been so rude as to fall asleep in company. Patting her hair into place, she noticed Lottie, who lived next door to her own home in Queen Street. She was dusting the sideboard with a feather duster before going to fetch a vase of pink camellia blooms complemented by sweet-scented, daphne making the whole room smell divine.

'*Yes, mum, no mum... niminiminim...*' Anna could hear the girl, no older than herself, chunnering away like a disgruntled bluebottle.

'Ma used to say they lock you up for talking to yourself.' Anna gave a rueful smile when she noticed the pink flush creep up to Lottie's cheeks and she hid her face behind the large crystal vase letting out a low embarrassed laugh.

'Pay no heed to me, Anna, I'm always chuntering away to myself. That's what happens when I have nobody to talk to any more.' Her hand flew to her mouth and Anna waved away her careless remark, knowing Lottie was the only offspring of her deaf, widowed mother. 'We really miss you and your family, the whole street does.'

'Thank you,' Anna said, her voice low.

'Your mum was a lovely woman, and your brothers, too. Me and Ma miss you all so much,' Lottie said, and Anna grew silent. 'Oh, there I go again, putting my size fives in and upsetting you.'

'No, you didn't,' Anna said, 'it's lovely to hear you talking about them. I'm sure Ruby thinks I will fall to pieces if I discuss my family, but there is nothing I would like more.' Anna wiped away a single tear, 'I miss them so much, too.'

'If they live in your loving heart, it means they will never die,' Lottie said and put her arms round Anna's shoulders, giving her a friendly hug.

'That's a lovely thought,' Anna whispered. 'I will remember your words when I feel overwhelmed. Thank you, Lottie.'

'You're growing stronger by the hour,' Lottie said, bringing a smile to Anna's face. Although Anna was devastated by the tragedy that had befallen her family, she knew she had to be resilient. Ma would not have it any other way and would be horrified to see her daughter mope around feeling sorry for herself.

'Do you like working for Aunt Ruby,' Anna asked, still a little self-conscious about calling Ruby her aunt when, in truth, they were no relation, but Ruby had insisted and who was she to go against her benefactor.

'I would rather work in the Emporium,' Lottie said, careful

not to be overheard, 'all that beautiful merchandise would brighten every day for me.'

'Is that what you really want to do?' Anna asked.

'It is my dream,' Lottie said, 'it would make Ma so proud. She is always saying to me – why don't you try to be more like Anna Cassidy?' Lottie gave an apologetic shrug.

'I'm sure you would make a first-class assistant,' Anna said. She knew Lottie and her widowed mother were well thought of in Queen Street.

'Do you think so?' Lottie asked, as a customary pink flush coloured her cheeks.

'I'm sure of it.' Anna liked Lottie, she was trustworthy, and her sunny disposition would be an asset behind the counter of the Emporium, if only she was more confident about herself. 'Would you like me to put a good word in for you?' Anna saw Lottie's eyes widen.

'Would you do that for me, Anna!'

'What's the commotion?' Ruby asked when she came into the sitting room.

'Lottie was just cheering me up a treat,' Anna said, giving Lottie a conspiratory smile.

'Oh, that's good,' Ruby said, 'it's lovely to see a bit of colour in your cheeks, maybe we can think about taking a little fresh air tomorrow after all.'

18

The sea on the journey from Liverpool was choppy in foul weather and Sam viewed the lashing waves enveloping the ship, reminding him of the young boy who threw himself over the side rather than spend another day at sea, which Sam could not fathom. He was a natural sailor, like his father, trusting he would have many a trip before his days were done. And, like his father, he loved to write letters home. The exception being, he had no family to send them to, so he wrote one to his mother's employer, Ruby Swift and would post it as soon as he could.

He and Daisy were good pals for the whole of the journey, keeping each other's spirits up. He told her all about his family, killed in a fire, and about his wonderful sister, Anna, who died in hospital from pneumonia, Mr Hastings had informed him on the day that he left Liverpool.

'I loved her as much as I loved my mother,' he said sadly, 'she looked out for me, and she was really good to us all. I will never forgive myself for being the cause of her death.'

'I'm sure she would have forgiven you for not being there,' Daisy said. 'You never said why you were late back to meet her.'

'I was beaten up by Jerky Woods, a local bully boy, and his cronies.' Sam did not meet Daisy's gaze as he continued. 'A kindly gentleman took me to his home and his wife patched me up, insisting I see the doctor, because my eye was bleeding and closed over.' Sam had never spoken so openly about the guilt and the pain he felt at losing Anna, but as the miles stretched between him and his former home, he felt able to discuss his worries with Daisy.

'I've heard of the tearaway, Woods,' Daisy said, 'he is well-known by many of the boys from Saint Simeon's.' She balled her little fists and took up the stance of a boxer making Sam laugh. She was such a delicate-looking thing, but she had the heart and courage of a lioness.

'You're the kindest girl I ever met, Daisy,' Sam said nudging her gently with his elbow when she took her place beside him and gazed out to sea. His wordless action spoke volumes. Her own story was no less tragic. Daisy was being sent to Canada because her ma could not cope with her and did not want her as much as she wanted a new man-friend. Although Daisy was eager for the great adventure ahead, she felt her mother's rejection keenly.

'I think it was Ma's man-friend who didn't want me,' Daisy said in that practical way she had about her. Sam thought it was a shame, because Daisy was the sweetest girl, made more so swamped in a heavy woollen coat, which was obviously meant for someone much bigger. 'We'll be pals forever.' Daisy looked momentarily scared. A rare chink in her armour. 'I'll look out for you.'

'Ta, Dais.' Sam followed her gaze across the sea and allowed his internal smile to break out on his lips. Daisy was only the size of twopenn'orth of copper, a saying his ma used, yet she was the bravest person he had ever met. Nothing was a trouble to her. She never complained, and she did not dwell on sad things too much, like some of them. Always convinced that the sun would shine tomorrow, Daisy was an everlasting hoper.

'There's no use worrying and fretting, it gets you nowhere,' she said in a voice far older than her years. 'Moving to a new country is a rare treat. At least I will have people who will look out for me. I won't have to sleep under a hedge.' Her voice dropped, 'Or get locked in the coal cellar.'

Sam turned her round to face him and the lump in his throat made him choke. How anybody could hurt someone as fragile, and gentle as Daisy. 'Oh Dais, I feel so sorry for yer.'

With a half-smile, she turned and looked out onto the ocean once more and suddenly her face lit up with her characteristic beaming smile. 'Look! It's Canada,' Daisy said as the new country came onto the horizon.

* * *

February was still part of the winter season and the ship was unable to dock at Montreal or Quebec they were told.

'The nearest ice-free Canadian port is Halifax, Nova Scotia,' said Father Wilson, one of the younger priests who were travelling as their guardians to make sure they arrived safely, 'and from there we will then travel by train to our destination.'

It came as a huge shock to Sam and Daisy when they reached Nova Scotia and saw the snow-covered prairies. Everything looked so white. So clean. Vastly different from the soot-covered streets they had left behind in Liverpool. Sam gasped in amazement at the beauty of it all when they disembarked, the blue haze of icy air took his breath away. In this country, they would be known as Home Children, said the young priest. And Sam realised he would need more than the woollen blazer and short corduroy breeches, which he was now wearing.

'Not sunbathing weather, hey Dais?' His droll remark made Daisy smile and he was glad because he remembered that scared glimmer. When they alighted from the train, she too was shivering.

'Mr Hastings told me that Mounties in red tunics protect the streets,' Daisy said as they put their suitcase on the glassy ground.

'Maybe they would lend us their coat.' Sam did not like the cold, no matter how beautiful it looked. Staring towards the snowy mountains, he sighed, knowing he would enjoy the diamond-glistening rivers more if it were warm enough for a bit of a swim. He could not voice the emotions he was now feeling. There were so many. They ranged from shock, to joy, to disbelief, to bewilderment.

'Come along now, don't dawdle.' Father Wilson gathered them together like sheep and herded them into a long, draughty wooden shed that said *Department of Immigration* on the board outside.

Huddling together on a wooden bench along the wall to try to keep warm, Sam and Daisy watched children being called to either one of two desks at the far side of the hut.

'God has planned this for you,' Father Wilson informed them with authority.

'I wish he'd planned it for somewhere a bit warmer,' Sam whispered, and Daisy giggled behind her hand.

'Somewhere like Australia, you mean?' she asked, and Sam nodded. Australia would be champion at this time of year. They sat in companionable silence for a short while until Daisy said, 'We'll get used to this place as long as we've got each other.'

'What d'you think we'll be doing?' Sam asked. 'I quite like the idea of building new houses and cutting down trees.'

'Well, the priests said we can be anything we want to be,' said Daisy dreamily, 'so I think I'll sing on stage and my adoring audience will stand as one, clapping and shouting: *Encore, encore!*' Daisy was out of her seat with one hand holding an imaginary gown as one leg swept into a wide arc behind the other. Taking a deep curtsey to an adoring fantasy audience, her other hand held an invisible bouquet like a newborn babe. Sam's enthusiastic smile slipped when her name was called.

'Daisy Flynn come over here please,' the young priest read from the register he carried always.

Giving Sam a little nudge in the rib with her elbow, Daisy went and stood in the crocodile line. Her wide smile could not hide the obvious apprehension she was feeling.

Sam watched her shuffling in line. Fixing her beret. Smoothing down her too-large collar. And gazing all round at her new surroundings. She looked younger than her years in the line of bigger girls. Moments later, the priest at the right-hand table told her she would be going to the Catholic Distribution Centre. And she turned to look for Sam, who quickly turned away so he could not see the alarm that made her eyes wide.

'What about Sam?'

'Know your place, Daisy.' Sam heard the priest say as she was pushed none too gently back in line.

Daisy turned, looking to him for reassurance and Sam saw the stark glimpse of panic in her eyes before she was marched towards the door marked exit.

Sam half-lifted his hand. He had prepared himself for this moment. He had heard two priests discussing their fate earlier. The older priest had said that Daisy was going to Montreal... He was not.

'Sam!' Daisy's voice was clear in the cold crisp air. 'Don't you forget me, Sam.' Through the window, Sam could see Daisy getting her legs slapped for calling out to him, and he flinched. The tears in her doe eyes had not yet fallen onto her cheeks.

He jumped up from the bench, but one of the priests restrained him and gave a warning shake of his head without saying a word.

Poor Daisy. All she ever wanted was a clean bed, a full stomach – and a friend.

'I've got nobody now.' Sam heard Daisy's defiant little voice echo in the ice-cold haze. 'Goodbye Sam... Goodbye.'

'Be strong, Dais...' Sam's voice cracked when he whispered, '... It's never goodbye.'

* * *

Sam knew that the priests who were responsible for sending him to this remote homestead in the middle of nowhere must certainly have been ignorant of the taciturn farmer, whose cold, aloof manner perfectly matched the freezing environment, because he was sure they would not have sent him here, to this hungry life of cruelty and back-breaking toil. He had never felt so alone and determined to get away as soon as he could.

Noah Jessup was a man of few words. So too his lumbering, slow-witted daughter, who eyed Sam's every move with suspicion. Sam was quick to discover, on that first day a year ago, when the farmer had nodded to the back of his horse-drawn cart without a word spoken, that the man was not as welcoming as the people he had already met when he stepped foot in this new country.

'Any chance of a bit of cover here?' Sam had asked, dragging at some sacking to protect himself from driving hailstones that bit into every part of exposed legs, hands, and face.

'That smart mouth won't get you anything here, boy,' the farmer had answered and, cautioned by an innate sense of survival, Sam had said no more. Knowing instinctively that if he did answer back, he may just come off worse. Huddling into the corner of the cart, he had tried to protect himself from the bitter wind that ripped at his clothing and stunned him with its ferocity.

Sam expected the new country to be a little strange at first, and the people would be different. He had never been on a farm in his life before, and the first thing he had to get used to, was the smell. Liverpool's dock road, one of the busiest main roads in the world, where horses clattered on damp cobbles and wagons groaned under the weight of produce from all over, was not blessed with sweet-scented air, more like smoke from steam-trains shunting cargo through heavy traffic. Where costermongers pushed barrow-loaded fish and fruit, and sailors staggered from one of the copious alehouses to another, all human life draped in soot and oil. But it beat the shit out of animal manure.

Nor had anyone warned him these farm people and this isolated place would be so hostile. When he had outgrown his breeches, he was given a pair of ragged pants that were far too big and nowhere near serviceable. Although Sam was glad of one thing when he first set foot on the farm – he had no idea he was about to endure this past year of living hell... If he had known what was in store, he would have made a run for it there and then.

He had been worked until he had little more to give. Out in the fields, he dug turnips with his bare hands and, dropping to his knees, his thoughts now turned to Daisy. He sorely missed her lively chatter and angelic voice. What would she be doing now? he wondered. Sam hoped she had found a wonderful place. Somewhere where she was well looked after and cared for. She deserved a bit of tender care, did Daisy. Looking to the low grey sky, heavy with the guarantee of snow, he vowed that one day soon he was going to get away from this place.

Farmer Jessup and his daughter, Noreen, were cold as winter. They thought nothin' of beating him for any small thing, real or imagined. Noreen was older than Sam and would stare at him for hours while he worked, saying nothing. Tilting her head to one side, her eyebrows furrowed like she was trying to make out what he was. Creeping up behind him and standing too close for comfort while he worked in the barn. She made eyes at him the moment he stepped foot onto the farm and scared the life out of him. Cornering him at every turn, in the barn, in the yard; when her father was not around and she was out of his beady-eyed vision, Noreen did things to him that surely must be sinful, yet he had no power to resist and was riddled with guilt after she took his hand and placed it firmly on her exposed breast, his excitement tempered by the urge to live, knowing Farmer Jessup was insanely protective of his daughter.

Sam had not stepped foot inside the farmhouse since the day he arrived. He slept in a barn with the animals, making it easy for Noreen to get at him. She promised he would no longer have to scavenge in dustbins for his food if he did what she wanted him to do. But her promises were quickly forgotten and each day he would be as hungry as the one before. If it were not for the frozen turnips, he snook into the barn and ate raw, he doubted he would have survived this long.

'Have you got that animal feed ready yet, boy?' Noah Jessup's belligerent tone sent an apprehensive shiver down Sam's aching back. Sam did not mind arduous work, he thrived on it, but this was downright slavery.

'What can you expect, Pa? He aint nothin' but cheap labour anyway.' Noreen ridiculed.

Sam looked out over the breath-taking prairie. This was a beautiful country, but a harsh one. Life was not easy in the sub-zero winter climate, and he longed for the days when he could weave his way in and out of the dockside courts, he once called home. Gazing over the ice blue yonder, he knew Canada was a healthy place to live, if you were well fed and suitably clothed. Neither of which applied to him.

Embarking on his new life, he had been told that someone would come out to the farm every six months or so to make sure that he was being well looked after. But he had been here more than a year, and on the one occasion somebody had come here, they were told he was out in the fields working, when, in truth, he was doubled up in pain in the barn after a severe beating.

'Yes, sir, Sam is making out real fine,' Farmer Jessup was heard to say, 'going to school regular. I will get him to write and let you know all about it.'

Sam, held down in the barn by Noreen's strong bovine arms, could hear the hooves of the departing horse crunching in the icy snow and he had fought to free himself and run out, tell the inspector he was not sent to school. But he no longer had the physical strength to fight her.

'Nobody's going to take any notice of a homeboy.' Noreen's biting remark caused his insides to shrink. 'And even if they did, there aint nothin' they will do about it. Nobody wants you here.'

'That's not true,' Sam said, feeling worthless and fighting to keep the germ of dignity that, against all the odds, remained. 'I've seen the newspapers full of advertisements. Farmers encouraged to apply for us to work the land?' His insolence earned him a stinging slap across the face. Sam had trained himself not to flinch, aware that it maddened Noreen. The drawback was that she would do it again. But he refused to give her the satisfaction of knowing she caused him pain. This humiliation was something he also had to endure since he came here. Noreen Jessup was worse than Jerky Woods - and that was saying something, he thought. Taking a deep breath Sam vowed that, the first opportunity he got, he was going to get as far away from this awful farm and these horrible people.

'You aint nothin' special,' Noreen had said through yellow teeth, and Sam believed her. Desperate for some much-needed sleep, he had spent every minute of the lengthening daylight hours out in the fields, knowing he would work even longer as the days lengthened in summer. 'You is less popular than the vermin you fail to get rid of.' Noreen sneered before leaving him to slump into the corner and close his eyes.

Sam had learned quickly not to argue. Even a sidelong glance could invite a razor strop across his back. He was a prisoner on this isolated farm. Existing in a country that did not want pauper children from a foreign country dropped on their doorstep. Farmer Jessup was not slow to take advantage of the free labour though, Sam thought, knowing the farmer's attitude was not to spare the rod and spoil the child.

In temperatures of forty degrees below zero, when frostbite could lose him an ear or a couple of fingers, Sam knew the one thing keeping him here this long was the certainty he would never get to another farm alive. He would bide his time. Summer would be here soon.

'You get here now, boy,' Noreen shouted down his ear, and Sam immediately jumped to his feet. Momentarily dazed by the sudden wake up call, he knew the voice did not belong to Ma or Anna. Then, just as quickly, he remembered. Kicking over the milking stool in his haste to do her bidding, Sam knew it was not a good idea to have her call him again.

'You put this coat on,' Noreen ordered, 'you's going into town with me.'

The thick snow had started to melt, and the watery sunshine seemed much brighter as Sam laced his arms through the threadbare coat, and pushing his hands into the deep pockets, he gathered the coat round his food-starved emaciated body.

'Put these on, over those you're wearing,' she held out a pair of too big corduroy trousers that were only marginally less tattered than the ones he had on. Sam was not concerned about that as he tied the string tightly round the waist. He was going into town. He was getting away from this hellhole. He would see people. People who could possibly help him. 'Don't you go gettin' any ideas 'bout runnin' off,' Noreen growled, 'd'you hear me, boy?'

Sam eyed her heavy coat, the fur-lined boots on her feet, and warm woollen hat that kept her tightly curled hair in place and he nodded cautiously.

'You remember what I told you about that other unfortunate.' Noreen said the word *unfortunate* like it was a curse. 'He was a homeboy too. Took a liking to me, he did. I told him to be careful. Then, Pa got wind of our little walks down by the lake.'

Sam said nothing as she repeated the ominous, oft-told tale that felt like a warning.

'I did not mean to tell Pa. It just slipped out...' She looked to the distance, as if watching something occurring down the bottom field. 'He whooped that poor boy 'til he could take no more.' She slowly shook her head and Sam did not realise he was holding his breath, waiting for her to finish. 'He went missing,' Noreen snapped her fingers, 'just like that.' Then, in true 'pennydreadful' style, she informed Sam the poor homeboy was never seen again. 'It was round about the time the new pine woods were being planted.'

Sam was terrified of *going missing*. Who would ever know? Out here, he was nothing in this isolated farm. Nobody except the Jessups knew who he was, while Noreen never tired of reminding him this place was the only farm for miles.

'Hup!' Noreen Jessup, as strong as any man, pulled on the reins as the horses halted in their shafts. Her father had stayed on at the farm while she came into town to collect supplies and mail from the post office. Turning impatiently, she called to Sam. 'Don't just sit there, boy, git down and help me.'

Sam hurried over and offered his hand. He did not let Noreen climb down by herself. He dare not. She was as mean as her father was, and Sam knew she would have no compunction in using the horsewhip. He helped her down from the cart as best he could but, ruddy-faced and a cumbersome fifty-six pounds heavier, Noreen was a heifer of a girl and Sam almost buckled under her weight.

There was a commotion outside one of the stores, and for as much as Sam itched to know what was going on, he knew he dared not leave her side. Nevertheless, the temptation was great. Starved of any news since he arrived in this country, he was fascinated to hear the latest.

'R.M.S Titanic has been sunk by an iceberg!' called the boy selling newspapers as interested, shocked people crowded round him. 'Titanic sunk on her maiden voyage. Many dead!'

'It doesn't concern us, boy,' Noreen said, her voice had a hard edge that shocked Sam, who, coming from a maritime port and being the son of a seafarer, felt every ship's loss keenly.

A ship had sunk! A big one too, if the picture on the front page was anything to go by.

Noreen headed towards the supply store, silently beckoning

him to follow. However, his insatiable curiosity got the better of him. What could Noreen do to him in a street full of people?

'Excuse me, Ma'am, can you tell me what is going on over there?'

The woman stepped away from him, wrinkling her nose like there was a bad smell beneath it. She did not answer him but turned quickly and hurried down the street. Sam knew he must smell bad to invite such a reaction, recalling how clean and fastidious he had once been, his shoulders hunched in shame. Ma and Anna would be appalled.

'Git over here right now! And keep your mouth shut.' Noreen's glowering expression told Sam he had overstepped the mark.

Accustomed to being mistreated over the last year, he was not prepared for the prejudice showed him when they heard his English voice.

'We don't need his kind here,' one woman told Noreen, pulling her child towards her as if Sam had some contagious disease. 'We don't need them Home Kids coming here, working for a pittance and taking the jobs that can be done by our own boys and girls.'

''Cept our boys and girls won't do the jobs that the Home Kids do,' Noreen retaliated, 'they think it's beneath them.'

At first, Sam thought Noreen was defending him and many like him. But when he gave her comments more thought, he concluded that she was not protecting him at all. She was protecting her father's reputation. What other boy would work outdoors more than sixteen hours a day in sub-zero temperatures – for no pay at all.

Before he came here, he believed the church and other charitable organisations were doing him and others like him an enormous favour. The Canadian government was desperate to populate western Canada with farmers to add production to the country, solve the railway problem, and help pay the national debt. They offered free homesteads to applicants who qualified, and Noreen had proudly boasted her father was one of those farmers. 'We were offered good money to settle on the prairies,' Noreen had told Sam when she was in a chatty mood. 'American farmers were wooed, along with farming men from Scotland and the North of England.'

'He looks like he needs a good feed,' said another bystander.

'He's just small-boned is all,' Noreen answered, completely oblivious to the shocking news of the sunken ship as she headed into the supply store followed by Sam.

Inside the store, she fingered a bolt of soft material in blue.

'You got this in red?' Noreen asked the storekeeper with a sneer, curling her lip and giving him one of her more contemptible looks. She continued her order in that haughty voice she used when she wanted to appear superior and Sam felt ashamed. She was making a fool of herself. 'These types of people do not make good pioneers.' Noreen did not lower her voice when she informed Sam. 'Not like my Pa.' Then, turning fully to Sam she looked him up and down like he was the runt of the litter. 'Nor, it seems, do fourteen-year-old boys from England, who is more trouble than they is worth.' Noreen picked up a perfectly good apple, pulled a contemptible face, and tossed it back on the pile., 'You is a drain on good Canadian food. You ought to be grateful we took you in, boy.'

Sam said nothing. Instead, he watched Noreen examine every item on her list in detail, before handing over any money. This was his best chance of escape, he knew. If he made a run for it, he would be away before she could untie the horses. While Noreen was busy, he decided that now was as good a time as any.

Without knowing where he was going or what he was going to do when he got there, Sam made a dash down the high street, passing startled women with wicker baskets and cursing men who he unintentionally bumped into in his haste to be free. Sam was way down the street before he heard her voice.

'You git back here,' Noreen Jessup hollered in the most unladylike fashion. 'You just git back here right now.'

Sam ran faster. He could not face going back to that farm out in the wilds, beyond civilisation. He could not. His thoughts were filled with fear as he ran blindly down the centre of the road and, his head down, he bumped into something soft and sweet-smelling. Before he had a chance to see what or whom he had bumped into he noticed a beautifully wrapped gift box rolling down the street.

Instinctively, Sam retrieved the box and ran back to the recipient. A vision in mahogany ringlets and pale blue coat. His lungs felt like they were going to burst through his ribs when he stopped running and then slid down a wooden post. Sam reckoned he had been going for a good ten minutes before he ran out of steam. Gasping and wheezing, he knew that before he left Liverpool he would have been able to go much further. But since he had been on the farm at the back of beyond his strength had left him.

'Are you all right, young'un?'

Sam lifted his head, and his jaw dropped to his heaving chest, when he saw the brilliant red tunic of a real live Royal Canadian Mounted Policeman. A Mountie. Sitting atop his glistening chestnut mare, he looked down at him. Sam felt his insides turn to jelly. The young girl was with a man whom Sam took to be her father. They had been talking to the Mountie. But that was not his greatest concern right now.

The Mountie had a gun! He raised both hands in the air. Just as he had seen the outlaws do on the pictures, back home.

Noreen had sent the Mountie for him. He was going to die for sure.

'I... I did not do nothing, sir. I just wanted to post this letter.' He held the letter in his hand, the one he had written before he got off the ship a year ago. Sam had saved and stashed away a few coppers to buy the stamp. This was the first chance he had to post it.

'You're going in the wrong direction for the post office, son,' the Mountie said helpfully, pointing in the direction Sam had just come from.

'You get here right now, boy.' Noreen Jessup's baying voice was more vociferous than ever as it front-lined the horses she was whipping to a frenzy.

'You done something wrong, son?' The police officer's voice was unhurried, and the kindest he had heard for a long time.

Sam shook his head.

'No, sir, I haven't done a thing wrong.' Sam did not voice the thought that he had been foolish to think he could ever have a better life in this country. 'I just wanted to post this letter.'

'Here, you give it to me, and I'll make sure it gets to the post office.'

Sam carefully kissed it before passing it and the money for the stamp to the Mountie's outstretched hand.

Taking it, the Mountie smiled and put it in his pocket, assuring Sam: 'Your letter will be on the next ship out.'

'Officer! You keep a hold of that wretched boy and do not let him go!'

The Mountie watched Noreen's rampaging approach and, turning back to Sam, he said in a quiet voice, 'I'd say you want to accompany that letter, don't you, son.' Before Sam got the chance to appeal to the Mountie for help, Noreen Jessup was by his side.

She managed to convince the officer that Sam was just fooling round, being in town and all. And as Sam headed back to the cart, under the whispered threats of what was going to happen to him when he got back, the officer's kind deed gave him strength and a great feeling of triumph. Nevertheless, it did not remove the dread of returning to the farm knowing he was going to pay dearly for his misdemeanour.

19

Ruby, flushed and breathless, hurried into the sitting room from the room below. She had run up every stair. And anybody who knew Ruby would confirm, she did not run anywhere. Her eyes were wide with horror.

'The Titanic has sunk!' Everybody knew the White Star Line employed many Liverpool men. 'It is so tragic. Mothers and wives are scrambling at the Town Hall in case there is any news of survivors.' Many Liverpool sailors were on the list of the dead or missing. The papers were full of it. People were clamouring for the latest news.

'We have all that black ribbon in the storeroom.' Ruby told Archie. 'We must put it in the display cabinet in the Emporium.' Ruby, aware of people's feelings of grief at a time like this, could be depended upon to gauge the local mood. Although the more cynical may say she could not let a profitable solution go to waste. 'Always anticipate. Never underestimate,' Ruby said, marching towards the storeroom.

'She'll be getting out those black silk bonnets from storage next.' Archie drew a lungful of pipe tobacco, and his eyes rolled heavenwards.

'I knew they would come in useful.' Ruby, ever the business-woman, went to fetch them and Anna's jaw dropped, realising that even amid deep, deep sorrow, Aunt Ruby saw an opportunity, knowing the White Star Line headquarters close to the Pier Head was the spiritual home of Titanic and recalled waiting there for Sam that Christmas Eve. Anna remembered every moment of that tragic day and could still recall her impatience. She had waited outside the White Star headquarters, known locally as the streaky bacon building, with its alternating rows of red and white bricks, before going into town to look for her brother.

'Titanic may never have visited Liverpool,' said Ruby, 'but Liverpool made a substantial contribution to her workforce.' By the end of the day, Anna knew Ruby was right. The black ribbon and the bonnets had practically flown out of the shop.

'Aunt Ruby you are incorrigible.' Words like incorrigible came easily to Anna these days.

'Supply and demand, my dear, supply and demand.' Ruby headed towards the women clamouring for news.

'We still need to eat and keep a roof over our heads.'

It was little wonder that Ruby had made a successful business out of practically nothing, Anna thought, reminded that the older woman never did stand on ceremony.

'Is she in here, Archie?' Ruby stood just inside the door of the pawnshop, with its high scarred counter, situated under battered boots hanging by tatty laces on the rope line above it. She looked all round the pawnshop, which was not as bright and glamorous as the Emporium, but it was busier, with hard-up women hocking the old man's suit or best boots because of the never-ending strikes that were concerning the whole area.

Archie, after pinning a ticket to a bale of bedding, lifted his head and smiled.

'I take it you mean our wonderful Anna, my sweet.'

'Less of the syrup, comic-cuts,' said Ruby, clearly pleased with his familiarity, 'I can always buy a guard dog, you know.'

Archie threw his head back and gave a hearty laugh. 'You'd be lost without me to carp at,' he said, and she nodded.

'Sometimes I wonder who's in charge round here, us or the young ones.'

'Oh, that'd be you, Miss Ruby.' Archie doffed his cap in mock servitude, and she shook her head, recalling the day when Anna expressed an interest in doing her mother's old job in the office.

Archie recalled how Ruby had told Anna: 'I have watched you working and noticed how discreet you are, never divulging the business of the customers, totting up in your head'. 'I would even say you are faster in your calculations than your poor departed mother, and she had a *very* keen eye for business.'

'You are offering me my mother's job?' Anna had asked and Ruby noticed the same look of pride in her eyes that she had when she talked of teaching. 'I would see it as an honour.'

Ruby hovered impatiently between door and counter whilst Archie, in his meticulously slow way, entered the last transaction into his book, whilst a queue of women customers watched the repartee with benign nonchalance. They liked Archie for his quick wit, and Ruby for her ladylike ways, and for all her bluff and bluster, they knew she had a heart of gold.

'She rarely comes in here these days. Not since she took over her mother's work in the office,' Archie addressed the waiting line of curious women, who loved a bit of gossip to liven their dull lives. 'It looks like we're not good enough for her any more.'

'Don't believe that for one minute,' Ruby declared, 'she gets along with everybody.'

'What do you want her for? And why are you so excited?' Archie casually gave the pawn ticket to a straight-backed woman from Audley Street as, intrigued, he hooked her bundle of bedding and heaved it high on a shelf near the loft.

'I've just been told she has something to tell me, and I'm eager to know what it is.'

'Oh, I think I know what it is.' Archie raised a mysterious eyebrow, whilst continuing to examine the merchandise that was being pawned.

'Well, come on, spit it out – it might be a gold watch,' Ruby demanded, but Archie said nothing. Instead, he leaned forward, looking over the counter to where she was standing and a hard-up housewife dallied, moving items round in her basket, not wanting to miss anything. 'You'll have to ask her yourself. I'm sworn to silence upon pain of death.'

Ruby's eyes trailed the long line. Archie obviously wasn't going to shed any light on Anna's news in front of this lot.

'I'll see you later,' Ruby called over her shoulder, leaving him smiling as she hurried next door.

'Ruby loves that girl like her own,' he explained. 'Anna's brought a ray of sunshine to her life.' The long snake line of women nodded sympathetically. He chatted easily to the morning women like he was born to it, knowing they lapped up the tale of little Anna Cassidy who had been saved by the lovely Ruby. 'I've never been so surprised, in all my life,' continued Archie, checking over a mantle clock, knowing that a bit of banter soon put a stop to any little bursts of impatience, 'I didn't think Ruby had a maternal bone in her body.'

'Neither did I,' exclaimed a fat woman with all her worldly goods wrapped up in a knotted sheet.

Archie looked up sharply. 'Don't let her catch you saying such a thing,' he admonished. Ruby was his world, and he would not have a wrong word said about her.

* * *

'There is nothing here to take my fancy,' said Mrs Sharp from one of the grander streets round the dock road, dithering between buying a vase or a teapot she had been looking at in the Emporium.

'Didn't I see your eye catch that beautiful Majolica vase, Mrs. Sharp?' Ruby asked as she came through the door and, without skipping a beat, went to fetch it from the window, her face wreathed in an expectant smile. 'Miss Lottie can wrap it very nicely for you and we will deliver...'

'Oh, I don't think so, Miss Ruby,' said Mrs. Sharp almost apologetically and watched Ruby's expression change to the stone-faced one she adopted when customers refused to buy. Lottie felt almost sorry for the unsuspecting customer. Everyone knew Ruby did not take kindly to people leaving the shop empty-handed.

'In that case I will bid you good day.' Ruby proceeded to grip the procrastinating customer's elbow and march her towards the door. 'Do come again, Mrs Sharp.'

Anna's eyes stretched wide with surprise as she came out of the office and saw her benefactor bundle the woman out of the Emporium and close the door behind her.

'You let her go without buying anything?' Anna knew this was a rare occurrence.

'I'll get her next time,' beckoning Anna to come forward she said: 'I think you've got something much more interesting to tell me.' Ruby waited with barely disguised impatience. And relishing her news, Anna went behind the counter. Then, unable to contain herself any longer she declared triumphantly,

'They've got him – again!' Anna's eyes sparkled, alight with glee. 'They took him away in the black maria. In handcuffs. The lot. And would you believe it?' Her words tumbled over each other in their haste to be set free. 'He actually had the temerity to scream his innocence even after they caught him red-handed with the money!' Anna watched Ruby slip the bolt on the door, ensuring complete privacy until Anna finished her news.

'Caught who red-handed?' Ruby tapped the counter impatiently.

'Jerky Woods.' There was a moment's pause. 'I was in the butchers when this hard-faced rapscallion pushed past me, nearly knocking me into the middle of next week.' Anna's eyes were wide, and her head spun from left to right, as if watching the escapade again. 'He flew out the back of the shop like Old Nick was after him. Quickly followed by two burly policemen who gave chase.' Her eyes were bright and her voice high. 'They floored him with a flying football tackle, Archie would have been proud.' Anna stopped her running commentary, took a deep breath, and clapped her hands with glee.

'The lying buck was screaming like a banshee. Saying he hadn't pinched the purses. But the bobby found them in his pocket.' Then, lowering her voice she leaned forward. 'They only let him out yesterday after pinching a purse last year, and he's up to his old tricks again today!' Then, without waiting for a response: 'Twenty pounds, he took. Would you ever believe it?' Her eyes were wide. 'Most families round here haven't got twenty pennies, never mind twenty pounds.'

'What happened then?' Ruby asked, obviously relieved that Anna's worst enemy was off the streets again.

Anna's chin was cupped in her palms, her elbows leaning on the counter. 'They carted him off in a paddy wagon. He will go away for much longer this time and no mistake. And when he does, I hope they throw away the key.'

'And for good measure, a few lashes of the cat wouldn't go amiss,' said Ruby, knowing Anna had suffered many nightmares about that lout.

'I'm not sure it will change that leopard's spots though.' Anna said, while Ruby gave a knowing lift of her finely arched brow.

'That is good news, but I can't say I'm surprised, the daily thrashing he received from his drunken father didn't do the slightest bit of good' Ruby said, taking the cash from the till and putting it in a cloth bag, ready to deposit into the bank on Monday morning. 'It's his poor mother I feel sorry for, Izzy doesn't have it easy. She might get a bit of peace now her oldest lad is off the streets.'

Anna breathed a sigh of relief when she heard Jerky Woods had been locked up. 'And people can walk down the street without fear of being molested by the troublemaker. He terrorised the neighbourhood,' she added.

'I seem to recall a feisty miss giving him a bit of a wallop, too.' Ruby said.

'Oh don't remind me,' Anna said, blushing to the roots of her hair as Ned came into the Emporium from the pawnshop. He had that twinkle in his eye that always made her feel a bit giddy and caused her pulse to race. He was looking at her now.

'Our Anna is quite the lady these days.' Ned laughed. 'Working in the office has refined her like no finishing school could ever do.'

'I've always known how to conduct myself,' Anna said in an

artificial haughty voice, while comically tossing imaginary curls from her shoulder. Because now, her beautiful, naturally curling hair was piled high on her head and it cascaded to the nape of her slim neck. She caught Ned's appreciative gaze and her heart soared. Thrilled, Anna laughed along with everybody else.

'I think he's got his eye on you,' Lottie whispered.

'Behave yourself, Lottie!' Anna's eyes widened. She and Ned were just friends.

'Well, I'm off now,' said Lottie, putting on her coat. 'See you on Monday.'

Ruby smiled as she followed Lottie to unlock and then lock the door behind her.

'I'm lucky to have such wonderful young people round me,' Ruby told the gathered throng. 'Ned, you are a good lad, a conscientious worker, and stronger than men twice your age.'

Anna laughed when Ned stood tall, chest out, chin up, like a Victorian boxer when he twiddled an imaginary handlebar moustache.

'That's what comes of working in the abattoir when I was younger,' he said, 'hulking huge sides of beef, lamb and pork. Back-breaking work.'

'I couldn't see all that strength go to waste when you could be working for me.' Ruby laughed.

'You're looking chipper today, Anna,' Ned said a few moments later. 'Getting prettier by the day, hey Aunt Ruby?'

'She is so, Ned,' replied Ruby, her pride bordering on maternal. He was wearing his beloved red and white scarf tied round his neck and carried a wooden rattle. It was Saturday, so he and Archie were going to the football match at Anfield this afternoon.

The previous week, Archie wore his blue and white scarf when they went across the park to Goodison to watch Everton. They each had their favourite team yet supported whoever was playing at home on Saturday afternoons. Then, later they would have a long, post-match discussion about every kick of the ball.

'Behave yourselves,' Anna said again feeling the heat rise to her cheeks. Having lived here for over a year she loved working in the Emporium, but not as much as working in the office on the business accounts, which gave her the privacy she sometimes needed when thoughts of missing her family overwhelmed her. Working in the office also allowed her to fulfil the promise, to ask Aunt Ruby if Lottie could be promoted to working in the Emporium.

* * *

Thinking of Lottie now, Anna recalled the conversation she had had with Ruby at that time.

'Lottie's a good girl, a credit to her mother,' Ruby had said to Anna's suggestion, 'she would be an asset to the shop.' Anna had smiled, glad she was able to repay Lottie's kindness. Lottie was extremely popular in the Emporium and Ruby was pleased with her work. 'She is such a loyal worker.'

'I'm so thankful to you,' Ruby told Anna later when Lottie left the shop that day, knowing not everybody from the dockside was cut out for the prestige of her Emporium. 'She is such a happy girl since she won a position in the Emporium.' Ruby's tone was light. 'She has the perfect temperament for the Emporium, and certainly for the well-to-do customers who frequent the shop. Lottie also has drive and determination. She would make a good suffragist.'

'Yes, she would. It is not right that to be considered half as good as men we must be twice as accomplished,' Anna said recalling how hard her own mother had worked.

'That is why we campaign for the vote.' Ruby liked nothing

better than a campaign but drew the line at the ferocious tendency of the more militant suffragettes, who smashed windows and chained themselves to railings.

'The reason women can't balance the books is not because they don't have the knowledge,' Ruby continued, knowing breeding and good manners commanded respect and obedience from the lower stratum.

'But because they haven't got enough money in the first place.' Anna added.

'You have hit the nail squarely on the head, Anna my girl,' Ruby said, rubbing her fingers and thumb together under Anna's pretty tip-tilted nose. 'One must not lose face. For that would mean elimination from society. Men have killed themselves for less...'

Anna, eager to know more, could not resist a low whistle, and blushed to the roots of her hair when Aunt Ruby gave her a gentle rebuke.

'A whistling woman and a crowing hen will bring the devil out of his den...' she said mysteriously and then laughed. 'Utter tosh, of course, but some of the less enlightened believe in such nonsense.'

'Is it nonsense though?' Anna asked, not believing a word of it either, but enjoyed playing devil's advocate.

'I don't believe in keeping people *in their place*,' Ruby said, 'while the bible-bashers take advantage of pagan superstitions.' Ruby was silent for a while after her little tirade against the church, the moneyed classes, and women who were put-upon because of their gender. 'One day women will have the vote and they will make a difference.'

'Wouldn't that be wonderful,' Anna said, clearing away the accounts for the day.

* * *

'It looks like a mother's meeting in here,' Archie came through to the shop via a side door behind the pawnshop counter.

'I was just saying how pretty Anna is these days.' Ned winked when Anna blushed to the roots of her hair.

'Leave the girl alone, can't you see you're embarrassing her,' Archie, turning to Ned, gave him a playful clout. 'Come on, young fella, we've got a football match to go to.'

When they left the shop, Ruby shook her head, smiling, then she said as if to herself, 'Archie will miss him when he...' She stopped talking, as if her words had fallen off the end of the sentence.

'Miss him?' Anna asked. 'Why, where is he going?' But Ruby said nothing, and Anna was puzzled. 'Where is he going, Aunt Ruby?' Anna noticed that the older woman suddenly became terribly busy, folding an already folded chemise. She put it in the drawer. Then she took it out again. And refolded it. 'Aunt Ruby...?'

'Oh, I'm sure Ned will tell you in his own good time.' Ruby looked flustered. Anna had never seen her look flustered before. 'I've said too much already.' Her face turned a deep shade of pink, which was most unlike her. 'I was just thinking aloud. He is ambitious, is Ned. Cleverer than anyone I know, present company excepted.'

'What's going on?' Anna asked. She did not like it when Ruby was being evasive.

'People should have ambition. I've always said so,' Ruby answered. 'He was never one to stand still.' She bustled round the counter to check the 'closed' sign was on the door. 'Never meant to stay long...' Her voluminous explosion of curls bobbed like coiled springs under a black straw hat.

Anna began to feel uneasy. Aunt Ruby was talking ten to the

dozen and making no sense. Ned had a liking for a laugh and a joke, but he also liked to keep stuff to himself and there was nothing wrong in that, she supposed. But why was Aunt Ruby acting so strangely?

Ned had confided in her about his childhood. His mother had died of typhoid fever when he was a nipper, and his father did everything he could to keep him well-fed and clothed, even resorting to illegal bare-knuckle fighting. Anna was saddened by his tale, if anybody had a good heart it was Ned.

When Ruby opened her home to him years ago, he gained self-respect and the urge to do more with his life than stay here in Liverpool. And she recalled his conversation on that ill-fated Christmas eve when he told her he wanted to see the world.

'Is he going away, Aunt Ruby?' Anna asked, but Ruby's lips were sealed, and Anna realised she did not want an answer, not if he was leaving.

Anna looked puzzled for a moment, then, she remembered what she had been talking about originally, and her eyes widened, as she lowered her voice conspiratorially, 'Do you remember when Lottie had her purse stolen from the market and Jerky Woods swore it had nothing to do with him?' Anna was eager to change the subject. 'Apparently, he has been dipping into ladies' baskets round the market for a long time, and today he was caught red-handed.

'I'm not surprised it was him that did it,' Ruby answered, 'it's his poor mother I feel sorry for. Poor Izzy has put up with a lot of heartache between her husband and her eldest son.'

'Yes, she has,' Anna said as she walked into the office and brought out a large ledger that contained the names of debtors and handed it to Ruby. 'Business has been brisk on new loans this week.'

'There has been an increase in borrowing from all classes,' Ruby told her.

'And glad of the service too, I shouldn't wonder,' Anna said, taking a soft cloth and polishing a particularly nice crystal vase, which had been exchanged in lieu of a late payment. 'My eyes have been opened since I came to live here,' Anna said, knowing there were men, bank clerks, teachers, political hunters, shipping clerks and the like who had been affected by last year's repercussions of the transport strike.

'Not to mention the gamblers who are too proud to tell their good lady wife that they cannot afford the new dining-room suite.' Ruby lowered her voice and cast her eyes towards the shop window, before continuing. 'The wives of those men who look as if they own the Empire can't be seen to be lacking in any way, especially when their husbands are aiming high in business and may receive a visit on the hop from their betters.'

'I can see by the accounts there are quite a few middle-class men who come to you for help?' Anna was amazed, realising she had been naïve to think that every well-dressed man and woman who stepped out of a hansom cab had the means to live a charmed life.

'There most certainly are,' Ruby replied with a nod of her head. 'And more of them than you would imagine. As an ideal hostess, the wife, who hasn't got a clue her husband is living on the never-never, is preparing a lavish spread in her newly decorated dining room, entertaining the boss and his wife – which does not come cheap if you want to make the best impression, my dear. So, that is where the Emporium comes in.'

Anna enjoyed being taken into Ruby's confidence as her benefactor led the way to the small back room and rang for Mrs Hughes to bring a nice pot of tea, and some of those fancy biscuits she had made earlier.

'This tea service belonged to a respected headmaster of a public boy's school,' Ruby said when Mrs Hughes left them to drink their tea from delicate porcelain cups. 'He was almost plunged into penury after being accused of a salacious affair with one of the masters' wives,' Ruby, in that pragmatic way she had about her told Anna, who fought to subdue the gasp that threatened to escape her lips. Her mother had never discussed such things within earshot of her offspring, but, obviously, Ruby held no such inhibitions. 'The headmaster did no such thing, as it turned out,' Ruby said, laying her dainty cup on a matching saucer, 'but the lying boy who admitted to starting the unfounded rumour had done enough damage to persuade well-to-do parents to extricate themselves from having anything to do with the headmaster, or his school.'

'How awful,' Anna said and Ruby nodded.

'The die was cast. And that is where I came in,' Ruby explained.

'Yes?' Anna hardly dared to breathe in case she missed a golden nugget of information. She had never heard the upper classes being spoken about like this before, but Ruby seemed to know an awful lot about them.

'These people want a champagne lifestyle on a jug-o-porter income.'

'Even the middle-classes live on tick?' Anna had seen the proof in the office files, but they were just figures, only Ruby knew the true story behind the rows of numbers. 'When I lived in Queen Street, I would see many women go into the corner shop and they had the price of their groceries put "on the slate" – you know, buy your food now and pay later when their old men got paid of a Friday,' Anna explained as if teaching Ruby something she didn't already know. 'They went and paid up – until Monday – and then would start all over again.'

'Yes. If truth be told,' Ruby said with a knowing nod of her botanical hat, 'the same can be said of the middle and even higher echelons of society, which is littered with social climbers, eager to outdo each other.'

'Well, I never.' Anna's eyebrows almost touched her hairline. 'Who'd have thought it?'

20

Looking at Anna now, Ned knew she was no longer the terrified girl, robbed of a feisty personality through grief. She was more of her old self; the girl he had taken an instant liking to the moment he'd met her back in Primrose Cottages all those years ago before Anna moved to Queen Street with her family and he was taken in by Archie and Ruby. Anna looked to him now and she smiled, her tender eyes lingering on his for just a moment longer than was needed.

'We are so lucky to be given this chance with these marvellous people, Ned.' Anna did not know where she would have been without her new family. Ruby and Archie were not the whip-cracking employers she had always believed them to be. They were kind-hearted and sensitive. And, although they could not prevent Sam being sent to Canada – of course they could not – Anna, Ruby and Archie did their absolute best to try to find out where her brother had been sent.

However, apart from the name of a children's home in Halifax, Nova Scotia, who would not give details, they had nothing more to go on. 'I will never stop praying for Sam's return,' Anna said, knowing her brother had not even had the chance to say goodbye.

'One day,' Ned said, 'one day we will find him, I know it. But, until then, we will hope and pray he is safe, and being well cared for.' Ned's words were a comfort to her, and Anna blessed the day she met him.

'You're all too kind to me, I don't deserve it.'

'If you want anything,' Aunt Ruby said, 'you only have to ask.'

Anna was not used to asking. Raised to work for what she needed, she assumed nothing came without a price. All she could offer was unstinting work and a fierce loyalty to this family, which would never weaken. Because even though she initially felt that nobody would replace her beloved mother and brothers, time and patience had convinced her that her heart was big enough to accommodate another family who, although not conventional, were loyal and loving and she would do anything for them.

'Didn't I say, Archie...?' Ruby announced later, from the opposite side of the table, 'My first impressions were right. Anna is doing an excellent job.'

Anna smiled at the compliment as she sewed one of the many beautiful gowns given to Ruby in part-payment for an unpaid loan. Ruby would later sell it for a fraction of the real cost to recoup her losses.

When the shops closed for the day, they gathered in the sitting room relaxing, chewing over the day's events. Archie and Ned invariably discussing the football they had watched earlier, and Ruby was regaling Anna with the latest news of what the suffragists were up to.

A proud member of the National Union of Women's Suffrage Society, which was led by Millicent Garret Fawcett, Ruby liked to campaign for votes for middle-class, property-owning women, who believed in peaceful protest unlike the Women's Social and

Political Union, the more militant campaigners, who took direct action for the cause. The N.U.W.S.S. were also the first wave of the campaign for women's votes.

'I have learned so much since I came to live here with you all.' Anna now knew the kind of things that were not taught in school.

'I know the Pankhurst woman has good intentions,' said Archie, who had been reading about the latest escapades of smashed windows and post box fires, 'but I fear she is going to get herself, and other women into serious trouble. The authorities will not stand for revolutionary action from women – it is not ladylike.'

Ruby remained silent, for once.

Archie smiled at Ruby's raised eyebrow and agreed times really were changing fast. But women had been calling the shots for donkey's years he knew. His Ruby was living proof that a woman could be successful in her own right. She had built up her business from nothing.

'Lottie tells me she would like to join the suffragettes,' said Ruby with a hint of disdain, 'I think maybe she has a few militant tendencies,' She added, placing her cup on the saucer.

'Oh, I hope not,' Anna said with a shudder, 'she's better off concentrating on her career. Lottie is lovely, although a little naïve, and she can be a bit eager sometimes.'

'Changing the subject, guess what day it is tomorrow, Archie?' Ruby looked to Anna, giving her a bright smile.

'Someone's birthday, perhaps?' Archie said.

'Yes, it is somebody's birthday.' Ned smiled.

'Please, don't go to any trouble on my account.' Anna knew that Ruby, Archie and especially Ned had done everything in their power to try to make her life better since the awful day when she lost her family. Yet, there was nothing to heal the gash in her heart. Birthdays were the worst: Ma's and each of her brothers, but also, even more so, her own birthday when she could not share the happy time with them all, as she used to do. The best present she could ever wish for was to have her family round her, but that was impossible.

Her thoughts turned to Sam, her lovely, feisty brother. Where was he now? Did he still think of them back here in Liverpool? She missed him so much. Nevertheless, she must not let her own selfish feelings spoil the cheery atmosphere at the table.

Smiling, she ignored the black cloud that hovered in the background, determined to settle on her shoulders. Tough little Sam, always dependable, he made the most of what he was given and always had a bit of fight in reserve.

If Ruby could have arranged it, Anna knew her brother would have been back home on the next ship. Nevertheless, try as she might, Ruby could not beg, persuade, or even bribe Father O'Connell to divulge Sam's whereabouts and she had her suspicions he had no clue what had become of Sam either.

Anna felt sick to her stomach at the thought of him being thousands of miles away and not able to communicate. However, she did not have time to ponder when there was a ripple of movement, signalling that their conversation was at an end. Archie and Ned went down to stable the horses, while Ruby finished her sewing in the sitting room.

21

'Oh, go on, Lottie, let me have the vase for sixpence, it will go lovely with my chintz curtains.' Lottie's aunt, Florrie, came into the shop every day to see what was on offer. In the hope she could wangle expensive household items for next to nothing, she would try every trick in the book, but Lottie was having none of her brass-necked cheek, wise to her wily ways.

After serving behind the counter for a while, she now had the measure of Ruby's customers, good and bad payers. This one was certainly one of the latter. Working with Ruby and learning her forthright ways had taught Lottie to be more assertive, and she was not shy in putting older women, who should know better, respectfully but firmly in their place.

Ruby was strict about people knowing their place, especially those asking for best quality at minimum prices. Some thought they could get one over on Lottie while Ruby was out on business. They were wrong.

'That vase is worth half a crown of anybody's money, and well you know it.' Lottie said assertively, proving that she was quite capable of minding the shop in Ruby's absence these days.

'Go on, Lottie, while her ladyship's out...' Everybody called Ruby 'her ladyship' due to her refined ways, including Florrie, who had a wheedling air of one who was used to getting her own way too.

Lottie, being soft-hearted, would knock a few coppers off an item if the customer was genuinely short, she had not forgotten what it was like to scrimp for every penny, but this one was downright hard-faced and was not short of a bob or two. Ruby had let her go with a generous pension. Unheard of in most households.

'This is not a charity shop, you know,' Anna said smartly when she came out of the office. Anna could not believe Ruby had once given this upstart a place in her employment and was thankful her niece was nothing like her.

'You've become a stuck-up little madam since you worked here, Anna,' Florrie Blythe said with an indignant shrug. Her nostrils flared and her mouth turned down at the corners. 'A right little jobsworth if ever there was one. I always thought you would be an asset in the Emporium, our Lottie. Go on, just a tanner. Her ladyship won't know.'

'But I will know, Aunt Florrie, and that is good enough for me. Two shillings and sixpence or it stays in the window. Miss Ruby has been good to me.' Anna could hear the determination in Lottie's voice.

'Good? Is that what you think?' Florrie Blythe's multitude of chins wobbled as she threw back her head and laughed. 'Oh that's a good one. I'll tell you something, shall I...?' A discernible hush fell over the shop as straight-backed women with an eye for a bargain discreetly stepped nearer the counter and Florrie's voice dropped a little lower. 'I know things about your *employer*,' she said the word as if it were a swearword, 'things that she would not like broadcast round the dockside.'

'In that case, I suggest you take your poison elsewhere,' Anna was not going to let this old harridan speak ill of Ruby.

'It might be better if you desist from gossip, Aunt Florrie.' Lottie said, walking round the counter, opening the shop door in the middle of the two bowed windows, and giving the older woman a practiced smile. 'And, if you do not have the wherewithal to make your purchase, I will look forward to seeing you when you have. I bid you good day.'

'I have never been so insulted,' Florrie complained to anybody who would listen.

'You do surprise me.' Lottie was past caring if Aunt Florrie was insulted. She was grateful to Ruby for giving her a steady job. However, the Florries of this parish would always try it on, always wanting something for nothing. She recalled seeing her aunt wrestle a half-priced ham from a woman in the butchers not two weeks ago. Her mother would be mortified.

Florrie stopped in the small black-and-white-tiled vestibule, and turning back, she said, 'You ask Ruby, she might even tell you.'

Half an hour later, after the last customer departed, the bell above the door tinkled and Anna sighed, she was hoping to get a well-earned cup of tea and sort through the morning's post. Then there was the weekly bookkeeping to do. Ruby's clients from the better-off districts sent their weekly repayments on their loans through the post. The money had to be recorded into the huge ledger, and receipts posted out.

Lottie was putting away the chemise she had been showing to the last customer and smiled, working in this shop had certainly opened her eyes to how the other half lived. She waved to the postman who had brought the second post of the day.

Among the pile of business envelopes Anna came to collect,

she was surprised and delighted to see one bearing the perfect copperplate handwriting of her brother, Sam!

This was the best day ever – a letter from her wonderful brother. Her heart was beating so fast at the sight of the Canadian stamp, it made her feel giddy. Although, when she was about to open the envelope, Anna noticed the letter was addressed to Ruby and Archie. Not her. Her heart sank. Holding it in her hands, she stroked the envelope and, putting it to her nose, she breathed in the paper's aroma, knowing it had travelled a long way. Reluctantly she put it on the shelf in the staffroom. It never occurred to her to open a letter addressed to somebody else.

Hardly able to sit still, Anna watched the hands of the mahogany wall clock crawl. Where was Ruby? She was usually back long before now.

Just before twenty to two, the doorbell rang again. Anna had never been so glad to see anybody in her whole life.

'Look what the postman brought,' Anna cried, grabbing the letter from the shelf and waving it in the air. 'A letter from Sam.'

Ruby looked as happy as Anna felt, not bothering with the letter opener, she ripped the envelope with her thumbnail. However, her smile faded when she looked more closely at the top of the page, 'Look at the date Anna? This was written more than a year ago.'

February 1911

   Dear Miss Ruby,

   We are almost in Canada, in a place east of Quebec. The journey was a bit rough, but we are all in one piece at least.

Ruby's eyes quickly scanned the page. She had closed the shop early so that Anna, Archie, and Ned could join her in the dining room upstairs. It had been so long since Sam left Liverpool, and everybody missed him, but none more than Anna.

When we arrived, we were kept in quarantine at the disembarkation station...

'Why did they have to go into quarantine?' Anna felt the rising shard of alarm hit her heart.

'Because of the typhus epidemic a few years back,' Archie said, 'it killed a lot of travellers.'

'How sad,' exclaimed Ruby, 'thank goodness Sam made it.' Ruby's eyes flew across the page and she paused. Moments later, she looked up to where Anna was standing by the window looking out, 'I think you'd better come and sit down, Anna.' Ruby's eyes were now full of tears and she obviously found it hard to continue.

'Please, Aunt Ruby, tell me.' Had something happened to her brother, and that was the reason the letter had taken so long to reach home?

She gave a gentle cough and continued:

'Father Quigley says I will be twice the size in a couple of years...'

Unashamed tears flowed freely down Anna's face and a sob caught her throat.

I must go now, Miss, but there is just one thing I would like to ask you, if I may? Would you do me a great act of kindness? Please put some flowers on Anna's grave. Mr Hastings, the head of the orphanage, said there was no time to do so before

I left Liverpool. It ripped my heart to shreds to hear that she had died in the infirmary…

   With profound respect,
   Samuel Cassidy xx

'Sam thinks I'm dead!' Anna's throat constricted and the fizz at the back of her eyes brought stinging tears. When she managed to ask why, her words were choked.

'I don't know why Anna, but we will find out.' However, Ruby did not have time to say any more when she saw Anna hurtling towards the door. Ruby knew she was going round to the church to have it out with Father O'Connell.

'You stay here, Archie and Ned, I have to go.' Within moments, Ruby had snatched her coat and was quickly following Anna.

* * *

Father O'Connell could not explain why the letter had taken over a year to arrive. Nor could he tell the two women where Sam was, all he did know was that he was happy and content with his *new* family.

'He has a family here,' Anna pleaded, 'he has me.' Her brother believed the barefaced lies. 'Why?' she asked. 'Why did they say I had died?'

'I don't know,' Father O'Connell answered, looking a little shamefaced. His complexion a little grey, his face pinched. He knew that some of the children sent out to the colonies were not orphans. Although Sam was, some poor wretches had nobody, and a life in another country was a fresh start. 'Samuel gained an opportunity he would never realise here, in this sooty town, with its blackened houses beside grimy docks. At least in Canada, he will have fresh air and wide-open spaces in which to grow strong.'

'We have wide open spaces in this country too, Father.' Ruby was livid but could do nothing. 'Anything could have happened to him.'

* * *

'They are not really man and wife, you know,' Lottie confided to Anna in a low, almost conspiratorial tones after breakfast the following day when Anna asked Lottie what her aunt had meant. If truth be told, she was trying to think of anything that would take her mind off the lies Sam had been told about her.

Lottie put her breakfast cup and matching saucer on the tray while Anna helpfully passed the milk jug and sugar bowl. Ruby was downstairs in the shop and Archie was in the pawnshop, while Ned was out on a collection. Anna waited patiently for Lottie to explain her strange announcement.

'Archie and Ruby?'

Lottie nodded.

'They're not married?'

Lottie nodded an affirmation and Anna's eyes widened.

'That is ridiculous! You'd better not let Ruby hear you talking such rubbish.' Frowning, she wondered what would make Lottie say such a thing. 'Of course, she and Archie are married.'

'That's what they'd have people believe.' Lottie nodded her head. 'But I know different.'

'You want to mind your own business.'

'They are living in sin,' Lottie said, heading towards the door.

'Fancy saying something as evil as that about the woman who gave you the job you always wanted.' Anna felt her hackles rise, 'Ruby has been good to you.'

'I am grateful, Anna, truly I am.' Lottie's pale cheeks were flushed pink when she turned back. 'But it's a bit strange they never talk of their wedding day or have any photographs.' Lottie was quiet for a moment and Anna could see she wanted to say something, and after a short while her suspicions were confirmed when Lottie said hesitantly.

'I saw the proof... When I worked for Father O'Connell.'

'What proof?' Anna could feel her agitation stir.

Lottie came back into the room from the doorway having made sure the coast was clear before she said in a low voice: 'I happened to look in the parish register, dusting and whatnot. I liked to look up people I know, see when they were married and when their children were baptised.' Lottie looked as innocent as a new-born babe, but Anna knew different. Listening to local gossip, even if she appeared busy doing something else, Lottie always had her ear cocked. Any morsels would then be relayed to her blind mother, if Anna remembered rightly from living next door.

'There were no weddings on that day,' Lottie said with an emphatic nod of her head. 'So Ruby and Archie could not have been married in Saint Patrick's church.'

'You'd better not let Ruby hear you spreading malicious rumours,' Anna warned, 'otherwise you'll be out on your ear.'

'You ask Ruby, I'm sure she'll tell *you*.' Lottie thought Anna was getting a bit big for her boots, what with being Miss Ruby's bookkeeper. Anna really had got above herself and had turned very *pound-noteish*.

* * *

'Anna, what's the matter?' Ned held Anna's chair for her to sit down. Ruby had put on a great spread for her birthday. 'Ruby thought you would be pleased about the tea, after getting the letter from Sam.' He suspected Sam's letter had knocked Anna for six – as it had all of them.

'I'm fine,' Anna said. Feeling Ruby's eyes study her from the other side of the table, she did not look up. She had been so happy here, both Ruby and Archie had made her very welcome, just like any loving aunt and uncle would. They had opened their doors and their hearts and had never asked for anything in return. But if Archie and Ruby were not married, they were living in sin. Only wicked people who would burn for all eternity lived in sin.

Anna needed to get out of here, go to her own room, think things over. Unable to concentrate on the happy chatter going round the table, the usual back-and-forth serving of the day's news, all she could think about was the possibility that two people she loved so very much, had been lying to her for the last year.

Shocked at the thought, Anna's body was tight as a coiled spring, her arms were like lead weights and, it was only when Ned gently prodded her arm, that Anna realised she was being spoken to.

'Hey, Dolly Daydreams, what's the matter, you are miles away?' Ruby asked.

'You haven't touched your trifle,' Ned was smiling now and usually her heart would melt under his gaze. However, glancing uneasily round the table, Anna felt so ashamed, her appetite had completely disappeared. How could she think such an evil thing on Lottie Blythe's say-so? Archie or Ruby had never given her any indication that they were morally corrupt in any way whatsoever. Everybody knew that you would go straight to hell if you lived in sin.

Saddened that she could even think that way, Anna did her

best to cheer up, if only for Ned's sake. These people had shown her nothing but kindness. Ruby and Archie had opened their home to her when she came out of hospital. Anna had never dared imagine living in such opulence. Ruby and Archie, oblivious to their lavish surroundings, cared only about her comfort.

'I know you miss Sam,' Ruby said in that motherly voice her customers would never recognise, 'is that what's troubling you?'

'Of course, I miss Sam,' Anna did not mean to sound so abrupt, 'I miss all my family, but...'

'You are unhappy here?' Ruby tried to hide her disappointment. She loved having Anna here to fuss over, as she would have done if...

'No, I'm not unhappy here,' Anna could not tell Ruby what Lottie had said. It would lead to the girl's instant dismissal for sure, and Lottie, like her own family a year ago, needed the money Ruby paid her. Although, she had no right to spread such lies. 'If I am being honest, Aunt Ruby, I am scared.'

'Why are you scared? Not of me, surely. Or, heaven forbid, Uncle Archie.' The very mention turned Ruby pale. 'Anna, please tell me what's wrong. You can ask me anything and I will answer you as truthfully as I know how.' Young girls needed the guiding hand of a mother, or the next best thing, a guardian who could steer them on the right path.

Taking a deep breath, Anna summed up every ounce of courage, knowing that what she was about to say might lead her to being thrown onto the street. 'I... heard something, today...' Her words were hesitant. There was a long pause, when the only sound was the soft ticking of the antique porcelain mantle clock.

'Go on,' Ruby said cautiously. She looked at Archie, knowing the letter had come as a shock to all of them, but she suspected it was not just the letter that was troubling Anna.

'I... I heard that you and Archie...' Anna could not go on. Even to voice such a terrible thing. They would be doomed to hell for all eternity.

'What about Archie and me?'

There was a slight pucker of Ruby's lips and Anna felt a chill pass over the room. She was the most ungrateful wretch for even repeating such a thing. A fleeting shadow crossed Ruby's attractive features, and Anna felt as if she had betrayed her in the worst way possible.

'Go on...' Ruby said gently, her shoulders relaxing now, as if she had made up her mind. She reached for Archie's hand, as naturally as breathing, Anna noticed. She watched Ruby carefully roll the corner of the cotton napkin without looking at it.

Anna chose her words carefully. 'Somebody told me that there were no weddings in Saint Patrick's church on the day you got married...' *A registry office.* Anna thought suddenly. In the eyes of the church, they were not married, but at least it would be lawful.

Ruby took a long deep shuddering breath of warm evening air. She so loved having Anna here. At times, she imagined the girl was her daughter. The thought was preposterous, of course, but she loved her as dearly as she would have loved her own daughter if only... If only she could voice the tragedy that had brought her to the dockside. If only she could say the words, to ease the ache in her heart.

'Ruby?' Archie stood behind her and put his hand on her shoulder, she reached up, covering it with her own, her gold band twinkling in the sun shining through the window. How could they not be married?

Anna could see they clearly adored each other. They slept in the same bed. They revered and had eyes only for each other. They were as married, as married could be.

Raising her eyes, Ruby immediately met Archie's loving gaze and she nodded.

Archie looked to Anna before saying in that rational, even-handed way of his. 'The jungle drums have been leaving little messages, I suppose.' He smiled and looked back to Ruby with such love in his eyes. 'It's time to tell her, my darling.'

'Tell me?' Anna could feel her mouth dry, and she looked to Ned, who gently took a deep breath and waited. Whatever it was Archie was about to tell her, Ned knew about it already.

'I have asked Ruby to marry me,' Archie's eyes never once left Ruby's, 'every day for over twenty years...'

'I cannot marry you while he is still alive.' Ruby's dark eyes were determined now. Although, it was a different determination from the one that Anna had seen before.

'...But what about the church...?'

'Ahh, the fire and bloody brimstone again.' Ruby threw back her head, and she laughed. 'Well, let me tell you something Anna, there are some women who marry for love and some who marry for folly.' She paused momentarily. 'Some walk down the aisle into their own private hell, and they have no way out once it is done. Death is the one thing they crave.'

Anna pondered on Ruby's words. She recalled the weary women who worked near the dockside from dawn 'til dusk. Toiling for their large families, with not a husband to be seen.

'I see the ones whose husband's go off to sea with a cheery wave,' Ruby said, 'the next day the wives are in Archie's place hocking the bed linen.' She looked round the table, 'The men come back, one, two, or sometimes many years later.' She slowly shook her head. 'On their return, they expect a loving woman to be waiting at the door in a clean pinny and demand to be waited on hand and foot.'

Anna knew women who had no say in anything they did once they married. They were tied, as surely as slaves, to wedlock.

'It is not like that with Archie and me, though,' Ruby said in the capacious dining room that was bigger than most houses round here, and the place Anna now called home.

'No, it is nothing like that,' Archie answered, taking Ruby's hand, 'but, you must trust that we love each other, Anna, and one day, when we can, we will tell you everything.'

Anna put her head down, unable to meet their tender gaze.

Unintentionally, she had been drawn into Lottie's narrow-minded views and now it was she who felt ashamed. She had no right to judge. People should be considered on their actions. Their kindness to their fellow man. These people were as close to her as her own family. Would she ever turn her back on her mother or Sam or James and Michael? Indeed, she would not.

'No. That is none of my business,' Anna said as a flush of heat crept up her neck and her cheeks. Wincing, she covered her face with her hands. She could not look her friends in the face and wished they could not see her. Her shame crawled over her like snakes. 'I'm so sorry. I should not have listened to the idle gossip of fools.'

'One day you will know.' Ruby accepted Anna's response with good grace. Then she said with a hint of mischief in her voice: 'Although, I never tire of hearing Archie propose.' Their eyes locked.

'And I never tire of asking.' A knowing smile played about Archie's lips, causing the familiar twinkle in his mellow eyes, telling Anna all she needed to know. They were good people. That is all that mattered to Anna.

'If you do get tired of asking, Archie, you just let me know.' The mellow light in Ruby's eyes changed quickly to amusement. 'Then there will be words...'

'As long as they end in "I will", that will do for me, my love.' Archie turned to Anna and winked, making her feel very privileged to be part of this family. For that was what they were now.

Moments later, Lottie entered the room after a cursory rap of her knuckles on the door, and the mood changed.

Anna gasped, causing the dainty crust-less triangle of bread to lodge in her throat. Her eyes filled with stinging tears as she tried to breathe, then she began to choke. The more she tried to draw air into her lungs, the more she gagged.

'Archie do something.' Ruby cried, throwing down her napkin.

However, Ned was already out of his chair and the gentle pat on Anna's back progressed to a hefty wallop. The backslap felt strong enough to break her ribs, but it did the trick, when the offending bread flew from her mouth, and landed right in the middle of cook's delicious, mouth-watering, sherry trifle.

'Oh no. I've ruined it,' Anna cried.

'Never mind that now,' Ruby jumped up and fussed over her, while Lottie disdainfully removed the bread from the trifle.

'As long as you are all right,' Ned said, looking relieved, 'that's all that matters.'

'I'm fine,' Anna made a triumphant effort to sound fine as she wiped tears brought on by choking from her eyes and vowed not to listen to Lottie's misguided gossip again.

22

Sam was crouched in the corner of the barn, his injured ribs had not mended, and he found it difficult to get up. He still suffered the effects of the awful beating he received over a month ago, after he got back from town. Noreen Jessup informed her father of his wild behaviour before she had even alighted from the carriage. Sam was dealt more severely than any other time since he got here.

At fourteen, he still had four years to serve his apprentice indentures and become a fully trained agricultural worker. However, Sam felt the expertise of staying alive, despite his mistreatment and starvation, was far more important.

Sam had quickly discovered that he had no say in his own life. He was a tool, in much the same way as a hoe or a fork. The workhorse was much better cared for than he was.

'There's plenty more like you, boy,' Noreen told him, 'and when Pa finds out what you've done to me, he's going to be mighty sore.'

'I haven't done anything to you.'

Sam was horrified when she opened the big coat she always

wore, showing her distended belly. He had seen women like that all over Liverpool, and working on a farm, he knew exactly how the lump got there. Nevertheless, no matter how much she enticed him, tried to corrupt him, Sam had always refused Noreen's temptation. He did not want to end his days under the pinewoods.

'You did this to me.' Her face was a spitting, purple rage and her bloodshot eyes now bulged in their sockets. She was as mad as a hellcat. He had to get away from here and soon.

'I did no such thing.' Sam felt his ever-flagging spirits completely sink. The welts on his back had not healed properly from the last beating. He doubted he would survive another.

'You did.' Noreen screamed in his face. 'You laid me down and you forced yourself on me.'

'I did not!' Sam felt tears of injustice well up in his eyes. No matter how many times she tried, he repelled her. She was twice the size of him and the stench of her made him feel sick. Whatever she was after was beyond him.

'Pa will believe me before you, *boy*.' The last word was said on a sneer and Sam tried to recall a time when she could have got off the farm to go and see someone. A boy who had a poor sense of smell, obviously. She had been friendly with the boy in the grocery store. But there were no other times that he could recall, apart from the day they went into town. Even then there was not enough time to, to... His stomach lurched. Oh, Lord, Noah Jessup would think he was the culprit.

'My daddy is going to kill you,' Noreen said with more than a hint of delight, her eyes alight, 'and he can, you make no mistake about it.'

'But I didn't do anything,' Sam protested as she circled him, knowing quite well Farmer Jessup was very protective of his *little girl*. He turned round, his eyes darting to the barn door and so did

Noreen's. Every muscle in his body went rigid. He needed to run but his muscles had become petrified stone.

'Well, I know you didn't do anything, you aint got it in you and you know that... but Pa aint gonna see it like that.' Noreen anticipating his objective, headed to the barn door, and Sam wondered if he should hurry after her, terrified of what she was about to do. But he could not move. As well as the broken ribs one of his legs was very painful and he struggled to put weight on it.

'Look, you are mistaken,' he added, knowing the boy in the grocery store had obviously had his wicked way, albeit very quickly. 'Do you know how babies are made?'

'Of course, I know,' Noreen scoffed, 'I'm not stupid. I raise cows and sheep. 'Cept I won't raise no baby. Daddy sees to that. And afterwards, he lets me stay in bed for a few days to build up my strength. No girl could wish for a more thoughtful Pa.' Noreen spoke in such a way that made Sam think about the other homeboy. The one who went missing.

'What do you mean?' Sam felt ice cold water coursing through his body. What did Mr Jessup *see to*? 'This has happened before?'

There was a moment's silence, as if she were trying to get the notion straight in her head. Then, like a child, she plucked at her fingers. 'Daddy says it don't matter 'bout the homeboys. They aint nothin' special. They just trash. They come from trash and will always be trash.' She held onto the handle of the barn door and started to sway. 'They can be replaced, Daddy says. But I can't.' Noreen had a coy, sickly grin on her face. 'I am special, I am Daddy's special girl. And you cannot tell no one. They won't believe a homeboy.'

It did not take long for the enormity of the situation to dawn on Sam. He had to get away. However, he needed to know the lengths to which Noah Jessup would go to protect his perverted activities. 'What happened to the homeboy who came here before me?' Sam was almost too afraid to ask, but he must, because whatever happened to the other boy was surely going to happen to him.

'He got real sick.' Noreen had a faraway look in her eyes. 'It came on sudden. Pa buried him up in the pinewoods... At the foot of the high mountain... A real nice spot.'

'What did he die of?' Sam asked cautiously.

'Pa said I wasn't to worry my pretty little head over it. He wouldn't be bothering me no more.'

'And did he *bother* you a lot?' Sam looked towards the door, if he could only get out of here, he would find the strength from somewhere to run and run and run, and never stop running until he reached civilisation. His body began to tremble, and beads of perspiration broke out, rolling down his collar, even though the barn was ice cold. The walls felt as if they were closing in and he could hear the rapid beat of his own heart.

'The homeboy didn't bother me anyhow, no more 'n you did. You English boys are dull. You aint got anything to offer a girl.' Noreen gave a coquettish giggle that turned Sam's stomach.

'When did your mother die?' His words were shaky and extremely cautious. If he could keep her talking, she might relax. Let her guard down. Take her eyes off the door.

'I was nine.' Noreen answered. 'Daddy says I look like her, but I don't remember her.'

'And how many homeboys have come to work on the farm since then?' Sam suspected Noah Jessup was looking for a scapegoat to assuage his guilt. 'Was there many homeboys who got sick?'

'You ask too many questions.' Noreen was getting jittery, possibly because she had never derived a conclusion before.

Then she was quiet. She would not look at him when she spoke. It was as if the realisation of what had happened in the past with other boys made her feel uneasy. She slowly lifted the latch on the door. Turning, she looked back at Sam, speaking hesitantly. 'I'm going to talk to Daddy. He will be along to see you presently, I 'spect.'

'I was thinking,' Sam said quickly, knowing he had to try to get her on his side. 'It must hurt really bad after. After your daddy... *sees* to you...' This kind of talk sickened him. But he knew he could not stop now. 'Maybe *I* could look after you instead?' He saw a flicker of something in her eyes. She took her hand off the latch.

'How will you look after me?' Noreen asked, curious now. She edged back inside the barn.

'I will marry you. We can be man and wife. Like your parents used to be.' *Where did that come from?* Sam would have offered her anything. Because he knew, once she went inside and alerted her ignorant father of her condition, Farmer Jessup would head straight to the barn. Even though her *condition* had nothing to do with him, Sam knew he would have to endure the worst of Jessup's anger. God alone knew what would become of him after that.

'Marry *you*?' Noreen's look of disgust made Sam feel worthless. 'Marry a *homeboy*? Are you out of your mind?' Turning, she slammed out of the barn to fetch her father.

Sam knew he was in for it now.

* * *

Sam realised he had ruffled Noreen's feathers when she forgot to put the outside bolt across the door, as she did at the end of the day to stop him running away. He had not given serious consideration to escaping before today. He knew there were many miles to the nearest town. A good half-day on horseback. It would be morning at least before he caught sight of another human being. But he had to try. If he were to survive and get back to Liverpool, he had to get as far away from this place as possible. He must find the strength to escape. Whatever happened to him after that was in the hands of the Almighty.

The creak of the barn door sounded like a rolling clap of thunder. Sam prayed that Noreen was still inside the farmhouse and made a dash towards the dirt-track road, dragging his emaciated body. He found strength to run, and run, and run. The thought of stealing a horse to make his escape quicker never entered his head. He had never stolen a thing in his life, and he was not going to start now. Even if, by taking a horse, it might save his life.

Even though he had been dragging himself along the dirt road for a long time, Sam had not got far when he heard voices. He dived into a ditch out of sight of the road, sure he could hear Noreen talking to someone. The male voice most certainly belonged to her angry father.

But there was more than one male voice and Sam feared Farmer Jessup had called the police, for sure. He would be treated as an absconder. Under sixteen years of age, Sam knew they would send him back to the children's home.

Being caught might be the best thing he could have done. Maybe it was one of the inspectors? His hope soared. They were supposed to come out every six months to make sure homeboys were being well cared for and looked after.

Nevertheless, there were so many like him that it would be time-consuming, maybe even impossible, to see them all. Many miles from anywhere. It would be so easy to lose boys out here. What if the other voice belonged to another farmer? One who was helping Jessup in his search to find him. The hope that Sam had clung to earlier, was beginning to slip from his grasp.

Cowering in the dark undergrowth, Sam heard the voices growing louder, coming closer. Jessup would be even more angry when he caught up with him. Fear fizzed through Sam's body.

Please, Lord, don't let him beat me again. He knew he could not survive another thrashing after he had been in that barn for days without a bite to eat, or even so much as a sip to wet his parched lips... Then, the voices were on top of him. And the light from a kerosene lamp hovered above his head, hurting his eyes...

'Come here, boy.' The voice did not belong to the farmer, but it had been a long time since anybody called Sam by his own name; he automatically answered to 'boy'. Edging forward his body was sore and stiff and as he supported himself on his right elbow, it collapsed under him. Sam drew in a stuttered gasp, and bit down the pain.

He said nothing, just stared blankly. His longing to get away from here was far stronger than his fear of strangers.

As his eyes grew accustomed to the light, he recognised the face as that of the Mountie he had seen in town. His legs, weak, unsteady could not hold up his fragile body and the infected welts on his back and buttocks made moving quickly so difficult, leaving Sam in danger of falling.

'What is your name, son?' Another man accompanied the Mountie, and Sam suspected he was in deep trouble for running away.

They edged closer. Straining to see him properly. Sam's weary eyes travelled the long length of the police officer, who looked seven feet tall.

'Sam, Sir. Samuel Cassidy.' His head was swimming and he felt sick.

'How old are you, son?' The other man spoke in a kindly

voice. And felt Sam's pulse. He instinctively sensed he could trust him. It had been so long since he heard a kind word. To his shame, Sam felt hot tears running down his frozen cheeks.

'Fourteen sir.' Sam could hardly breathe, his chest felt tight and his vision blurred.

'I did not think he would be this bad,' the police officer said. Then turning back to Sam, he said, 'You remember me, son?' Sam nodded. 'I remember you too, in fact, you looked so ill that day in town, I got in touch with my brother, here. Doctor Warburton.'

'You're a doctor?' Sam was only vaguely aware of the relief he felt.

'How long have you been here in Canada, Son?'

'I've been here over a year sir.' Large plumes of opaque air scattered into the night as he tried desperately to quell the racing gasps of air he so needed.

'We have no record of you,' the doctor said to the officer. 'Why is he not registered? He's in a bad way.'

'Please don't send me back to the farm, sir.' Sam would rather die than go back to the farm. 'I am strong, and a good worker, but I can't go back there.' The doctor and Officer Warburton nodded. '*She* told me there was another boy and now he's buried in the woods.' His words shot from his lips in case Noreen silenced him. Sam could not bear the thought of what would happen to him if he had to go back to the farm.

'Whatever this boy has been through is cruel in the extreme.' Sam heard the officer say. Then, the officer explained: 'You may have been strong when you came here, son, but you need urgent help now. And plenty of it.'

'We will make sure you get the care you need,' the doctor said as the sound of buggy wheels crunched to a halt, and his next words were intended for the occupants of the buggy. 'Your time here is done.' Jessup's face was dark and angry when Doctor Warburton held the kerosene lamp aloft.

'That boy has been interfering with my daughter,' Jessup pointed to Sam, his words full of anger, 'and when he gets back to my farm, I'm gonna whoop him *real* good.'

'This boy has not got the strength to interfere with anyone or anything,' Doctor Warburton said, 'and the only place he is going is to the hospital. And you'd better pray this boy survives.'

'Because if he doesn't,' said the police officer, 'you are up on a murder charge.'

Sam felt a furnace grow inside him in the cool night air. He was being lifted from the ground. The voices, full of concern, were dwindling... He no longer had the strength to care. A shroud of blackness enveloped him.

23

'I have a collection in Southport at eleven,' Archie said, 'Ned will come with me as the writing bureau is a two-man item.'

Before Ruby could reply, there was a cacophonous racket down in the street outside the Emporium, disturbing their breakfast. The room filled with the ear-splitting noise as Archie and Ned's cutlery clattered on their plates. Quickly they got up from the table and made their way over to the bay windows.

'What the hell is that noise?' Archie said, pulling back the lace curtain and pushing up the sash window. Leaning out, he peered over the windowsill and down into the street. 'Don't you know people are trying to eat their breakfast, here,' he called to the begoggled driver as his admiring eyes stroked the gleaming bottle-green Crossley 15 motorcar.

'Wow,' breathed Ned, looking out of the corner bay that allowed views of two streets, 'that is some motorcar, hey Archie?'

'It is, Ned,' Archie answered in matching tones, 'but Mrs Watson looks like she wants to knock some sense into him with her brolly, he's making enough noise to wake the dead.'

'A motorcar, you say?' Ruby looked to Anna, her eyes filled

with curiosity. 'Every child within hearing distance will be buzzing round it like bluebottles.' Motorcars were not an everyday visitor to the people who lived round the courts and streets along Vauxhall Road.

Ruby laid down her napkin, rising elegantly from the table. Today was her day off from the shop, so she was not in her formal black and white uniform. Anna noted how much younger she looked in the pale duck-egg blue chiffon dress with its soft floaty skirt draping elegantly over her slim hips. At thirty-eight, Ruby pooh-poohed the latest craze of the 'hobble' skirt, telling Anna, she had no wish to tether the legs like an unbroken horse.

'He's coming here?' Ruby said, looking over Archie's shoulder to see the young man in a pale, ankle-length driving coat walk straight-backed towards the shop. The bell at the side door leading up to their private quarters signalled the arrival of the visitor and sent Mrs Hughes hurrying down the stairs.

'I'll be giving him a piece of my mind, you just see if I don't,' Mrs Hughes chuntered as she headed down the wide staircase, 'making that unholy noise at this hour of the morning.' Opening the side door to the driver, any further retort was silenced when the driver removed the driving gauntlet and proffered a pale, slim delicate hand. 'Oh, my goodness! You are a woman.' Mrs Hughes's mouth slackened, and her eyes opened wide. Not usually lost for words, she could only gawp from the driver to the car as the young woman removed her goggles and unbuttoned the pale buttermilk coloured coat.

Mrs Hughes understood the clothes were a status symbol of an elitist group of young people rich enough to afford those outrageous machines. But, if asked her opinion, she would tell anybody that those noisy, smelly contraptions would never take on. Nothing could better the more ladylike horse and carriage.

'Is your mistress at home?' the young woman asked in clipped tones.

'Do you have an appointment?' Mrs Hughes asked equally formal. She was sure the mistress would not take kindly to being disturbed at breakfast. Even if it was by a car-driving woman. To knock at a person's door at this hour of the day, after driving one of those monstrosities. Well, it really was the limit! 'If you will take a seat.' Mrs Hughes waved to the high-backed Louis the four-teenth chair positioned near the front door. 'I will see if Mrs Swift is taking callers this *early* in the day.' She gave a small, almost imperceptible sniff.

'Mrs Swift?' the young woman asked, her brow creasing in puzzlement. Eleanor's mother had told her that her aunt had changed her name to Ruby but hadn't been told that she was married.

'That is what I said,' Mrs Hughes confirmed with a nod. She was not quite sure what to make of this young woman, who was probably no older than nineteen or twenty, and obviously had more money than good manners. 'Who shall I say is calling?' Mrs Hughes paused, her hand on the highly polished bannister, trusting her first impression was correct.

'My name is Eleanor Harrington,' the young woman said and looking at her now Mrs Hughes caught a determined look in her dark eyes that was vaguely familiar. 'She will know who I am.'

Mrs Hughes gave a curt nod of her head and began to make her way upstairs. She had never heard the missus mention anybody called Eleanor Harrington. Nevertheless, she had no time to ponder when she saw Ruby standing above her on the landing. And if Mrs Hughes knew anything, she would say the missus was going to faint as all colour drained from her face.

'Are you not feeling well, Madam?' Mrs Hughes asked, but Ruby said nothing, only gazed over the housekeeper's shoulder and silently beckoned the young woman upstairs. Then, as quickly as she appeared at the top of the stairs, she headed back into the breakfast room.

Anna, still sitting at the breakfast table with Ned, watched Ruby go immediately to Archie's side at the mantelpiece and search for his hand.

'Eleanor is here!' Ruby said simply, and after giving her hand a reassuring squeeze, Archie put his arm round her shoulders, drawing her to him while Anna and Ned exchanged puzzled glances, but said nothing as they both eyed the door.

Mrs Hughes showed Eleanor Harrington into the morning room and Ruby said nothing. Looking at the girl who bore a striking resemblance, nobody said a word until Ruby broke the elongated silence.

'Hello, Eleanor. How lovely to see you after all this time.' Ruby went to their young visitor and hugged her. Then, holding her at arms-length, she said: 'This is a wonderful surprise, let me have a look at you.'

'Hello, Aunt Ruby.' The girl smiled, and then addressing Archie, her voice became a little softer. 'Hello, Archie. Mama has told me so much about you both.'

Anna studied the fresh-faced girl, who looked to be around the same age as herself, amazed at how much she resembled Ruby, with her dark hair and her large doe-eyes. Ruby never talked about her family.

'How is your mother?' Ruby's voice sounded stiff, like it did when she was talking to a customer.

'She's fine,' Eleanor answered with the ghost of a smile and her sharp features softened, 'I think she deserves a medal, if truth be told, you know what Father's like.'

Oh yes, Ruby knew exactly what Giles Harrington was like:

sneaky, greedy, a man who would stab you in the back to get his own way. Really not a good look for a country vicar.

'Although Mama keeps herself busy with *churchly* activities.' Eleanor gave the word *churchly* the same disdainful intonation Ruby applied to anything relating to the religious.

Anna, feeling they would like some privacy, made her excuses as she cleared away the breakfast things, while Ned carried the tray to the kitchen. 'I'll go and ask Mrs Hughes to make more tea.'

'Thank you, Anna,' Ruby said quietly and waited for Anna and Ned to leave the room before she returned her attention to Eleanor. The situation must be serious, Ruby thought, and of the utmost importance if it brought Eleanor to her door for the first time. Ruby knew her sister, May, had never allowed contact between herself and Eleanor on the orders of her husband. So, to Ruby's way of thinking, either Giles Harrington was dead, or her sister had suddenly developed a backbone.

* * *

'Ruby looked shocked when Eleanor came in,' Anna told Mrs Hughes as they were, getting the tea tray ready, and Mrs Hughes went to the cupboard to fetch the deliciously dainty tea biscuits, she had baked the night before.

'Given the pasty look of Mrs Swift,' Mrs Hughes said, with the air of one who knew about these things, 'she might want something a bit sweet.'

'Let us wait and see.' Ned, a rock of common sense, knew when to keep out of the way. He was not one for idle gossip, reckoning Archie and Ruby would soon tell them if they wanted to let them know.

'You're so sensible, Ned,' Anna said. 'I wonder what's brought

her here so early. She must be rich to own a car like that one.'
Anna voiced what everybody was thinking.

'It's a grand car and no mistake,' Ned agreed.

* * *

Ruby felt numb listening to what Eleanor Harrington was saying.
She was explaining the outcome of the sinking of R.M.S. Titanic
and what it meant for the family.

'Everybody said she was unsinkable...' Ruby mouthed the
words. The ship was embarking on her maiden voyage and the
world had watched in awe and admiration. But in just a few short
days that admiration had turned to horror and, for a lot of Liverpool families, grief. Rich and poor had died together when
Titanic sank, and death paid no heed to status. Famous and
anonymous were washed up alongside one another.

'His body was recovered from the sea by a passing ship,
R.M.S. Carpathia...' Eleanor said. 'Grandfather was drowned
when the ship succumbed and sank south of Newfoundland in
Canada.'

Ruby listened without saying a word. She could not speak. Her
silence mistaken for a stoic demeanour that hid the fact she felt unex-
pectedly stunned. Silas Ashland, one of the wealthiest ship builders
in Europe, had been invited to travel on the ship's maiden voyage.

'He sold his shipbuilding empire and was going to retire to
the Lake District...'

'And the funeral?' Ruby needed to sit down. Her mind
retracing every step taken from the moment she got up this
morning until being given this news. She was frozen to the core.
Her chest tight.

'I'm afraid it was yesterday,' Eleanor plucked the skin on the back of her hand, her stilted words full of remorse. 'I did tell Papa that you would want to say your own goodbye.'

'Obviously, he did not take a blind bit of notice.' Ruby's words were brittle.

'Please, Eleanor, do sit down.' Archie took in Eleanor's straight-backed slender frame, her familiar dark eyes, and the wisps of ebony curls that were now escaping a tortoise-shell comb.

'I am sorry to be the bearer of such sad news,' Eleanor said in that whispery church voice, reserved for moments like this.

Ruby did not say anything for a moment. Her lips compressed together, lest she utter something trite, or worse, acerbic, and irretrievable. She felt a rage building inside her. Her father had gone. No goodbyes. No resolutions. No justifications for her years of torment. And she had also been denied the chance to see him laid to rest.

'I had been staying with Grandpa before his voyage, in fact, that is his car outside,' Eleanor explained, 'I was going to be his companion, but I caught chickenpox and was not allowed to travel.'

'The Lord moves in mysterious ways,' Ruby said as Mrs Hughes brought a tray of tea.

'Mother sends her love,' Eleanor said simply, breaking the silence as she took in the elegant furnishing. Aunt Ruby's spacious living quarters were a breath of fresh air. The pale-coloured chintz sofas and sweet-pea floral wallpaper were the height of modern living, and such a surprise.

To hear her father talk, Eleanor had expected Ruby's home to resemble something akin to a courtesan's boudoir. But this place was lovely and so tastefully furnished.

What a shame she was here on such sad business, Eleanor

thought, she could imagine many a jolly conversation in a room like this.

Ruby silently watched Eleanor and recalled catching a glimpse of her as a child. She had been holding on to May and Giles's hands when they entered a smart tearoom in Lord Street, Southport. Even now, Ruby could still feel the slicing pain that shot through her when her brother-in-law pulled the girl towards him and ushered his wife and child from the tearoom.

'I suppose your mother expects me to live in a hovel, under the eaves of a garret,' Ruby said, taking in Eleanor's obvious interest in her home. She watched her pretty features for signs of surprise at such a remark, but the young woman appeared unfazed, and for the first time since she arrived, Eleanor smiled.

'She said nothing to me,' Eleanor replied, after Mrs Hughes had left the room, but she did not mention her father at all.

Ruby admired her discretion but, nevertheless, she felt more than a little put out that her sister had sent Eleanor to give the news of their father's tragic demise.

'Did she not think it proper to come and tell me herself?' Ruby knew she was putting the girl into an unforgivably awkward situation. However, she assuaged her guilt by assuming a hard-hearted woman would have refused her niece entry altogether.

'She is grief-stricken,' Eleanor explained, 'especially as Father persuaded Grandpa that a maiden voyage trip on the new ship would be good for him... The sea air...'

'Oh dear, the sea air most certainly did not suit him this time,' Ruby's acerbic tone caused Archie's eyebrows to raise slightly. How dare Giles Harrington say who could and who could not go to her father's funeral!

Ruby apologised to Eleanor, for making her feel uncomfortable with her seemingly callous remark. However, she could not forgive her father in death... In much the same way, he could not forgive her in life. She was angry that he had died. Because now they would never get the chance to make amends.

'Will we see you at the house?' Eleanor asked, unperturbed. Buoyed with a vibrant spirit that horrified her father and deliciously shocked her mother, Eleanor realised that in the short amount of time she knew her, she really liked Aunt Ruby. She was not the painted lady her father purported her to be.

'The house?' Ruby asked. 'Are you all staying at the house?'

'Yes, the reading of the Will is next Friday. Three p.m.'

'Did your father send you to tell me?' Ruby asked, knowing she and Giles Harrington had never been on good terms.

'No,' Eleanor said honestly,' in fact, he did not want me to come here at all.'

'I'm sure he didn't.' Ruby could not stop the words, but Eleanor did not seem shocked or even fazed by her assumption.

'I vowed never to set foot in my family home again,' Ruby said, leaving her tea untouched. 'However, I now realise people, and feelings change. Nothing stays the same forever.' If that jumped-up little pipsqueak Giles Harrington thought he was going to lord it over her and keep her from the reading of her father's Will, he was wrong.

24

A stay in the small town hospital preceded lodgings in the home of Doctor Warburton, his wife and family. They had visited Sam every day until he was strong enough for discharge from the hospital.

'If you'll have us, son,' said the doctor, 'we will show you what good Canadian hospitality is, for sure, and we would welcome you into our home for as long as you wish.'

Sam was so grateful. He would be staying with them, and their fourteen-year-old twins, Albert and Millie, who, even though they were the same age were much bigger and stronger than Sam was. Doc Warburton assured Sam that, with a lot of tender loving care, he too would be as strong one day.

Over the next weeks, Sam regained his strength and for the first time since he arrived in Canada, he knew he was with good people. Salt-of-the-earth people, who had his best interest at heart. They looked after him better than he had ever known.

'Jessup has been prosecuted for what he did to you,' Officer Warburton came to tell Sam. 'Furthermore,' he lowered his voice, out of earshot of his homely sister-in-law, 'his daughter has been sent to an institution for wayward girls. Her father had the temerity to say she was out of control, throwing herself at every man she saw.'

Sam had seen Noreen's antics at first-hand, but he was not sure her behaviour was all her own doing. Living in the back of beyond without any motherly guidance was bound to send the girl a bit strange. 'I feel sorry for her if the truth be told, she didn't know any different,' Sam said, relaxed for the first time in years, feeling stronger every day, with good nourishing food and kind-hearted people round him; he was beginning to thrive. 'She didn't stand a chance.'

'You have a more forgiving nature than most boys your age,' Doctor Warburton said.

Sam was thoughtful for a moment, glad now, that he had gone to town with Noreen and bumped into Officer Warburton, who searched for many days to find him. Jessup's farm had been a last resort, and Sergeant Warburton had brought his brother, knowing if he was at the farm, Sam would need to be checked over.

'I am so lucky you both found me, and ever so grateful.' Sam smiled 'I was losing hope.' Smiling was becoming a regular occurrence these days. He had almost forgotten the reason to smile. Nevertheless, now he had plenty of them. 'God only knows where I would be today.' *Under a mound on the back field probably.* He shuddered visibly.

'I was shocked when I first saw you, I won't lie,' Officer Warburton said, 'with your wasted appearance, so different from our own children... You got inside my head and I knew I had to get Charlie to go and have a look.' He was quiet for a while. 'I kept thinking, without help, this boy is going to die. I could not let that happen.'

'It took ages to get any information,' the doctor said in that low rolling timbre, 'we were wondering if you had just dropped off the earth. We dreaded to think what you were going through.'

'I know I don't have any identification papers, no birth certificate or official documents to prove who I am or where I came from,' Sam pondered.

'And having no identification will make it difficult to get a passport home,' Doctor Warburton said in that low, rolling timbre, 'if you ever decide to go back home, that is.'

Sam had not dared dwell on going home. He had not even thought of trying to get a passport. It would take years to save for a ticket Sam thought.

Little did he know that something was about to happen that would bring him hope.

25

Ruby did not want a huge affair with frills and furbelows. Now her father was no longer alive, she wanted to be a married woman when she re-entered Ashland Hall.

Anna, Ned, and Mrs Hughes were the only people invited to the West Derby registry office wedding at Brougham Terrace. Ned was Archie's best man and Anna was Ruby's maid of honour and Mrs Hughes supplied copious happy tears. After the simple ceremony, they were all treated to delicious afternoon tea, served in a private reception room at the huge North Western Hotel facing St George's Hall.

A beautiful but simple two-tier wedding cake was brought to their table by Chef, and Archie had organised a harpist to play in the background. The whole day was a celebration, made possible by special licence.

'To the outsider, this would seem like a disappointment of a wedding,' Archie said to the small intimate gathering, 'but let me point out one thing.' He looked to Ruby, who smiled indulgently. 'I have been celebrating every day since I met my darling Ruby. We do not need grand gestures to prove our love.' He paused momentarily and smiled. 'Ruby told me to say this – and now we are properly married nothing will change, she is still the boss.'

Everybody laughed, knowing there was more than a smidgeon of truth in Archie's words.

'Bravo, my darling,' Ruby said, delighting in his little speech. They fell in love as soon as they met when Ruby – then named Rowena – was just sixteen years old, but society and her father would never countenance such a match. As soon as her father got to hear about their relationship, he sent Archie packing and refused to allow her to marry.

Nevertheless, Ruby was determined. She could not live without Archie. The only choice she had was to run away from home to live with her man. May was the only person who knew where she was.

Ruby recalled her father telling Archie that if she ever married him while he was alive, Silas Ashland would disinherit his oldest daughter and leave everything to the church. 'You do know, my love,' Archie said in an intimate whisper as the waiter filled their glasses, 'if you ever do want a grand gesture or two, I will oblige – with bells on.'

'I know you would, my darling,' Ruby said raising her glass. *That is why you, my darling husband, will accompany me when I go back to Ashland Hall.*

Ashland Hall was set in five hundred acres, its walled garden bordering a glorious beach which boasted breath-taking sand dunes. Bordering the Hall, the sweeping coastal pinewoods, planted by Silas Ashland when he and his new bride moved into the Hall thirty years earlier, were surrounded by lakes, pasture and a nature reserve.

'It certainly lives up to its reputation of being one of the biggest private houses in the North West,' Ned said as he manoeuvred the horse and carriage onto the winding drive leading up to the steps, 'it is huge.' The majestic house combined the elegance of a country estate with the luxury of a grand hotel.

'It looks like we are not the first to arrive,' Ruby said, looking out of the carriage window to see her father's motorcar haphazardly parked at the foot of the steps, and she bit her bottom lip as she edged forward on her seat, her hands clasped on her knee, avoiding all eye contact. Anna, watching Ruby now, rightly suspected Ruby was more nervous than she was letting on.

'Is that a tennis court?' Anna's eyes widened. She had never seen one except in a book.

'May and I played a lot when we were younger...' Ruby said remembering a time long gone and her voice trailed when Ned brought the carriage to a halt.

'They look a bit scary,' Anna said, alighting from the brougham and shielding her eyes in the afternoon sunshine while looking up to the stone gargoyles, gazing down from a pale sandstone balustrade over the imposing portico entrance.

'They come alive at night and hide under your bed,' Ned kidded, 'and when you are asleep, they come out to tickle your toes.'

When Anna shuddered, he threw his head back and laughed, just as the front door opened wide, and Eleanor came hurtling down the steps in an unladylike fashion towards them, dodging the butler and the footmen in her haste to get to the bottom of the wide stone steps. Ruby and Archie exchanged a silent glance that was impossible to fathom.

'Who does she remind you of?' Archie asked and Ruby smiled, knowing exactly who Eleanor reminded her of – she was just the same at that age.

'I never dreamt I would come back here,' Ruby said, taking in the green apple smell of newly cut grass.

Archie nodded, holding her arm close to his body when she linked it through his. Her new wedding ring glinting in the afternoon sunshine the day after their simple wedding ceremony.

'It is so wonderful to see you back home, Aunt Ruby.' Eleanor did not call her aunt, Rowena because Ruby made it plain that she did not answer to the name since she left Ashland Hall all those years ago and took the name of Archie's beloved aunt. Hugging them all in turn, Eleanor indicated to the front door, chatting nonstop. 'I'll show you your rooms, and then we can have tea. Grandpa's solicitor, Mr Swanne, is coming to read the will later...'

Ruby noticed there was no sign of her sister or her pompous brother-in-law.

'Mama is in the library with Pa.' Eleanor sounded almost apologetic, as if reading her thoughts, and obviously embarrassed at her mother's lack of hospitality. 'She is waiting for you.'

'I am so relieved she did not hire a brass band to greet me.' Ruby smiled, aware that everybody present, staff included, knew the story of her past, but she did not recognise any of the staff. Giles Harrington had fired the old guard, according to Eleanor, and hired new staff. Ruby remained tight-lipped, valiantly trying not to reveal how she really felt.

'You lived here?' Anna gasped in the awkward silence, observing the two women who were amazingly similar, in word and deed. Their clipped enunciation and light delivery almost identical.

'I did,' Ruby answered, 'and strange as it might seem now, I was incredibly happy,' she looked to her husband, 'weren't we, Archie?'

'Aye, lass,' he said proudly in a strong mock-Lancashire twang, 'we were that.'

Watching them, Anna's overactive imagination began to conjure all sorts of what-ifs.

'Give me a moment, Archie.' Ruby's voice held a rare note of hesitation. Coming back here after being away so long felt a little peculiar as memories flooded uninvited. She felt like a visitor. Trees had grown in places where once there were saplings. The house itself looked a bit unloved. The windows were grimy, neglected. Not the sparkling glass she remembered. And although the lawn either side of the winding path had been cut recently, the grassland further afield was unkempt and overgrown.

Perhaps her father was less strident in old age, she thought. Time moved on. People change. Mellow. Become complacent. Although she could not imagine her father ever being so. He was known for being a tough nut to crack. A strong-minded businessman who did things his own way. After all, as they said back in Vauxhall Road, she did not lick her shrewd business acumen off the floor. Ruby felt the longer she delayed her meeting with May, the better.

'She is eager to see you,' Eleanor said, standing on the bottom step, half turned to go back into the house.

Ruby raised her chin and the unconscious movement told Anna that Ruby was on her guard. Her natural defences were up. Prepared to do battle if necessary. Anna had seen the actions many times when she was dealing with an awkward customer.

'I cannot think why...' Ruby knew May was not one for effervescent displays of affection since she began walking out with pious Giles. A cold fish if ever there was one. Ruby suspected the vicar had browbeaten her docile sister into marrying him and was even more sure she knew the reason why.

Giles Harrington had his eye on Ashland Hall, from the day he set foot in the place. He made no secret of the fact. Ruby also suspected Giles loved Ashland Hall more than he loved her sister. Compliant, dutiful, submissive, May, married the vicar the year before Ruby had been banished.

Older by ten years, Giles treated May like his pet, happy only if she complied with his ever-increasing demands on her time. May, eager to oblige a good man, was a soft touch. Ruby could see right through him. It came as no surprise that her sister was not here to greet her. Giles would never stoop to welcome the prodigal daughter back into the fold and would persuade his wife it was her duty to stay by his side. Duty meant a lot to Giles.

'Maybe you prefer a little walk?' Archie said. 'Reacquaint yourself?' He understood exactly what she was going through. Ruby nodded, her grateful eyes speaking for her. Admitting to himself he was not eagerly anticipating coming face-to-face with Giles either, Archie would keep a civil tongue in his head for Ruby's sake. But for how long? He could not say. He was sure that Giles had something to do with her father's discovery of Ruby's whereabouts, all those years ago.

Ruby and Archie were at church on the morning the pastor came and took away their beloved child on the order of Ruby's father. Ruby, unmarried and under twenty-one had no say in her baby daughter's welfare. Silas Ashland held the upper hand. Aided and abetted by Giles and the church.

'You don't mind if we meander, Eleanor?' Archie asked, knowing the family solicitor was not due for another hour. 'Aunt Ruby is feeling a little bilious after the journey.'

'I will let Mama know,' Eleanor answered, loving the fact that her aunt flouted social niceties, and did her own thing. 'Of course. She will understand perfectly.'

I doubt that very much. Ruby's smile did not show her true feelings and she decided she would stay only until she heard what Papa had to say. For she knew there would be plenty.

Father always had the last word.

* * *

'The house is amazing,' exclaimed Anna, knowing the Grecian statues would not look out of place outside St George's Hall. 'I've never seen a private house so remarkable in my whole life.' She could say words like *remarkable* now without feeling as if she was betraying her working-class roots; Ruby had taught her a lot.

'You've visited a few then?' Ned smiled. They had both come a long way from the days of living hand to mouth in the dockside streets of Liverpool.

He took in the banks of vibrant, cerise-coloured rhododendrons, watching Archie and Ruby stroll through the gardens, letting their memories flow.

'Ma would have loved this,' Anna said wistfully, knowing such a place would usually be out of bounds to the likes of them. Then she smiled, 'Michael and James would have run the legs off themselves in these grounds.'

'I can imagine Sam having a kickabout on those lawns,' Ned agreed.

Anna turned away from him then and suddenly found the surrounding trees and flowers fascinating.

'Poor Sam,' she whispered, feeling guilty for enjoying her new surroundings. 'I wonder where he is. If he's happy.'

'Don't upset yourself, Anna,' Ned said as they sat on the wide semicircle of steps. He smiled and gently nudged Anna's arm with his elbow, 'Look at the face on him.' He nodded towards a straight-backed haughty footman awaiting Ruby's return. 'He looks like he's lost a shilling and found a penny.'

'I wouldn't feel right, going in there without Ruby,' Anna nodded, looking over her shoulder towards the house, 'the servants seem stuffier than the toffs.'

Ned laughed.

'Some of them think they *are* the toffs,' he said, 'you'll see what I mean when you meet them face-to-face.'

Anna's astonished eyes took in a lion's stony prowl atop the extensive sandstone steps. 'I am so glad *they* aren't real,' she said, enjoying the nearness of Ned, and the warmth of his easy-going nature.

'Me too.' He smiled. 'Otherwise I would have to fight them off to save you.'

They sat in companionable silence for a while, taking in the stunning view of the grounds and gardens. He was glad Anna was settled. She had travelled a long dark road. The scars, both inside and out, caused by the death of her family, had been made worse by Sam's exile and took a long time to heal.

There had been times he feared she would never get over the tragedy. But thanks to Ruby's loving care, and Archie's cheerful good humour they had both found peace in the family fold. Even if they were the oddest kind of family. At the same time Ned's increasing affection for this beautiful girl, the most special person in his life, was in danger of destroying his ambition to see the world.

He had always treated her like a sister. Someone he could lark about with and have a laugh. Then, suddenly, one day when they were unloading the collection from a defaulter in the middle-class suburb of Gorsy, Anna put one of the fancy, silk dresses under her chin, as she had done a hundred times before. Only, this time, it nipped in and covered her slim figure in all the right places. Ned could not drag his gaze from her neat curves.

'You're doing it again,' Anna said, bringing Ned out of his reverie and causing him to start.

Tugging his stiff shirt collar, he realised he was getting hotter.

'Doing what?' Ned was not used to being all spruced up on a weekday and suddenly found the trees remarkably interesting. 'I haven't done anything.'

'Yes, you were,' Anna exclaimed, 'you were staring at me like a capon in the butcher's window again.' She liked it when he looked at her like that. Although she would never say.

'You've something in your hair,' Ned gently removed a fallen leaf from her curls. Being so close, he had an irresistible urge to kiss her now. She returned the look of tenderness that made his heart sing. However, as he moved closer, a small cough made him aware that Eleanor was waiting at the top of the steps.

Another time, hopefully.

'Do you think Ruby will keep the shops on now her father's gone?' Anna asked. 'After all, she has all this to manage?' She was sure Ned was about to kiss her and so wished he would.

'I don't know,' Ned answered, returning to his usual self.

'Do you think she'll want me to carry on working in the Emporium?' Anna suddenly realised the enormity of this new turn of events. 'What if Ruby sells the shops, we'll be out of a job and a home!' Anna folded her arms and leaned forward, resting her chin on her knees. The thought made her blood run cold.

'She will want you with her, you are like the daughter she never had,' Ned explained, standing up when Eleanor beckoned them forward. 'Although it won't make much difference to my circumstances.' He had not yet told Anna what was on his mind and threw little clues like flat stones skimming water, watching the ripples of realisation dawn on her face.

'Why? What do you mean?' Anna asked as a strange, unspoken notion caused her insides to tighten.

'I'll tell you later,' Ned reached the top before she did, his long limbs devouring the steps. Twisting his cap, he lowered his eyes under the footman's gaze. He hoped Ruby would still want the girl from the dockside. A broad-minded free spirit, Ruby might be, but the staff would not take kindly to waiting on the working classes. They might see Anna as an interloper, an upstart, trying to better herself. And he would not be here to reassure her. There was nothing wrong with trying to better yourself, he thought. He intended to do that very thing. That was why he had joined the Royal Navy.

Deep in thought now, he knew that previously, when he considered leaving Archie and Ruby, he reckoned it was tantamount to a betrayal after all they had done for him. However, now he knew. Now he was certain. He was going to follow his dream. He was going to see the world. Anna would understand.

* * *

Standing at Archie's side, Ruby linked her arm through his as they both looked beyond the huge, waterlily-festooned lake. 'I vaguely recall seeing a fountain in the lake when I was a child,' Ruby said, not taking her eyes from the high plumes of water shooting up into the balmy afternoon sky.

'Your father would not allow the fountain to be turned on, as I recall,' Archie answered. They both knew the cascading water held a magnetic fascination for Clive. Heir to Ashland Hall. And was where her seven-year-old brother drowned when Ruby was only four years old. She quickly turned to walk back to the house.

'We will leave immediately after the reading of the will,' Ruby said. 'There is nothing for me here now, Archie. I will not hang round for scraps from May's table. By God, no.'

'Do you think you and May will ever be able to reconcile your differences?' Archie asked, watching the pain wash over her beautiful face, knowing they used to be so close.

Ruby sighed, before saying quietly, 'I doubt it, Archie... she did such a terrible thing when she told Giles my secret.'

'She had lost her own child only days before,' Archie said, knowing the long separation had hurt Ruby more than she would ever admit.'

'So, she thought because she was a married woman, she was entitled to take my child, is that it?'

'Not at all,' Archie answered, suspecting Ruby was going through her own living hell right now.

'I doubt I can ever forgive her.'

'By three thirty, this place and everything in it will belong to me... Us,' Giles Harrington told his wife as they waited for the prodigal daughter's return.

'I would have liked to go and greet her, welcome her home,' May said gaining courage from her father's portrait behind her husband's balding head. 'I would have liked to...

'Oh, you would have liked,' Giles words were forced through his teeth, 'but we are not here to do what you would like, May. We are here to inherit what is rightfully yours, for bringing up her child and raising Elleanor to be the good, upstanding woman her mother never was.' He leaned back in the chair and surveyed the riches that surrounded him. There was plenty of money to pay off his gambling debts, and the arrears on the mortgage he had taken out on the vicarage before anybody found out. When he took charge of Ashland, he would give up being a man of the cloth for a lord of the land.

* * *

Ruby took in a long stream of warm air before going into the library, where May, seated in the chair near the fireplace, turned to greet her. However, she did not rise. Giles, almost lost in Father's chair behind the six feet by four feet mahogany desk, lifted his head, quickly shutting one of the drawers on the left-hand side.

Clearing his throat, Giles stretched his back, his hands now pressed against the green leather top of the desk, indicating he had been sitting there for a while.

'Ahh, Rowena, there you are,' Giles said in a high-handed manner that made Ruby want to baulk, 'do come and sit down...'

How dare you tell me what to do in my own home, she thought watching his stubby fingertips follow the pattern of gold tooling round the edge of the desk. Making no attempt to reach out his hand in greeting, Giles, much to her irritation, looked every inch the cat that got the cream.

Ruby's eyes could not resist taking in the huge painting of her father's benevolent expression over Giles's shoulder. The painting held a morbid fascination, and Ruby could not drag her gaze from it. She had not seen it before and his tired, rheumy eyes followed her to the waiting chair in front of the desk. He had grown so old.

'He commissioned it last Christmas,' Giles said with the air of one who was in the know. Ruby said nothing. She felt she was attending an interview with her bank manager. May had not spoken yet. 'Such a mild-mannered man...' Giles Harrington had lost none of his pious pomposity. 'We shall repair to the drawing room. I will order tea.'

Will you, indeed? Ruby watched him possessively hold May's elbow like one would hold a cup and saucer, and she gripped her tongue between her teeth to stop herself from saying something she knew she would regret.

Mild-mannered? Giles was obviously not talking about the same man she called her father. The same one who threw himself into his business empire after their mother died, leaving the two girls to fend for themselves.

'He was ruthless.' Try as she might, Ruby could not hold her tongue any longer, knowing she could not sit here listening to this jumped-up bible-basher talking about Silas Ashland as if he were a saint.

She saw May, bolt upright staring straight ahead, as if she had been instructed to say nothing. Because why else would she allow her husband to play lord of the manor before the will had even been read. Maybe Giles knew something nobody else did.

As they walked to the drawing room, Ruby watched May's tears silently rolling into the fine lines that prematurely webbed her stricken face. It was obvious that harsh words had been exchanged between May and her husband before Ruby even got here.

May cried easily, Ruby remembered. She felt things deeply, and tenaciously held onto a grievance. Although, she was hardly recognisable as her father's favourite daughter these days. She looked more like a withered old woman who was too scared to open her mouth.

Ruby felt a momentary pang of remorse for being so blunt. However, unable to remain silent, she continued: 'Pa did not get where he was by being mild-mannered. You saw only the best of him. I may not have been the son and heir he craved,' Ruby's voice rose slightly, 'but I am as good in business as he ever was.'

'Yes, I heard you were in trade.' Giles looked like something putrid had just crawled under his nose. He held up his hand for silence when Ruby rose to retaliate. However, she knew it was futile to continue the feud today. This was not the time to open old wounds. No matter how much she longed to set the record straight. She would bide her time. Something she had become accustomed to doing. Twenty years practice had stood her in good stead for this day.

Moments later, the parlourmaid apologised for interrupting and said there was somebody in the lobby asking to speak to Mrs Swift. Ruby stood up, smiled, and walked towards the door, satisfied her shocked sister had only just realised she had married a man out of love, not coercion.

When she reached the marbled hallway, Ruby was surprised to see their old family housekeeper, Archer's aunt, waiting to speak to her. The aunt whose name Ruby took when her father threw her out without a thought for her welfare. Apparently when her father perished on the Titanic, Giles had sacked her. So that was why the place looked as if it had not seen a duster or a scrubbing brush lately.

Ruby was delighted when given the latest piece of news. She thanked the housekeeper with a hug and told her she would sort everything after the reading of the Will, knowing her mother had hired the housekeeper, who had since given forty years of impeccable service to the Ashland family.

Returning to the drawing room Ruby saw her brother-in-law standing at the imposing Palladian chimneypiece, looking quite at home with his arm resting on the marble mantelshelf. She watched him snatch a crystal glass from a nearby tray and pour two fingers of finest malt whisky greedily down his throat in the blink of an eye.

'That did not quite hit the spot,' said the Anglican lay preacher, who puffed up his rotund chest, 'but it will have to do for now.' He rubbed his hands together when they were called to Father's office where the Will was to be read.

26

'Ahh, tea,' Ruby said when they reconvened in the drawing room after the reading of the Will, 'or something a little stronger for Giles, perhaps?'

Ruby noticed her sister had said nothing when Mr Swanne informed them of their father's wishes. If truth be told, Ruby thought May looked relieved.

Giles downed a large whisky. *For shock*, Ruby hoped gleefully.

'I am as surprised as you are, May,' Ruby told her younger sister after the family solicitor departed, 'I expected you would inherit Ashland Hall.' *And so did Giles, by the look of him*, she thought.

'The old goat told me he was going to change the Will in May's favour,' Giles said in a disbelieving tone, his face puce with rage. 'He did not say he would do it when he returned from New York.' His voice had a sneering edge. 'You have no right to this place,' Giles spat the words and Ruby noted the white spittle forming in the corners of his mouth, reminding her of a rabid dog. 'May should have got the lot.'

'And what makes you think that? Giles,' asked Ruby, enjoying his downfall immensely.

'Your father said he would disinherit you if you married Archie,' Giles answered, imagining he had Ashlands all sewn up.

'Indeed.' Ruby said, knowing that, for a man of the cloth, Giles Harrington was the most mean-spirited fellow she had met in a long time. 'But there is one part you left out, a very important part, actually.' Ruby took a schooner of sherry from the silver tray. 'My father said he would disinherit me if I married Archie *in his lifetime.*' she nodded to Archie who took a long envelope from his inside pocket and retrieving the document within, he handed it to Giles.

'Ruby and I were married yesterday.'

'Yesterday?' If he did not have the proof in his hands Giles would never have believed it. 'May has suffered so much.' His words were as tortured as the practiced expression on his face. 'She visited your father every week.'

Hardly, according to the housekeeper. Ruby was made aware of the fact that May, having moved to Scarborough when she married Giles, had rarely visited. The only person who visited, was his granddaughter, Eleanor. The irony was not lost on Ruby.

According to the housekeeper, whom Giles sacked after her father drowned, Giles went through the house like a magpie. Her sister's husband always did have his eye on the main chance. Father was nearing his eighties, and recently diagnosed with a concoction of illnesses that, although not life threatening, were proof he was not as strong and as powerful as he had once been. The situation was ideal to a gold-digger like Giles.

Ruby caught her brother-in-law's look of disdain as he waved his empty glass to the unobtrusive butler. *What did May see in him?* She knew May had never been energetic. Ruby was the feisty one. She and Archie eloped to a small village cottage, while timid, submissive, May, married the cleric and raised her child.

Looking to her younger sister now, the notion May had betrayed her illegitimate pregnancy to their father was absurd. Especially considering what Ruby had learned before the reading of the Will.

'What would May have to gain by doing such a wicked thing?' Mrs Swift, more of a mother to Ruby than her own, had said. 'Giles knew May could not have any more children.' Putting her hand on Ruby's arm, there was no mistaking her insinuation. 'The only people who knew about you and Archie and the baby, were me and Giles, and I didn't tell.'

'Of course.' Ruby had nodded. When she had got back from church on that fateful day, she was horrified to be told by Mrs Swift that her father had arranged to have her newborn daughter adopted.

Ruby knew for certain that Giles was involved and that *her* daughter had been brought up by May and Giles as their own, and not adopted.

Looking to her sister now, Ruby knew she should pity May. But she did not. Not any more.

'Another sherry, my love?' Archie held up the decanter and Ruby, as if coming out of a daze, shook her head. She knew by the tender look in his eyes that her husband was silently supporting her.

'That she should be given so little is an outrage.' Giles spoke about her sister as if she were not present in the room. His fury was almost luminescent and certainly not the serene expression of a country parson.

Ruby looked to May while her sister sobbed quietly, knowing that when they were younger, she would have moved heaven and earth to protect May.

'I am sorry you are upset,' Ruby told her sister, ignoring Giles, the odious pocket dictator who reminded her of a puffed-up garden gnome, with his red cheeks and manic stare. For a moment, she thought May was going to say something, when she opened her mouth to speak. Then, as if undecided, she closed it again, reminding Ruby of a freshly landed trout. 'We will talk a little later, perhaps?' Ruby said pointedly. Suspecting May could not air her own opinion in front of her husband, her suspicions confirmed as May turned to Giles, who gave a small clearing of the throat, which Ruby assumed was a warning to his wife to say nothing. She so hoped Giles was not going to be difficult. However, by the determined look on his face, she doubted it.

'We have to get back to Saint Ninian's for Matins,' Giles said emphatically, obviously trying to force Ruby to talk now, 'so we shall leave this evening.'

Having met his type in business, Ruby knew he was trying to force her hand. He wanted part, if not complete tenure, of Ashland Hall, clearly considering the house his wife's rightful inheritance. Giles's direct glare said it all. May did not bring shame on the family by giving birth to a bastard. Maybe not, thought Ruby. But what Giles Harington did was far worse. He was a thief and a scoundrel. Mrs Swift, the housekeeper had told Ruby about his gambling debts.

'I have all the time in the world,' Ruby said evenly to her sister, cutting across Giles's words. 'We can talk another time.'

Let battle commence. Ruby matched his unflinching glare. Smiling sweetly, she treated him with the contempt he deserved and was concerned when she saw the light dim in May's eyes. A faint tinge of pink coloured her neck and cheeks, in the same way it did as a child, when promised a treat that was not forthcoming.

'I can stay for a couple of days?' May looked beseechingly to her husband.

'Oh, that would be excellent,' Eleanor was delighted, 'there is so much I want to know about your lives together.' She hoped the two sisters would now be reconciled. Eleanor adored Aunt Ruby, even though she had seen very little of her over the years, and so wanted to get to know the *rebellious* aunt her father openly despised.

'Be quiet, Eleanor.' Her father's brusque tone made her hackles rise. Eleanor hoped he was not going to cause a scene and belittle Mama, as he usually did to bolster his own shortcomings. Although, by the determined set of Aunt Ruby's jaw, he may not get all his own way this time. 'Out of the question, my dear.' Giles's tone was lighter now he realised all eyes were upon him, although he ignored May's silent beseeching. 'Your mother has an appointment at the bank.' It was obvious to Ruby this man bullied her sister. May had no say, whatsoever.

'I will be here for the rest of the week,' Ruby said, 'it has been so long since I was here last.' She did not want to dwell on that night so long ago. 'I want to reacquaint myself with the house.' She had decisions to make. Household accounts to consider. She must contact her father's servants whom Giles had dismissed. Some had been here since she was a child. There was a lot to ponder. The house, although beautiful, held unhappy memories. But she had Archie, Anna, and Ned to help her this time. The last time she was here, she had nobody, except Mrs Swift, who was in no position to defy Silas Ashland.

Eleanor, to lighten the atmosphere and perhaps learn more about her aunt's and mother's childhood at Ashland, said: 'Mama told me you would both slip through the perimeter fence to play with the village children,' Eleanor told the gathered company. Breaking into Ruby's thoughts, who was amused at May's anecdotes and pointedly ignored her brother-in-law's bored demeanour. Happy that her sister had remembered the good times.

'I think it was that perimeter fence that ignited Ruby's rebellious spark.' May smiled.

'You forget to tell everybody that, at the age of ten, you ran away from home.' Ruby laughed, aware Giles was growing increasingly irritated.

'I went to the nearest railway station and bought a ticket to Liverpool.' May's eyes widened at the memory. 'I intended to earn my living as a servant.' She laughed, and for the first time since their arrival, Ruby saw her sister relax. 'I was caught that very same night.' May, animated by the conversation, was giving everybody a glimpse of the girl she once was.

'You were so determined,' Ruby said in a quieter voice, 'what changed you, I wonder?'

Archie's fingers curled round her hand. His most precious gift to her was his love. Thank goodness, he was nothing like Giles, she thought. And for the first time in many years, her heart ached for her poor sister.

'That was the year Mother died...' Ruby said, feeling the raw anguish that initially defined her, making her the stoic, resilient woman she was now. However, a loud sigh of irritation showed Giles was obviously tired of their childhood reminiscences and interrupted their nostalgia. Ruby smiled indulgently, excusing her brother-in-law's obvious bad manners. His retribution was rapidly approaching. Of that she was certain. 'I will arrange the evening menu with Mrs Swift,' Ruby told the gathered company. 'Oh, did I forget to tell you I reinstated her, Giles?'

'Giles!' May looked horrified. 'You dismissed Mrs Swift?' She did not fail to notice the glowering expression on her husband's face. 'That really is the limit.'

'You will stay for dinner, Giles?' It was an expectation, not a question, and by the look on his face, Ruby knew he wanted to be anywhere except this house right now. At the reading of the Will, May was informed she had inherited only a hunting lodge and took the news in her stride. However, Giles was almost apoplectic his wife had not inherited the sprawling country house. Making his feelings clear when he stormed out, quickly followed by May, who tried to pacify him, Ruby had watched him push May away, his unconcealed anger as obvious as the fat nose on his face.

How the mighty fall. Ruby thought, knowing Giles would have revelled in being lord of all he surveyed, given the chance. Watching him now, she caught a look of intolerant contempt in his piggy little eyes, so far removed from the altruistic homilies he spouted from the pulpit, as it was possible to be. Did Giles honestly think the great Silas Ashland would entrust his hard-earned wealth to poor, spineless, meek May, who bent to Giles's grasping nature.

The look on his face reminded Ruby of the time father's cocker spaniel lost a bone to a feral bitch. The miserable dog lay watching every mouthful disappear, not even allowed the discarded remains.

Ruby had discovered her sister had not betrayed her. Giles had played a major part in her child's disappearance. She had waited patiently... Her day had come. She silently raised her glass and, nodding her head, she smiled. *Rot in hell, Giles Harrington.* Eleanor was her daughter. Not his, or May's.

27

Anna heard Ned's words and she felt her fingernails digging into the palm of her hand. They had been having a lovely time, helping Aunt Ruby and Archie choose the new décor for the drawing room. Ruby wanted light and bright, while Archie wanted something a bit more substantial in wood. Ruby would win, Anna knew, she always did – and Archie let her. They were such a lovely couple. Made for each other. Like her and Ned... So, she thought. Obviously, he had other ideas.

'Leaving?' Anna asked. She looked round the table, to Ruby, to Archie, and finally to Ned. What she was looking for she did not know. 'Leaving here? Leaving us?' She could not take her eyes from Ned, sitting opposite her.

He gave a silent nod, as if forming the words were too much of an effort, his face devoid of expression. Anna took a long slow intake of air. As she picked up her cup, it trembled on the saucer.

'I always said I would leave one day.' Ned did not take his eyes off her, she noticed. 'Didn't I always say that?' His eyes were beseeching now, as if he was silently asking for her approval.

He said he would always be here. He said... He said...

'I didn't think you meant it.' Her words sounded fractured even to her own ears. 'I thought it was just a silly notion. That you'd get over it.' She could not drag her gaze from him.

Rising now, Ned scraped back his chair and came round to her side of the table. Hunching down beside her, sitting on his heels, Ned reached for her hand.

Anna could not look at him as brimming tears threatened. Ned was her best friend. Her soulmate. She loved him with every beat of her heart. Swallowing hard, she tried to push down the threatening sob. Anna should not let him see her so upset. But she could not help it. They had been friends for so long. Did he think she was going to let him go without showing any emotion whatsoever? It was like losing her family all over again.

'I got you this.'

Anna stared straight ahead. If she looked at him now, she would surely lose what little dignity she still had. Ned did not move, when Anna's eyes sought the square-shaped gift, beautifully wrapped in blue tissue paper. Perversely, she wondered if he had wrapped it himself, or had somebody else gift-wrapped the beautiful present? However, this was not the time for silly questions.

Anna reached out and picked it up, turning it over, barely able to comprehend the enormity of the situation. Ned was going away. He was joining the Royal Navy. He would return after travelling the world, conquering oceans, and seas, doing what men did. She did not want to see what was inside the packaging. Nothing was going to take away the pain of his leaving. Nothing.

'Shall I help you?' Ned asked as if talking to a child, and for a moment, Anna wanted to scold him. No. Of course not. She did not need him. She was not helpless. No matter what he thought.

'I can manage,' she said crossly, pushing away his hand. Instantly she regretted her quick retort. Opening the tissue paper with as much care as she could muster, so as not to rip it, her eyes devoured the small book of poetry. When she opened the ivory leather binding, she felt it was like opening her heart. Quickly she wiped her tears that fell on the cover. She knew Ned liked pleasant words, and he liked to read a lot. Nevertheless, she never imagined he liked poetry.

'There is a particular favourite of mine,' he said quickly, taking the cream-coloured book from her hands. 'It's by Matthew Arnold and it is called "Longing". I remember you used to like it.'

Anna closed her streaming eyes when he opened the book and in his rich melodious voice began to recite the poem.

> 'Come to me in my dreams, and then,
> By day I shall be well again
> For then the night, will more than pay
> The hopeless longing of the day.'

However, it was too much for Anna. She could not keep her feelings to herself any longer, and tears ran freely in rivulets down her cheeks.

'Oh, Anna, please don't cry,' Ned begged, taking her face in the palm of his hands, 'I can't bear it.'

'And I can't bear the thought of never seeing you again.' The words were out of her mouth before she could stop them, and Ned held her to him, regardless of Ruby and Archie sitting at the table. As far as Ned was concerned, they were the only two in the whole wide world.

'Of course, you will see me again, sweetheart.' Ned smiled, trying to placate her, but it was useless, she was beyond calming.

'How long have you had this planned?' She knew there was no use skirting politely round the issue now. She had already disgraced herself. She had no dignity left.

'You know I want to see the world,' Ned said gently, 'remember that night, when you gave Jerky Woods the pasting he deserved?' He waited until Anna nodded. 'I told you then, that I wanted to see what was on the other side of the water.'

Anna was bewildered. 'I thought you were happy here.'

'I have never been happier, Anna, I'm not leaving forever, but we all move on eventually. Even you.' His words were like a slap in the face. Nevertheless, it was not right that she should expect everybody else to do what she wanted. She knew that. Taking a deep breath, she tried to stem her tears. Knowing such a thing did not make it easier though.

'Of course, you must follow your dreams,' she gave a shaky smile, her chin wobbling slightly as she opened the little book. Anna noticed, in perfectly neat handwriting, Ned had written:

My Dearest Anna,
   Please think of me sometimes, and the friendship we share...
   I will see you when I come home. Until then, take care,
   Fondest love, from your best friend,
   Ned xxx

'I'm not much of a poet,' Ned looked sheepish and his gentle eyes danced, making her smile as he always did.

'I know,' she answered, and then she hugged him, 'I'm just being selfish.'

'The world is changing so fast I want to grab it by the tail, hang on for dear life and gallop along for the ride.' Ned's eyes lit up as he spoke, and she knew how he felt.

Anna eased her shoulders, letting her hands fall limply on her lap. She examined her neatly manicured fingernails, which were quite different from the rough, calloused fingers of a few years ago, when she worked all the hours God sent, just to keep body and soul together. It was unfair of her to put Ned in this awkward situation. He was her friend, not her nursemaid, and she had no right to embarrass him like this.

'I'm sorry, Ned,' she said, her lips trying for another wobbly smile. 'I shouldn't have said those things. It was the shock. When you've made your fortune, come back and share it with the rest of us.' She was aware of the nervous laughter from Aunt Ruby and Archie.

'Hear, hear,' said Archie stoutly, 'and if I find a lad who's anywhere near as good with the horses as you, Ned, I'll be a lucky man, because I've never known—'

'Shush, Archie.' Aunt Ruby had tears in her own dark eyes now, 'Don't set her off again.'

Archie cleared his throat, 'Aye, well it's best you told her, lad.'

Ned tenderly took Anna's hand, 'I was going to take the coward's way out and leave you a note but...'

'No, we couldn't be having that,' Archie said in that blunt, no-nonsense way. 'I said, didn't I, Ruby...'

'Not now, Archie,' Ruby said, wiping away another stray tear, giving Ned an encouraging smile. Anna was confused...

'Tell me what?' she asked, suddenly afraid.

'I'm leaving tomorrow.' His voice was almost a whisper, but the impact his words had on Anna, he might as well have roared it from the rooftops. His silver-blue eyes searched hers. She felt stupefied. Vacant. They were all staring at her. Waiting.

'Archie, you must stop him,' Anna said, desperate now. It was too soon.

'I start training on Monday.'

Anna gave Aunt Ruby a murderous look, she had not even hinted.

'It is a fantastic opportunity for him,' Ruby said, 'he will make his fortune.'

'Is that all you think about, Aunt Ruby?' Anna asked, her heart ripping so savagely, she did not care that her words were harsh – and unjust. 'There is more to life than...' The news was like a body blow.

'I should have gone years ago,' Ned said gently, stroking her hair, 'but I couldn't leave you. You had lost your family.'

'I'm sorry I held you back,' Anna's voice held a note of sarcasm, 'it must have been awful for you.' She could not help it. Unsurprisingly, she wanted to hurt him. Like he was hurting her.

Quickly excusing herself, Anna hurried for the door, almost falling down the stairs in her haste to be out of there. She ran blindly through the grounds of Ashland Hall, not knowing exactly where she was heading. Her feet skimming the ground as the chilly air robbed her breath. In the little clearing near the lake, Anna sat shivering, thinking things through, letting the news that her best friend in the entire world, was about to sail out of her life forever. He caught up with her. Neither of them speaking.

When he saw her crestfallen features crumble, he took Anna and folded her trembling body in his strong arms as they sat beside the water's edge.

Lost in the nearness of him, Anna could feel the thundering beat of his heart. She knew she could never hold him down. Nobody could. Ned was a free spirit. He had to be out there, roaming. Free as a bird...

When she came down to breakfast the next morning, he was gone.

'If ever there was a more wilful, single-minded determined girl then I haven't met her.' Ruby rose from the pale silk Chesterfield chair and went over to the window. Viewing the panoramic shoreline, her back to the door, her fingernails drummed impatiently on her folded arms.

'Why I ever agreed to you coming to live here, I will never know.' Ruby remained standing at the window, her back to Eleanor to hide the uncontrollable smile that lit up her face.

'Because this place was so dull before me, Aunt Ruby.' Eleanor, delighting in Ruby's mock irritability, knowing her aunt loved having her here. Ruby told her so, every day. But being so alike, they instinctively knew each other's failings. Anna smiled at their inability to listen to anybody else's ideas except their own when she caught the tail end of Ruby's exasperated tones.

Ruby had taken her rightful place at Ashland Hall to stop Giles moving in, knowing Giles was desperate to inhabit the Hall. And he was so incensed when he heard the Will read out he immediately refused to step foot inside the cottage, left to May, and headed back to Scarborough. Ruby had a sneaking suspicion he thought her heart belonged to the docklands and she would never return to Ashlands. However, Ruby had ideas of her own, she had no intention of leaving Ashlands empty so Giles could sidle in with May.

Not one for sitting still, Ruby left the Emporium and the pawnshop in capable hands until she had sorted the mess her father had left.

* * *

'If only the customers in the back-street shops could see all this,' Anna said on entering the brightly lit drawing room to the sound of Eleanor's capable tones.

'It's a fantastic idea, Aunt Ruby, and well you know it.' Eleanor, whom everybody called Ellie, had been an active member of the suffragist movement before turning her attention to nursing. Ellie, fancying herself as a modern-day Florence Nightingale, could not move away from the claustrophobic clutches of her father quick enough and moved into Ashland Hall the day after the reading of the Will. Much to Ruby's delight.

'Anna needs to do something useful, not vegetate in this huge house.'

'I suspected you would get bored not going to the shop every day,' Ruby answered, turning to greet Anna with a nod of her head.

Ellie, sitting on the elegant sofa opposite the imposing marble fireplace, was rolling bandages and smiled when Anna sat beside her and picked up a long strip of material to roll another bandage.

'Is that really what you want for her, dear Aunt? To be a shop girl for the rest of her days.'

'Don't be such a snob, Ellie,' Ruby countered. 'I was a shop girl. It stood me in good stead, as well as putting bread on my table.' Ruby was in no mood to yield, Anna could tell.

'Is there a slim chance I have any say in the matter?' Anna asked the two women, so alike, who were having another one of their friendly exchange of views. Anna liked Ellie. She was lively, opinionated and, according to Aunt Ruby, would cause war in an empty house. Never having had a close friend, Anna realised it was lovely to have somebody near her own age.

'I love the sound of nursing,' Anna said when Ellie explained Aunt Ruby's latest cause of disagreement. 'I never thought about it before, but it is such a worthy pastime,' Anna added, knowing girls from her part of the dockside world did not train for work, or graft buckshee for worthy causes, as Ellie did. They were too busy trying to keep body and soul together, earning a meagre copper here, a penny there.

However, the idea of nursing thrilled her. Swanning through this huge house, no matter how beautiful, or working in the office at the Emporium was not something she envisioned doing for the rest of her life. She wanted excitement, just like any other young person.

Nevertheless, Anna felt as if she was betraying her benefactor when she saw Ruby's lips set into a straight line, a sure sign she was irritated. Although, being polite, she would never say so. Anna watched Ruby's dark brows pleat ever so slightly. They had settled into the house with more ease than they had first imagined.

'I think nursing is a marvellous idea. Anna and I have discussed it in detail,' Ellie said, 'she knows it is not easy, and yes, she will have to clean dirty backsides.' Anna watched Aunt Ruby wince, but Ellie was not going to stop now. 'She doesn't mind, do you?'

Anna shook her head, knowing Ellie's remark was a statement, not a question.

'Look how determined she is, Aunt Ruby.' Ellie's voice became excitedly louder, 'Anna won't shirk.'

Anna hardly needed to offer an opinion as they gathered round the polished walnut table in the sunny drawing room.

'Ignore Ellie as best you can.' Ruby looked to Anna now. 'That pestiferous mouth may be contagious. No self-respecting young woman should be allowed within a mile of her... Anna what are you laughing at?'

Anna could not speak as tears of mirth ran down her cheeks, knowing Ruby enjoyed having '*her*' girls round her. Since she had moved here, Anna noticed a discernible glow in her patron's cheeks that had not been there before.

'That word, *pestiferous*...' Anna laughed. 'It reminded me of another time...' The laughter suddenly died on her lips, as memories of her other life came flooding back. She never imagined in her wildest of dreams that she would be in a sumptuous drawing room, drinking tea in the afternoon, discussing her prospects. More likely, she would have been too busy teaching children to read and write by now. '...So much has happened since then.' Her family... Poor Sam...

'I know, my dear.' Ruby patted her hand. 'You were a smart young girl, who hit the ground running. Feisty and determined if I recall.'

'I thought I had nothing but an ache in my heart and a dark future,' Anna replied. 'Then you and Archie saved me.'

'You saved us, Anna,' Ruby continued, 'you brought light into our lives.'

'I can't think how.' Anna, put melancholy thoughts back in that little part of her heart she reserved for when she was alone. 'I was such a bother.'

'You most certainly were not,' Ruby declared, then, she was quiet for a moment before saying: 'You will never understand how much joy you brought to Archie and me.'

'I have a lot to thank you for and I do not want to let you down, Aunt Ruby.'

'You will never do that, Anna.' Ruby reached out and clasped Anna's hand in hers. 'You are free to do as you wish.'

'I could never even dream of nursing in the backstreets of Liverpool,' Anna said, 'most girls scratch a living anyway they can.' She smiled broadly now, allaying Ruby's apparent concern. 'I will never be able to repay you.'

'Pfft.' Ruby dismissed Anna's words with the wave of her hand. 'You are a delight, my dear.'

'Whereas I am such a trial,' Ellie said, putting the back of her hand to her brow in her best Lillian Gish impression. 'I have brought nothing but headaches and sorrow to my sainted family.' Her fun-loving nature was in complete contrast to her downtrodden mother and maudlin father, Ruby knew.

'You do everything you can think of to irritate your parents, as I did, at your age,' Ruby said, knowing Ellie was an enthusiastic rabble-rousing suffragist, although not as militant as some, she did not listen to a word her father said.

'It is such a hoot,' Ellie claimed, 'and to think, if Father had ignored them in the first place, I probably would have lost interest in the suffragist movement. He is his own worst enemy.'

'Your mother says you are overbearing and impossible to live with.' Ruby laughed and looked fondly to the daughter she lost as a baby and who only knew her as a forthright aunt who delighted in shocking her parents. 'So like me at your age.'

'A compliment, indeed, Aunt Ruby.' Ellie threw her head back and laughed. 'Although, I have to say, if it is all right, I blame you for everything.' She gave Ruby a knowing look.

'This is better than any music hall act.' Anna decided unaware how accurate her suspicions were. Ellie and Aunt Ruby, she thought, were so characteristically and physically alike they could have been mother and daughter.

'Sometimes, when I am not in the same room and you are both talking,' Anna said, 'I find it difficult to tell you apart.' She watched Ruby's eyes lose a little of their sparkle now and she felt immediately repentant. 'I'm so sorry, Aunt Ruby, did I say something wrong?' Anna would not upset Aunt Ruby for the world.

'No, Anna, you did not, but there is something I think you deserve to know.' Now that she had the two girls together, Ruby felt she could now tell them and then went on to describe the time her father had her baby daughter taken away. That awful day when her father turned her back on her. That night when Archie took her from Ashland Hall and helped her make a new life for herself. 'We could not marry,' Ruby continued, 'I was only eighteen and my father would never give his blessing to me marrying *one of the staff*.'

'Archie was far and above, much more of a gentleman than my father or many of his associates.' She went on to tell Anna and Eleanor the whole story of how Silas Ashland had disowned her and her baby, who was only ten days old, and had her taken away to be adopted. 'He gave generously to the orphanage next door, such was his hypocrisy.' Ruby inhaled deeply, allowing herself time to steady her emotions and stopped short of actually telling Ellie that she was indeed her daughter. What good would it do now, she wondered. Ellie loved May as her mother. While she was as close as any blood relative could be. Ellie lived under her roof. There was no need to upset the apple cart with grand announcements. If ever Ellie needed to know, she would tell her. Until then, it was best to let sleeping dogs lie.'

'I am so sorry, Aunt Ruby,' Anna said, hugging her now. This wonderful, forthright woman, a businesswoman without equal, who had been through so much heartache.

'You would have been the best kind of mother,' Ellie said, causing a tightening in Ruby's throat.

'Whatever experience does not kill you,' Ruby said now, 'certainly makes you stronger.'

'I'm sure it does,' Anna and Ellie replied, feeling honoured Aunt Ruby had taken them into her confidence like this.

'Do not let anybody stand in your way, or tread on your dreams,' Ruby said, 'not even me.' She smiled now, accepting the girls' praise with an unusually quiet response. 'You would make a wonderful nurse, Anna,' Ruby said, 'you have that quiet way about you, a soothing stillness, which cannot be taught. Ellie is more forthright, a born campaigner for patient's rights.'

'She so wants to do it.' Ellie's face was alight with enthusiasm, 'I can get her a place at the hospital... I know somebody.'

'You always know somebody.' Ruby laughed, picking crumbs from a slice of Cook's delicious cake. 'Is it something you really want to do, Anna?'

'I don't want to seem ungrateful...' Anna would love nothing better than to nurse, '...you have done so much for me...' She looked to Ellie now. They were going to have such fun.

'I will make sure she doesn't catch anything fatal,' Ellie said quickly, as Ruby put up her hand to silence the protests.

'Anna, you are free to make your own decisions,' Ruby said, 'go to it. That's my advice.'

'Oh, Aunt Ruby, you are wonderful.' Ellie threw her hands in the air, clapping them together before coming round the table to hug her aunt. Then, turning to Anna, she said with a flourish, 'Right, now that is settled, when do you want to start?'

* * *

Two weeks later, Anna took her place as a probationer nurse at the infectious diseases' hospital over six miles away, at Fazakerley.

'If they think they will be in for an easy time, they are sadly mistaken,' Ruby told Archie when he got back from taking Anna, Ellie, and their luggage to the nurses' accommodation. She would miss their lively conversations now they were 'living in'. 'It is so quiet without them,' Ruby said, 'I cannot recall the time when Anna was not part of our family.'

'The shops will keep you busy, my love,' Archie said fondly, knowing if there was one thing Ruby could not abide it was being idle, 'and they will be home on their days off.'

'I've offered Lottie the position of sales manageress at the Emporium. All we need is somebody who will work the pawnshop.' Ruby told Archie.

'You will never guess who came into the pawnshop asking for work the other day?' Archie said, 'Izzy Woods!'

'Izzy Woods?' Ruby's eyes widened, 'I heard about her no-good husband, he fell into the dock and drowned, didn't he?'

'He did,' Archie answered, 'they fished him out two days later, dead as a dinosaur and what with Jerky Woods locked up in Walton Gaol, there's only Izzy and young Nipper.'

'I heard Nipper is good with horses,' Ruby had a twinkle in her eye and Archie rolled his eyes to the ceiling. Here she goes again, he thought. 'Are you sure you want Izzy and Nipper working for us?'

'Better the devil we know, Archie,' Ruby answered. 'I cannot have Izzy working in the Emporium, she does not have the same way with customers that Anna and Lottie have had, but she knows the pawnshop business like the back of her hand...'

'Doesn't she just,' Archie agreed. 'She can tot up the value of a pledge faster than I can. So, what do you think?' Archie knew

Ruby's loyalty went beyond the tolerance of most employers. She smiled.

'Everybody deserves a chance, Archie,' she said, 'and with this talk of war, there are rumours abound that when the men are called to fight there will be plenty of work for women, although I can't see it, myself.'

'Lottie Blythe, you are such a giddy girl these days,' her mother told her, knowing that for Lottie, the world was full of promise and romance. Lottie was better paid than most girls her age, managing the Emporium, she could treat her mother now and then. She did not want to discuss the threat of war with her, though. She was far too excited about the August Bank Holiday Fete in the grounds of Ashland Hall.

As things stood, even though Austria-Hungary had declared war on Serbia, and Germany had declared war on Russia, Ruby saw no reason to cancel the merrymaking – in fact, she had said, the rumours were even more reason to have some fun.

'Miss Ruby's biggest worry is that the gathering clouds do not ruin the big day with rain.'

* * *

'We must do our best to push away the awful news with gaiety and song,' Ruby said when she declared the event open and as if to quell any doubts, the storm clouds parted to reveal bright sunshine and a gentle breeze. A carnival rolled up along the wide stretch of golden sand on the shores of Liverpool Bay, and Ruby gleefully clapped her hands, 'Enjoy this paradise at the bottom of the garden,' she said as the band struck up a lively tune.

'Oh, I do wish Ned could make the fete,' Anna said, gazing out to the gentle rolling waves glinting like diamonds in the afternoon sunshine. She wondered where he was right now, missing him so much.

Anna and Ellie were lucky enough to get time off from the hospital and parade not only the grounds of Ashland Hall but also the shore, enjoying the crowds, shielding themselves from the now blazing sunshine with parasols over their shoulder. Anna wondered if Ned would get leave as he promised. She hoped so. He loved a Summer Fete as much as she did, but with news being what it was, Archie said all leave might be cancelled.

Ruby watched Lottie step down from Archie's horse and carriage, dressed in all her flouncing finery and dainty shoes. Not boots. The shoes had been a present from Ruby, especially for the day.

One of the musicians sang to Lottie as she walked past. He even called after her, 'I'll treat you right, my beauty.' However, Lottie did not speak to him, Anna noticed, instead she tossed her head, looked neither right, nor left and carried on walking along the sun-drenched shore, swarming now with merrymakers. To Anna's dismay, Lottie had caught the attention of a lad.

'You don't want to have anything to do with him,' Anna warned, but Lottie was not listening. She only had eyes for Jerky Woods, who had been released from Walton Gaol.

'He is ever so sorry for the things he did in the past,' Lottie told Anna. 'He has mended his ways and promised me he will find a job and live a good and wholesome life.'

'And the band played *believe me if you dare,*' Anna murmured, knowing Lottie liked to see the good in people, but doubted Jerky Woods had it in him to change.

Woods gave Lottie a lazy smile as he leaned against the harbour wall, chewing a spent matchstick. Anna prayed Lottie would not yield to his bad-boy reputation. However, filled with dismay, she saw Lottie go straight up to him. No doubt Lottie's helpful nature was working overtime when she said the letters, she had sent him in prison, changed him for the better.

Anna gently shook her head as she watched Lottie chatting happily to the local bad boy, and even more so, when she heard her say in a low, self-assured manner: 'I know you have changed. Everybody deserves a chance.'

It was obvious Lottie was drowning in Jerky Woods cheeky smile. He had obviously cleaned himself up and put his best foot forward. His herringbone cap was pushed haphazardly to the back of his woolly head, and dressed in his Sunday best, his leg was bent, so the sole of his polished boot appeared to hold up the sandstone wall. Anna worried for Lottie, especially when she heard him say with indolent self-assurance: 'Meet me at the back of the bathing huts.'

He had something other than bathing on his mind for sure, Anna knew, when Lottie whispered something in his ear, obviously thrilled at his audacity.

'We don't need to go behind the huts,' Lottie whooped as he caught her round her shapely waist and pulled her towards him.

'You're a defiant one and no mistake,' Woods grinned, wasting no more time and in full view of anyone watching, he pulled a giggling Lottie, so blindly keen, into a bathing hut.

Anna felt her heart sink...

* * *

Gazing out at the coral sky, Anna breathed in the salty air, as the sun began to dip. Enjoying the cooling rays, she was imagining pictures in the cotton-wool clouds. A dog with a lolling tongue. A maiden surrounded by locks of flowing hair. A fairy-tale castle...

She felt as serene as the white billows drifting by. A gentle, whispering breeze caught the curling wisps from her loosely bound chignon. They tickled her cheek, and she brushed them away absentmindedly. Lost in romantic thoughts of Ned, she did not hear anybody coming up behind her.

'Penny for them?'

Turning quickly, Anna was thrilled to see him standing behind her. Unselfconsciously she jumped up and threw her arms round his neck.

'You made it,' she cried.

'I said I would, didn't I?' Ned laughed, thrilled to have his girl in his arms. 'Are you cold?' he asked, taking off the navy-blue jacket of his naval uniform, and slipping it round Anna's shoulders.

'Not any more,' she sighed contentedly, the warmth of the garment and Ned's masculine scent cloaked her in security. Her fingers dancing, first over the lapel, and then at the delicate lace on the square collar of her fine lawn blouse, Anna felt strangely nervous now. A sentiment so unfamiliar, she almost told him.

'Let's sit down here for a while, catch up,' Ned said, guiding her to a sun-bleached rock. The evening sun dying now to a golden glow. They talked nonstop for a long time. Each eager to give their news. Then, with the sun dipping further into the sea, they became quiet.

'I was making pictures in the clouds,' Anna said quickly, not willing to voice her fears. His eyes, as blue as the cerulean sky, searched her face and she felt the familiar tingle of love course through her veins. She could not whinge about him being away. She must show pride in his choice.

'I do that,' Ned said, smiling, his teeth whiter, against the natural golden tan of a man whose skin had been windblown by salty air. 'I stand for hours just watching the sky, thinking of you, and what our future together will be like, it is one of my favourite pastimes.'

'Is it, Ned?' His masculinity took her breath away. Ned could do nothing to irritate her. He was her champion and her strength. Since he went away to join the Navy, they had exchanged letters almost daily, their intimate thoughts revealing their true feelings for each other. So when Ned came home on leave it was the most natural thing that their strong feelings for each other went far beyond friendship.

'I adore you, Anna Cassidy,' Ned whispered into her hair, securing her dangerously welcoming body in his embrace. With a delicate touch, he lifted her chin, raining kisses over her face, her eyes, her neck, and her shoulders. Trance-like she gazed up into his handsome features, drowning in the worship that was so nakedly visible in his eyes.

Nestled in the valley of the sand dunes, Ned's powerful body protected her from the gentle brackish wind, both watching the sun dip its golden reflection into the sea and burst into a myriad of vibrant colours: pinks and mauves and lilacs. All reaching out to the last of the perfect blue of a radiant sky. Anna sighed contentedly, wishing it could be like this forever, an enjoyable day made even more perfect with Ned beside her.

'I've never been so happy,' Ned said in a low, contented drawl 'Sitting here with you is better than anything I've ever known.' He leaned down to her upturned face and kissed her softly yielding lips. 'Nothing stirs my blood and has it racing through my veins quite like you do, Anna.'

'I'm sure I could introduce you to a good doctor who can prescribe something,' Anna giggled, shifting her body slightly in the soft sand to try to relieve the yearning inside her. It would be so easy to yield to temptation. She was in paradise. And she never wanted to leave.

'There is only one kind of treatment I can think of to cure this wonderful affliction,' said Ned, shifting in the sand to lie at her side, trying to quell the growing unease within him. 'I would do anything for you.'

Anna raised her face, offering another sweet kiss, and he experienced that familiar stirring that tormented him every time he looked at her. The stirring that was becoming more difficult to ignore. Especially now. Nonetheless, he would never take advantage.

Slowly, reluctantly, he straightened from her embrace and, sitting upright, he hugged his knees. Looking out to sea, he dared not meet the confusion in Anna's eyes.

'What's wrong, Ned?' she asked, lifting herself onto her elbow, her face cupped in her hand, unable to see the haunted look in his eyes.

'I must tell you something.' Ned knew this would spoil the rest of their evening together, but he had no choice. Now was not the perfect time. There would never be a perfect time.

'Tell me, Ned,' Anna's worried voice broke the silence between them both as her eyes followed his gaze towards the last dusky beam of the sun's rays illuminating the water, mesmerised by its shimmering light, hypnotised by the tranquillity that seemed a million miles from a troubled world, until now. A shiver of foreboding clouded her perfect day.

Ned always had and always would be there for her, she knew. However, her confidence was shaken by his next words. And she found them almost impossible to take in.

'I will be going away soon, Anna...' Ned's words were blunt and to the point. Like a slap in the face. She knew what this meant. The navy was on stand-by for war. She and Ned had talked about it. Nevertheless, she did not think such ugly news could happen on such a beautiful day. She had not intended to react as she did, and when the audible gasp escaped her lips, Ned put his strong arms round her, and he held her so close she could hear his thundering heartbeat. Gentle shushing echoed in her hair as he rocked her back and forth as fearful tears streamed down her face.

War was imminent? The mere thought of it was madness. The day had been bright and full of happy people. Parading on the shore. Enjoying ice cream. Delighted children taking donkey rides and engaging in three-legged races.

Anna wanted to hold Ned close and never let him go, she wanted to climb inside his skin and lose herself. Suddenly desperate, she longed to feel his lips on hers. Ned granted her unspoken wish when he lowered his head and tenderly brushed her lips with his. His huge gentle hands supporting her head as indulgent tears rolled down both their cheeks.

'I'm only on short leave from Eagle,' Ned's voice was thick with emotion and Anna knew exactly what *short leave* meant. In case of war, all ships' company must be within a twelve-hour radius.

'When?' Anna's voice held a note of panic.

'Who knows if I will still be here when you get up in the morning.'

Anna was scared that he would not be. She watched as he plaited three strands of star grass, engrossed in the activity.

Ned tried to find the right words, but he could not as his eyes lingered on the gentle sway of grass poking its sharp head through the golden sand, whispering its goodbye on a balmy breeze while the strident cry of gulls carried and swooped along the ebbing tide in sympathy.

Shifting slightly in the concave of sand, he pulled Anna towards him. Basking in the glow of love for this woman whose salty tears he let dry on his lips.

'Our beloved country is actually going to war?' Anna's terrified voice was barely a whisper and Ned gave a silent nod. Yes. Then he put his fingertip to her lips, stilling the words that would rip at his heart. Anna kissed it and her eyes betrayed her fear for him.

'It will all be over by Christmas, so we've been told,' Ned said, trying to make light of the situation, knowing that she too would be called back to the hospital before her summer leave was over.

'Where will you go?' It was a stupid question, and she knew he could not answer, but she felt the need to ask anyway.

'Anywhere I am needed.' Ned could not meet her gaze. He could not bear to see her disappointment. 'I have no choice.'

Looking at him now, she could see Ned had a troubled, faraway look in his eyes and Anna's stomach churned, the thought of him being away for even the shortest time terrified her.

'Don't go putting yourself in harm's way,' Anna's voice was barely a whisper, her eyes bright with unshed tears. Then, rising quickly to her feet, she ran up the beach, her hair billowing in the breeze. She had to get away. Tears blinded her as she ran towards the house, hoping the milling staff would not notice her. She did not want them to see her cry.

'Anna. Anna.' Ignoring Ned's anxious call, she flew up the shore towards Ashland Hall, but Ned was quick and right behind her. 'Anna, wait.' Ned caught her arm, and pain etched his handsome blue eyes. 'Anna I'm so sorry.'

'Sorry?' Anna could hardly think straight. 'Ned you have nothing to be sorry about.'

'I love and adore you.' Ned looked truly contrite when he said: 'When I hold you in my arms, I lose all sense of reason.' He sighed now. 'I should have told you we were one of the first ships to sail. But I could not find the right words.'

'Let me tell you what you should have said, shall I?' Anna's heart was breaking now. 'You should have said, *Anna, I am going to war and I might not come back.*' Then she broke down and cried body-shaking sobs until she felt sick.

Ned managed to calm her with many kisses, while Anna unable to resist, yielded to his touch as if she would never let him go. Eventually, gazing into his very soul, she knew she could not be angry with him for long, and soon his lips worked their magic once more. She was powerless to resist.

'Let's stay out all night,' Ned whispered between kisses as they ambled along the shore, 'just you, the moon and me.'

'What about Aunt Ruby?' Anna felt pleasure she did not think possible.

'No,' Ned answered, 'we don't need to invite Aunt Ruby.'

A gurgle of mirth rose to Anna's lips, and before they could stop themselves, encircled in a loving embrace, they were laughing helplessly, uncontrollably, unable to let each other go. If he was leaving soon, Anna thought, she needed to be close to him, for as long as was humanly possible. If that meant staying with him all night, then so be it.

'We can write,' Anna said eventually, knowing she had to be strong now. She could not allow her emotions to get the better of her. She had a duty to nurse injured men and women, while Ned had a duty to his country.

'It's just a skirmish, nothing serious.' A cool wind blew in off the sea and Anna shivered again. Ned put his arm round her and drew her close. It was as natural as breathing. 'We will do what is needed, Anna, we always have.'

'You are the bravest man I ever met. You are afraid of nothing.'

Ned gave a little self-conscious laugh. His biggest fear was never seeing Anna again. Worse, being so severely injured he was worthless to her.

'Being brave has nothing to do with it, Anna,' he said, choosing his words carefully, knowing there had been times in the past when he had been terrified out of his wits when his father was alive, but knowing Anna was a few yards away, in the next house, he would not allow his cries of pain to escape. Ned was considered the toughest lad in Queen Street, and all for the love of a girl with the beautiful smile.

'I will miss you when you go,' Anna whispered, her words choked as her throat tightened. She must not cry. She must not let him see her weep again. Parting would be difficult enough.

'Not seeing you every day will rip my heart to pieces, but imagine the reunions.' He was laughing now. 'We will dance and sing and enjoy ourselves.'

Anna wished she could rid herself of this dark cloud of foreboding, which was hanging over her. When he pulled her to him once more, she clung to him, as she had never done before.

'Do you remember when you said you wanted to see the world beyond the Mersey?' Anna asked, feeling his secure arms round her as they both looked out to sea.

Ned's heart was too full to allow him to answer, but he nodded. He remembered it as if it were yesterday. It was the day he knew for certain that Anna Cassidy was the only girl he could ever love. The only girl he ever wanted to love. And the knowledge that she felt the same about him was all he ever wished for. This was the best and the worst day of his life.

'It will all be over by Christmas,' he whispered. If he were one of those soaring gulls that wheeled across the water, he could wrap his wings round her and keep her safe.

'When you go, I will write every day,' Anna promised, wishing this moment would never end. Content in the loving arms of the man she had loved with all her heart for as long as she could remember.

'Me too,' Ned followed her gaze across the River Mersey, wondering when they would get another chance to be like this. He was determined to hold on to this wonderful memory forever.

30

Anna's eyes inched open in her room at Ashland Hall as the morning sunshine threatened to blind her. Ned had walked her back to Ashland Hall before he left her to join his company back at H.M.S. Eagle, the fifty-gun frigate based at Brunswick Dock.

Ellie came into Anna's room without knocking.

'Get up! Get dressed!' Ellie ordered, flinging a dressing gown onto the bed.

'Ellie! What's wrong?' Anna jumped out of bed and pulled on her dressing gown and Ellie headed towards the bathroom without a word. Then pointed to the sink full of water.

'Hurry!' Ellie cried. 'There is no time to bathe! Make do with a cat's lick this morning.'

Anna did not ask questions, surmising that it must be something serious to get Ellie so het up. However, when she reached the dining room, Ruby and Archie were sitting at the table. Archie was reading from the daily newspaper, his face grim.

'Listen to this, lass,' Archie stalled momentarily.

'Yes? Go on!' Anna dragged the chair from under the table and sat down, fearing the worst.

'They are leaving in droves!' Ruby wailed. 'The troops are marching down London Road as we speak.'

'Oh my God! Ned?' Anna's face drained of all colour. Ned did not say he was leaving today. They had not slept at all. They had talked right through the night. He did not mention it would be soon, and it terrified her to ask.

'I'm sorry, lass,' said Archie, 'he said...'

Anna did not hang round to hear any more. Ned must have known when he kissed her goodbye that it would be their last kiss, for God only knew how long! She looked at the clock on the mantle. What time was the troop train leaving? Nobody knew!

* * *

'Let me pass.' Anna grabbed her cape and headed for the door. She wanted to keep their love a secret, but it was impossible. She could not remember a time when Ned was not there for her. He had helped her through many a crisis. She doubted she would have got through life without him. In moments, she, Ellie, Ruby and Archie were hurtling along in Ellie's motor car and heading to Liverpool.

London road was choc-a-bloc with people and vehicles and, sure he was catching the Plymouth train, Anna impatiently jumped out of the car. Running through the major road was unseemly, Anna knew, so she took the narrow back alleyway to the railway station. Ruby and Archie, who had followed her, were caught up in the tangle unable to catch up with Anna as she headed towards London Road. Khaki uniformed soldiers from Seaforth Barracks marched towards the docks and train station.

Anna prayed she was not too late. There were thousands of men on the steps of St George's Plateau. Lime Street was swarming with uniforms. Army. Navy. Infantry. Cavalry. Ned could be anywhere!

All night they had stayed awake, holding each other, watching the sun go down, whispering in the darkness that followed and then as the sun broke through the morning clouds, they had strolled hand in hand along the shore. They had shared their hopes and dreams for the future. Ned was the perfect gentleman. If she had only known what the day would bring, she would have said to hell with what *nice* girls didn't do!

Running along the line of marching soldiers, indifferent to the irate glare of matrons and unmarried women, Anna strained to glimpse her beloved over the heads of crying wives and sweethearts. However, Ned was not in the line of men about to board a train or march off to war. There was no sign of him anywhere.

Anna could hardly believe it! Less than two hours ago, she had kissed him goodbye. Now they may never see each other again! Ned told her how much he loved her and every innermost secret. Except one. That he was going off to war – today.

'Is the Plymouth train in?' Anna's voice was high with anxiety. She must see him. She had to see him. Desperate now, she was giving little thought to her actions. 'Have you seen Ned Kincaid?' she asked a sailor clad from head to toe in navy blue. 'Ned Kincaid, have you seen him?' She was making a fool of herself, and Ruby would have something to say on the matter when she returned to Ashland Hall, but Anna did not care.

A jagged pain sliced right through her ribcage. Gripping her side, she took shallow breaths, but she did not give up. She had to go on. Someone said the troop train was ready to leave at nine o'clock. It spurred her on to get there quickly. It was ten-to, now.

Anna reached the sandstone entrance of Lime Street station. At a run, she entered the domed mouth and wove her way through the sea of khaki and navy-blue uniforms that lined the platform. They were standing, hands in pockets, laughing, chatting, putting off that heart-ripping moment when they had to say goodbye to wives, girlfriends, mothers.

'Ned!' His name impaled the heightened atmosphere and cut it like a blade! He could not go yet! Not like this. People turned. They viewed her with pity. The mothers. The sweethearts. 'Ned!' Unashamed tears ran down alabaster cheeks and settled in the salty crease of her down-turned lips. They stared. Dismayed. Disapproving. In equal measures, sympathetic. Knowing...

A sharp wind whipped her ankles, sent an icy shiver through her spine and, rising, almost toppled her straw boater. Clamping it to her honey-coloured hair, she saw a large woman with a child on her hip kiss a young soldier long and languorously. The boy, barely a man, was not her son.

'Ned!' Anna was not here to judge or to suppose. She was here to tell Ned she loved him. Wanted him with all her heart. She would always love him. She would wait forever.

'Ned...' her voice was low, beseeching, *'come to me in my dreams and by day I shall be well again.'* The poem saw Anna through much grief. It was not just a piece of poetry now, though. It was a plea.

Would she ever see Ned in this crowd? There were too many people. The train whistle sounded again, and the noise brought tears to the eyes of every woman, saying goodbye to their loved ones. The soldiers and sailors, seeing their distress, gave a cheerful smile.

'We will be home next Christmas!' they called, waving like demented windmills.

'Anna! Anna, I'm over here!'

She heard Ned's voice and cursed the tears that were blinding her. Above all others, she heard his voice. Loud and clear. Wiping her eyes with a handkerchief, she looked up to see him leaning out of the rolled-down window, head and shoulders above others.

'I love you, Anna Cassidy!' Ned shouted over the station noise, causing tremendous cheers from his travelling companions. She scrambled through the throng and accepted his loving kiss goodbye. Their last kiss for who knew how long.

'I love you too, Ned!' Anna answered, unashamed as a woman in a flowery hat put brawny arms about her shoulders, hugging Anna, crying all over her best coat.

'*Lord, watch over him, while we are absent from each other*,' Anna said, reciting a phrase becoming more popular with wives and sweethearts now. She was still standing on the platform when the train was just a dot in the distance.

31

'The morning paper said enemy troops have moved into Ypres,' Ruby said, 'its streets are packed full of soldiers, horses and carts.' She read the article, aloud: '"the locals said 10,000 troops had arrived. Soldiers are billeted in schools, the army barracks, the waiting rooms at the railway station, and in the houses of local people!"'

'Have they taken over the whole of Belgium?' Anna felt light-headed. And suddenly cold, although she could not explain why as Ned, being in the navy would not be there. Ruby continued in tones more urgent.

'It says here there is damage to the railway station, German soldiers are stealing from local people and drinking until they fall.'

'That was earlier in the month,' Archie said, reading another paper, 'since then, French and British Armies have arrived in Ypres.' His face was grim, not wanting to discuss it in front of Anna. Nevertheless, she insisted he continue. 'Our boys passed through the town to the east, taking up defensive positions, holding up the advance of the German Army.'

'Oh, my word, it is so real.' Ellie hugged Ruby. 'Nurse Fletcher's fiancé was killed...'

'They say this is going to be a war to end all wars,' Ruby said, 'it will certainly not be over by Christmas.' Anna and Ellie looked at each other. Ellie's new beau, Rupert, was off to Belgium today!

'Time is getting on,' Anna said quickly, trying to remain positive while their mood was becoming more sombre. Matron had taken them all to one side and told them that the chairman of the Port and Sanitary Committee, Doctor Utting, had granted military authorities' permission to use the hospital. And the West Lancashire Territorial Association took formal command of The First Western Hospital, as it would be known from now, and had plans in place for rapid expansion if need be.

It sounds serious,' Anna whispered, but Ellie shook her head.

'Mountains and molehills, my dear. They will be back home soon.'

'Then tell me this,' Anna was not so sure, 'why are the authorities appealing for the loan of a potential convalescent home?'

'What kind of convalescent home?' Ruby's interest piqued, mentally sizing up Ashland Hall for recuperating officers if the need should arise.

'Us girls could help. It would be fun!' said Ellie.

'It would certainly be a worthwhile thing to support the war effort,' said Ruby, 'and perhaps while we help to mend their broken bodies, we could do a lot to make the men happy.'

'Don't you think you have enough on your plate?' Archie asked his lovely, but meddlesome, wife who loved nothing more than to be out fundraising for tanks or whatever.

'Do be quiet Archie, I'm thinking...'

Anna and Ellie rolled their eyes to the ceiling, when Ruby was *thinking* they would really rather not be there.

'Here, put these on, Archie will take you both to the hospital this morning.' Ruby said in a surge of patriotic fervour, fussing over her ministering angels like a mother hen gathering her brood. 'We must not be late this morning, our brave boys need us!' She handed the two girls their dark cloaks and urged them towards the door.

'*We?*' Ellie whispered while Anna silently shrugged, 'I didn't know you were coming to help at the hospital.' She planted a kiss on Ruby's cheek while Anna knew her light-hearted banter hid deep concern.

'I'm not. Yet!' Ruby said with a smile. Anna could see her mind was working, plotting more like, but Ruby was not telling. Instead, she shooed the two girls out of Ashland Hall. 'Come along... Busy, busy, busy! Do not work too hard! Eat properly!'

'Of course, Aunt Ruby... No, we will not work ourselves into the ground... Yes, we will eat properly.' Anna answered Ruby's orders in turn, as she gathered her black leather bag, inserting her unopened letters into it, then headed towards the door with Ellie. Anna wondered what Ruby was up to but did not have time to find out. When they got to the front door, Ruby hugged them both in turn.

'I know about wars,' Ruby said, clinging on to Anna and Ellie.

'They will be late, Darling.' Archie's light touch on Ruby's shoulders told her she must let them go, and Anna gave him a warm if somewhat grateful smile. She knew Ruby could be a touch dramatic, but now was not the time to lose one's head.

'Find her something to do Archie,' Anna said over Ruby's shoulder, 'keep her busy. Send the errand boy to the hospital... I'll have some material sent over, so she can roll bandages, or knit balaclavas.' With that, she and Ellie kissed her cheek and hurried out. Archie dropped them off from the carriage on the corner, at their insistence. A frosty morning, the air woke them up like nothing else, and it gave them a chance to chat before starting their duties.

'I don't mean to sound callous,' Ellie said as they hurried along, making the sign of the cross as they passed the local church, 'but I'm excited about the prospect of nursing wounded soldiers.'

'Ellie you are priceless!' Anna laughed. 'Trust you to make the outbreak of war sound like an opportunity to meet young men.'

'Oh, they don't have to be so young.' Ellie said with a twinkle in her eye.

32

As a Dominion of the British Empire, Canada was automatically at war with Germany upon British declaration, and the patriotic people of Canada anxiously waited on the quayside, listening to the distant left, right, left, right thump of boots in the dockyard. Young girls were waiting for the honourable soldiers to pass, eager at a run to put a sprig of lucky heather in their hatbands. A departing troop train whistled in the distance, and the noise brought tears to the eyes of the mothers saying goodbye to their sons. The papers warned of the bloodshed to come...

Sam did not care about bloodshed. He reckoned if he could survive Liverpool docklands, then survive the Jessups, he could join the Canadian Expeditionary Force and survive anything. Not being eighteen years old was not a problem as his papers were barely glimpsed when he signed up. Doctor Warburton had made it his business to retrieve Sam's particulars and provide him with the necessary documents so he could legally remain in the country or travel outside of it.

'You write now, do you hear me!' It was an order, not a

request, and Sam nodded. Doctor and Mrs Warburton had been good to him and he was grateful.

'Don't get hurt, will you, Sam?' Millie Warburton had grown to be a beautiful girl and her gentle eyes held a look of trepidation, when she planted a small goodbye kiss on Sam's cheek. Sam lightly touched the place her lips had been. He was not in the habit of being kissed. He could feel the heat rise to his face for the first time in years, his throat tightening. The shipyard brought back many memories. The place where he said goodbye to Daisy Flynn, the little songbird who made his passage to Canada so bearable. It seemed so long ago now. Yet it seemed like yesterday.

'No, Mil, I won't get hurt,' he said, his voice a little gruff, exchanging a gaze that was longer than necessary. She had grown over the last couple of years, and her gentle nature soothed him in times of anxiety, which he still experienced sometimes. 'I'll write to you.' Sam did not think he would feel this way. His head had been full of the journey home. The war was a consequence he must endure until he could see his family again.

'I will write every day,' Millie whispered so her parents could not hear, 'is that all right?'

'That is perfect,' Sam said, feeling a little ashamed. He had not told them he did not intend to come back to Canada. The Warburton family had welcomed him into their home, built him up to be a fine, upstanding member of the community, and this was the way he was repaying them. Doctor Warburton had even taught him first aid, which enabled him to join the expeditionary force as a medic. He should say something. However, looking at Millie's sweet face now, he was torn.

'Will you come back to Manitoba?' Millie asked.

Sam knew he had to be honest with her. She and her family deserved that much. Pushing back his cap, he hesitated, looking round the crowded dockyard.

He had joined the Canadian Expeditionary Force without hesitation, the moment they asked for volunteers. He desperately wanted to get back home. The old place. Queen Street. In his memory, it was now a gauzy, cleaned-up version of the place he left behind. He looked over Millie's head and said to nobody in particular, 'I will never forget you or your family. You have all been so good to me.' He gave a little cough. 'I will be forever grateful.' If he saved from now until he was fifty, he could never afford his ticket back to England. Sam knew that the quickest route home, back to Liverpool, was going to be via France or Belgium. If he had to have a bit of a scrap on the way, then so be it.

Forever the optimist, Sam did not believe in defeat. He was going back to his homeland. He could hear the uproarious notes of a female singing, *'Pack up you troubles in your old kitbag and....'*

'I'll see you again, Sam, I know I will,' Millie said.

Words would not come as Sam slung his kitbag over his shoulder and boarded. Another ship, another adventure, he thought, waving over the rail to the throng of people below. He would miss the Warburton family. Most of all, though, he would miss Millie, now waving frantically on the quayside. 'I'm sure we will.'

'Does anybody know anything about this place called *Wipers*?' a female voice called over the hubbub of milling soldiers standing on deck.

Wipers? Sam rolled his eyes. 'It's not *Wipers*, its *Eep*,' Sam answered, 'spelled Y p r e s.'

'Well, aren't you the clever one,' said five feet two inches of female daring, pressing an ambulance driver's hat to her windswept canary-coloured bird's nest of hair. Rolling her eyes heavenwards, she shook her head. 'There's always bleeding one.'

Sam instantly recognised the unmistakable Liverpool twang

in her words. His heart beating faster. 'As I live and breathe,' he said, stooping to peer under the rim of the young lady's hat, 'if it isn't Daisy Flynn...'

ACKNOWLEDGMENTS

I would like to thank Nicki, my daughter, and my first reader for her patience and her insight.

Who knows where my stories come from? They pop into my head and stream onto a blank piece of paper in an undignified scramble. However, to make them the best they can be, I am lucky enough to have the expert talent of the Boldwood team alongside me.

I would like to thank Amanda and Nia, who are not only keeping this happy ship afloat – but have also cut through the choppy waters of 2020 with unwavering alacrity.

A special thank you to Caroline, Jade and Sue for their proficiency, their drive and their dedication, which is second to none, and to Megan and Ellie, who ensure the world knows about our books.

Also, thank you to my wonderful family for your love and support, and to Zoom for bringing us all that bit closer.

Love and hugs

Sheila xx

MORE FROM SHEILA RILEY

We hope you enjoyed reading *The Mersey Mistress*. If you did, please leave a review.

If you'd like to gift a copy, this book is also available as an ebook, digital audio download and audiobook CD.

Sign up to Sheila Riley's mailing list for news, competitions and updates on future books.

http://bit.ly/SheilaRileyNewsletter

Why not explore the *Reckoner's Row* series, another bestselling series from Sheila Riley!

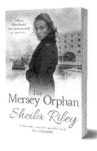 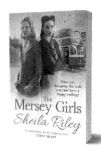

ABOUT THE AUTHOR

Sheila Riley wrote four #1 bestselling novels under the pseudonym Annie Groves and is now writing a saga trilogy under her own name. She has set it around the River Mersey and its docklands near to where she spent her early years. She still lives in Liverpool.

Visit Sheila's website: http://my-writing-ladder.blogspot.com/

Follow Sheila on social media:

f facebook.com/SheilaRileyAuthor

🐦 twitter.com/1sheilariley

📷 instagram.com/sheilarileynovelist

BB bookbub.com/authors/sheila-riley

ABOUT BOLDWOOD BOOKS

Boldwood Books is a fiction publishing company seeking out the best stories from around the world.

Find out more at www.boldwoodbooks.com

Sign up to the Book and Tonic newsletter for news, offers and competitions from Boldwood Books!

http://www.bit.ly/bookandtonic

We'd love to hear from you, follow us on social media:

facebook.com/BookandTonic

twitter.com/BoldwoodBooks

instagram.com/BookandTonic

Printed in Great Britain
by Amazon